Silver Moon

HAVE A COLLECTION
OF 60 GREAT NOVELS
OF
EROTIC DOMINATION

If you like one you will probably like the rest

A NEW TITLE EVERY MONTH
NOW INCLUDING EXTRA BONUS PAGES

Silver Moon Readers Service
c/o DS Sales Ltd.
PO Box 1100 London N21 2WQ

Silver Moon Books Inc
PO Box 1614 New York NY 10156

Distributed to the trade throughout North America by
LPC Group, 1436 West Randolph Street, Chicago, IL 60607
(800) 826-4330

Silver Moon Books of Leeds and New York are in no way connected with Silver Moon Books of London

If you like one of our books you will probably like them all!

Write for our free 20 page booklet of extracts from early books - surely the most erotic feebie yet - and, if you wish to be on our confidential mailing list, from forthcoming monthly titles as they are published:-

Silver Moon Reader Services
c/o DS Sales Ltd.
PO Box 1100 London N21 2WQ

or leave details on our 24hr UK answerphone
0181 245 0985
International acces code then +44 181 245 0985

<u>New authors welcome</u>
**Please send submissions to
PO Box 5663
Nottingham
NG3 6PJ**

www.silvermoon.co.uk
www.silvermoonbooks.com

Church of Chains first published 1999, copyright Sean O'Kane
The right of Sean O'Kane to be identified as the author of this book has been asserted in accordance with Section 77 and 78 of the Copyrights and Patents Act 1988

CHURCH OF CHAINS
By
SEAN O'KANE

Free first chapters of all Silver Moon & Silver Mink novels
at
http://www.silvermoonbooks.com
Decide before you visit the shop or use our postal service!
Electronic downloads also available

This is fiction - In real life always practise safe sex!

PROLOGUE

Father Burton's gaze swept round the courtyard of the monastery as the girls of the new intake, the novices and the initiates were shepherded to their quarters for the night. There had been two formal punishments to administer that evening. It had rained heavily during them, but it hadn't mattered. He had surveyed the faces of the other girls during the floggings, and all of them had seemed suitably fearful as they stood; legs apart, hands behind backs and watched as the rain had plastered their scant clothing to their bodies and their hair to their faces. Apart from the occasional flick of a head to clear the hair from in front of their eyes, none had dared move a muscle while the sentences were being carried out. Of course it was forbidden for them to look away during punishments and the brothers had patrolled the ranks to make sure none did.

In fact Father Burton felt the rain had added to the spectacle. Once the girls had been chained naked to the whipping post, it had made their palely exposed flesh gleam very pleasingly. And the whips of the brothers charged with carrying out the punishments had cracked down with an interestingly wet, smacking sound, sending sprays of rain and sweat up from the helpless bodies. Also it had added to the picture of utter dejection and defeat the girls had presented as they hung in their chains when they had taken their lashes, hair matted down and the panting, moaning bodies running with water.

The public humiliation of these floggings had denied, was specifically designed to deny the girls the usual pleasure their sex had been ordained to take in being dominated by their masters. As he watched now the two victims struggled to carry the heavy whipping post back into storage, just as they had earlier sweated to carry it out. The brothers' whips played mercilessly round their thighs and calves to encourage them.

The Father felt well pleased. The work of the Church was progressing fast, all round the country, monasteries like this one were quietly being established and those who could not live by the laws espoused by the Church were being purified and redeemed. The wickedness of society was being beaten out of it in various ways. But here was where he belonged, here with these errant girls, it was the task the Patriarch himself had bestowed on him. And Father Burton knew he was equal to it.

In only a few nights' time there would be yet another new intake of girls. He strode back into the monastery, yet again he would see to it that they were purified, every trace of their previous, sinful lives expunged. He couldn't wait to move the great work on.

1.

WPC Paula Cheever gave herself one last critical examination in the mirror of the ladies' toilets before going on duty.

The bright red lycra dress hugged every curve of her body. Her full breasts which were naked under the thin material stood out proud and firm, the nipples thrusting into little peaks at their tips. The plunging neckline bared a daring expanse of the creamy skin at her cleavage. The skirt was short enough to leave her stocking tops invitingly visible and it clung lovingly to the neat swell of her taut buttocks. She had been allowed to grow her hair for this assignment and now it fell in gleaming black waves to her shoulders.

Pretty good Paula, she told her reflection smugly, whoever christened this 'Operation Honeypot' knew exactly what they were doing.

When she reached the Vice Squad office with its desks piled up with paperwork that needed attending to, and would be one day, and its dingy walls covered in polaroid snaps of girls who were persistent offenders she found the Chief Inspector was waiting to give them a pep talk.

The Chief Inspector was Margaret Barfield, a good looking woman in her mid-thirties and tipped to go right to the top. She was sitting on the front of the Inspector's desk, her shapely legs being secretly appraised by the men sitting on the rickety chairs that were the room's only other furniture. They were wasting their time, Paula thought, her tastes didn't run to men. And several WPC's had had their careers blighted by refusing to hit the sack with her.

As Paula entered CI Barfield gave her an ironic smile. "Well WPC Cheever, should police work ever lose its appeal, I don't think you'll lack for alternative employment," she said.

The men sniggered and Paula groaned inwardly. For one thing she was getting tired of the snide comments from the men; for another she was terrified that CI Barfield would propostion her, she had already seen her eyeing her up. But the Chief Inspector moved on briskly and everyone settled down.

She briefed a group of four officers who were on the trail of a new pimp who had recently moved into the area and they left to set up their observation point. That left Paula and the two officers who were to man the mobile unit which would back her up.

Her job was to pose as a prostitute on one of the city's streets which was regularly used by kerb crawlers. She would have a small microphone attached to her dress and when she was propositioned the man's voice would be recorded in the unmarked van parked just round the corner from her. At the crucial moment the van would pull round and he would be arrested and brought in.

"You both know the drill," the CI told the men. "Don't leave Paula out there any longer than you have to with a punter. Just get the evidence and then go in and get her; and him. And there's an added reason why that's important at the moment. Anyone ever heard of the Church of Ultimate Purification?"

They all shook their heads, and then Paula remembered a documentary she had seen some weeks before. "Aren't they some kind of fundamentalist sect that's setting out to reform society?"

"That's them," Margaret Barfield nodded seriously. "They've got some pretty far out ideas and some questionable methods. Up north we're trying to infiltrate them. Amongst other things, known prostitutes are vanishing off the streets. We think they're behind it, and what's more we think they may be about to start operating down here. So you," she addressed the men, "keep a close eye on Paula."

They acknowledged their orders and left to pick up the van from the depot downstairs. The CI said she would drop Paula off at the agreed corner on her way home. It was an uncomfortable drive, Paula tried to use body language to convey to the other woman that she wasn't interested but Barfield just smiled. The bitch is biding her time, Paula thought.

It had been thought best to keep the decoy as far apart as possible from the van until the very last moment. When the van did arrive, a couple of minutes after Paula had taken up station, she would simply lean in at the driver's window as if she was negotiating with him. She would be fitted with the mike and the van would take up a discreet station and wait to see who fell into the trap.

Paula shivered a little as she climbed out of the car. Margaret Barfield leaned over before Paula could shut her door.

"You show a lot of........promise Paula," she said, managing to make the word 'promise' sound like Paula had asked her to leap into bed with her.

"When you've finished your attachment to Vice, we really must have a drink together. I like to get to know promising young officers."

Paula managed to make some non-committal reply and closed the door. The Chief Inspector's car pulled away and left her.

"Oh bloody great!" She muttered after it, "I either get felt up and laid by a creepy lesbian or stay as a PC for the rest of my career!" She knew there was no earthly point in reporting any proposition, Margaret Barfield could do no wrong in the eyes of the brass hats. Well it was a problem she would have to face in due course. She sighed and summoned up all her professionalism to concentrate on the job in hand.

The evening was chilly and the cold air cut through her thin clothes. How the real tarts stood it in all weathers she would never know.

She checked her watch and tried to stand in the shadows of the trees which overhung the high garden walls behind her. The van, a big, white, unmarked Transit, would be along any minute but if she could avoid being approached before it reached her, then so much the better.

The minutes passed. A couple of cars cruised by; the only traffic on this quiet street. The drivers looked hard at her, but the fact that she was standing well back from the kerb made them uncertain and they drove on. Paula wasn't concerned, she knew they would go round and round the kerb crawler's circuit. Once she had been miked up she would make it very plain that she was touting for business, then they would stop and the trap would spring.

She checked her watch again, a small frown on her face. The van didn't normally take this long. The road was very quiet, all the big old houses set back behind their stone walls seemed deserted. A small shiver of alarm went through her. She felt very much alone.

Where the hell was the van?

Suddenly the silence was broken by the sound of a vehicle turning into her road off the main street. It sounded like something larger than a car. Paula stepped out of the shadows to get a better look as the lights approached her. She watched anxiously as the vehicle made its way slowly towards where she was standing. It was only a few yards away when she breathed out a sigh of relief and hailed it.

It was a large, white, unmarked Transit.

In the vehicle depot the two Detective Constables were searching frantically for jump leads. Over the weekend the van had been parked with its lights left on and the battery was dead. By the time a set had been located and a car manoeuvred into a position from which the leads would reach the van, they realised that Paula had been out for half an hour with no back-up.

They drove across town as fast as the van would go but their hearts sank as they turned into the quiet road on which Paula was keeping station. Even though the street lights cast pools of shadows under overhanging trees, the road looked deserted. They drove slowly along peering into gateways and every dark corner which could be hiding her, but at the end of the road they exchanged grim glances.

The driver picked up the radio and raised the desk sergeant back at the station.

"Operation Honeypot here Sarge. We've got a

problem."

As soon as the van pulled up beside Paula, she approached the driver's door.

"About time!" she began. "Where the hell have you. . . ?"

She got no farther.

The door was suddenly pushed open violently, hitting her with savage force and knocking her backwards off her feet. She lay on the pavement, fury and bewilderment roiling in her dazed mind. But before her head could clear a cloth was pushed firmly over her nose and mouth and held down hard. It had an overpowering smell which was somehow familiar. Chloroform? Even as she began belatedly to struggle a part of her mind wondered professionally who would be using that stuff in this day and age? A young man's face came into view above her, he was looking down with calm disinterest and it was the image of his clean-cut features, so at odds with the situation, that Paula took down into darkness with her.

And when she came round she was sitting in darkness, but it was a swaying, moving darkness. She blinked her eyes until they began to focus and tried to bring a hand down to rub them but found she couldn't. She tugged harder, what were her hands doing above her head anyway? There was a pain in her wrists as she struggled and she heard the clink of metal. She was handcuffed!

In a panic she tried to move her feet, but again there was the discomfort of restraint and this time a rattle of chain. She tried to cry out and finally became aware of the fact that she was gagged as well. Fighting down her fear, she concentrated on trying to get her eyes to adjust to the gloom and slowly her surroundings fell into place.

She was in the back of a large van. Suddenly images

of her abduction came back to her. But if the van which had pulled up beside her wasn't a police van, whose was it? She turned her head, at least she could do that. There were several other girls imprisoned with her. They were all seated on benches which ran the length of the van, down either side of it. Their hands were handcuffed to two, long metal bars which were bolted to the roof and ran above the benches, their ankles were manacled and a heavy chain ran through steel rings on the manacles so that they were all chained to each other. All the girls were gagged. The back windows of the van had been crudely painted over, and only an occasional glare from the headlights of following traffic penetrated the dark.

Paula couldn't make out any of the facial features of her companions, but she got a general impression of uniformly short skirts and revealing tops, or short dresses like hers and high heels. As her head cleared she realised that these were other girls who had been taken off the streets by whoever it was. They were prostitutes like she was pretending to be, except that her abductors had thought she was a real one. Her head fell back in despair as she put the rest of the picture together.

Chief Inspector Barfield had said that the Church of Ultimate Purification was taking girls off the streets. Something had happened to her back-up, her cover had worked too well and she had been taken for a real prostitute and abducted by a bunch of fundamentalist loonies for God knew what purposes. Even in her despair she found a grim humour in her own choice of phrase.

She tried to remain professionally calm and review her position. No-one knew where she was or what had happened. At all costs her abductors mustn't find out who she really was. Her training came back to her; in a hostage situation never allow yourself to be seen as a threat to your abductor. She would have to maintain cover and hope someone caught up with her, and also hope that none of these girls recognised her.

Suddenly the van started to slow and then made a sharp right turn which threw all the girls on Paula's side forward against their handcuffs. Then they were on rough ground or a track of some kind and were thrown all ways, making muffled protests into their gags. After some minutes of jolting the van stopped. Paula heard the cab doors open and close and then the back doors were thrown open.

A powerful torch was shone into her eyes and a man's voice addressed them.

"Right then you sluts. You've got a long way to go yet so we're going to let you out for a moment. But don't get any ideas. You'll still be shackled and you're a long way from home. Sister Lavinia will release the hands of one row at a time. When your row is free you will be able to come out and relieve yourselves. If there is any disobedience or struggling, both of us have whips and will punish the offender here and now."

Paula hardly registered the more outlandish parts of this speech, she was using the torchlight to look at her fellow captives and was greatly relieved to find that she didn't recognise any of them. They must have been brought in by that new pimp the squad was trying to nail.

Somebody climbed into the van and Paula felt her hands released but then immediately cuffed again in front of her once they were clear of the bar. She looked at the figure which stood over her. It was a woman dressed in a long dark skirt and a white blouse which gave her an almost Victorian look. She passed down the line of girls and when all were free of the bar the man told them to stand up and they shuffled clumsily out into the night, dragging the heavy chain at their feet with them like a nineteenth century line of convicts. They stood for a moment shivering in the night air. The van seemed to have stopped on a hill. All round them was open moorland as far as Paula could tell, and far below them were the lights of a city, but which one? She was given no time for thought though. The woman told them to follow her and they stumbled after the pool of light her torch provided. A little way from the van they were halted and told to squat down and relieve themselves. Paula realised that now it had been drawn to her attention she was desperate. The woman stood over them, a long whip trailed down beside her. Paula looked at it and decided against trying to wrench off her gag and scream. It was difficult with their hands cuffed together but with much pulling at recalcitrant knickers, all the girls managed and made the best of the humiliation of having to perform in a line, chained together.

It was when they returned to the van so that the other line of captives could be freed that Paula got her first taste of what was in store.

The captive ahead of her, a slightly built, mousy haired girl balked at getting back in and began to scream into her gag. She tried to swing a clumsy two-handed punch at the woman who slapped her hard across the face and pushed her to the ground. Immediately the man was there, standing over her. He was very close to Paula and she could see his whip. With no hesitation he flicked the lash out and began to whip the girl on the ground. Paula reeled back as the whip sang close by her ear when he pulled his arm back. It was a brutally long whip and bit through the white material of the girl's blouse at almost the first blow while she writhed and screamed on the grass trying to escape the beating but only succeeding in spreading the punishment across her arms, ribs and thighs. Paula had no idea of how many lashes the girl had taken when she heard the one sound she had been praying for: the sound of a car coming up the track.

To her amazement however neither the woman nor

the man paid any attention. The punishment went on, the whip cracking across the girl's back as she now lay exhausted, face down and hardly squirming any longer. She was only capable of sobbing and screaming at each blow, bruised flesh showing through the rips in her clothes. Desperately Paula turned to the car for help and her heart leaped as it stopped, the driver's door opened and the figure of a policeman emerged.

But her hope turned to complete horror as the policeman sauntered up to the man who was now calmly recoiling his whip.

"Evening Brother Davis. See you've had good hunting then, another load of sluts to be rescued and redeemed."

The man with the whip smiled. "Evening Brother Willis. Yes it's a good haul but there's always one who needs a little extra redemption."

The men laughed as Paula watched in wide eyed bewilderment. They bent and hauled the gasping victim to her feet, then urged the line of girls back to their seats while the other line was taken out and then returned. This time no-one protested at getting back into the van.

When the woman, Sister Lavinia, Paula supposed had finished re-handcuffing the last of the captives and joined the men, the policman took her by the arm.

"You don't mind waiting a few moments do you Brother?" he said.

The other man grinned at him. "Of course not. It'll do this lot good to see how a properly redeemed slut conducts herself."

Sister Lavinia herself smiled and went willingly with the policeman. Paula saw him settle himself comfortably against one wing of his car and then in a single graceful movement, Sister Lavinia knelt in front of him. All the girls watched as she opened his trousers, took out the stiffly erect member and gently took it into her mouth. She was obviously well practised and took her time licking and sucking at the sex, bringing it slowly to its climax, her head moving gently backwards and forwards. At times she had almost the whole shaft in her throat, at others she just had the head of it and teased at it with her tongue. At last they saw the man dig his hands into Sister Lavinia's hair as her head went rhythmically, faster now, up and down the shaft and they heard him gasp as he thrust himself hard, again and again, into her mouth. Even when he sagged back against the car and sighed in satisfaction, she didn't stop. She licked and kissed the quickly shrinking sex until she was quite sure it was clean. Finally, long after his hands had relaxed their grip on her and with that graceful movement in her long skirt, Sister Lavinia stood up.

"Thank you for allowing me to pleasure you Brother Willis," they heard her say and then she walked back to the van. Paula could see that she was smiling proudly.

"While we're here I think I might sample the goods myself." Brother Davis said.

Paula had been the last girl they had picked up and was sitting next to the doors of the van. His torch shone straight in her face.

"Come on you! We'll start your training right now."

He climbed in and released her hands again but this time re-fastened them behind her back. Her ankles were freed from the chain and she was pushed out roughly to land on her knees in the grass. Her heart was hammering. She knew what was coming and kept repeating to herself that she had to do whatever it took to keep her abductors happy.

Brother Davis approached her, his hands working at his trousers. When he stood right in front of her his sex was rearing up before her face.

"You can either have the whip first," he told her,

"and believe me you'll do it afterwards, or you can suck me now and save yourself a beating."

He bent over her to release the gag. Once she was free of it, Paula shook her head to flick her hair back from her face and made no protest.

"Good girl. Now let's see if you were worth your money."

He gripped the back of her neck and she had no choice but to open her mouth wide and take him in. He went straight for the back of her throat.

Paula had never enjoyed giving her boyfriends oral sex. She felt there was a large element of subservience in it, and apart from that she disliked the salty taste of the sperm which she always tried to spit out if they came in her mouth.

But she had never encountered a man who simply didn't want the caresses of her lips and tongue. He just wanted to use her mouth and throat the same way he would use her vagina. She nearly gagged as the engorged head thrust in as deep as it could and then withdrew only to thrust in again. His hands held her head immobile and her imprisoned wrists left her helpless to stop him. All she could do was open her mouth as wide as possible and try to relax her throat to prevent retching. Relentlessly, and arrogantly careless of her discomfort he rammed himself in time and again until at last the moment she was dreading arrived.

She felt his shaft swell to an even greater size and the pumping begin deep inside it, and his hands tightened their grip. She made a desperate, muffled protest and then it began throbbing and jerking in her wide stretched mouth. She heard Brother Davis gasp and he pulled her head forward as he went for the very depths of her throat. Spurt after spurt of hot semen splashed out and fighting down her revulsion she began swallow it. But he came too fast and hard. Paula began to choke and splutter but he ignored her and held her tight as she fought to get his emission down, and keep it down.

Just when she thought he would surely suffocate her, he withdrew and left her to gasp for air and spit out what she hadn't been able to swallow. She heard the men and Sister Lavinia laughing.

"Whatever she charged, they didn't get their money's worth," Brother Davis said and retied the gag before bundling her back into the van.

The policeman shouted to Brother Davis that their way ahead was clear but if there was a problem, he should use the false ID. Then the doors were slammed and their journey continued.

Paula felt the eyes of the other girls on her and glanced round. As plain as day she could read the contempt she saw. A prostitute who couldn't give a blow job?

Paula tried to come to terms with everything. Obviously the Church of Ultimate Purification was very well organised and had infiltrated more places than anyone had realised. Apart from that they were plainly brutal in their methods. They didn't make threats, they simply said what they would do and then did it. Paula shuddered, she would have to play the part of a street tart much better. She was terrified of what might happen if they thought she was an informer. And she hadn't got off to a very good start.

They drove on and on. Paula managed to doze from sheer exhaustion but her arms were hurting savagely and the other girls moaning as well when at last the van stopped once more.

The doors were thrown open and this time it was early morning. Brother Davis grinned at them.

"Rise and shine my lovelies. Come and see your new home!"

Sister Lavinia, whom Paula could now see was a

tall blonde with a trim figure but voluptuous breasts came along the rows. This time she cuffed their hands behind them but unlocked the loops of chain which had shackled them and pulled them free of their manacles. At least this time they would be able to walk properly Paula thought.

They stood in a miserable line across the back of the van and stared round them. They were in the most spacious courtyard Paula had ever seen and one which was surrounded on three sides by two storey buildings and on the fourth side by a huge Gothic house with many towers and crenellations, it looked like a cross between a church and a fortified manor house. The whole complex was plainly home to many people, people who, even at this early hour were getting about their business. Paula saw many more men like Brother Davis, well set up young men in black trousers and white T shirts, all with a large red X on the front. Some of them, like Brother Davis carried coiled whips while others had riding whips or leather straps tucked into their belts.

There were plenty of girls as well. Some of them wore simple, very short brown shifts of rough looking cloth. Some wore equally short, spotlessly white dresses, a little like tennis dresses, except these were worn with three inch heels. Their skins were tanned and healthy looking against the white. There were also slightly older women all dressed like Sister Lavinia. The long skirts, Paula could now see were a deep midnight blue but the blouses were crisp and white with strangely high collars but deeply cut V necklines. Everyone seemed to go about their business in almost complete silence she noted. They all seemed to know where they were going and made straight for it. There were no spoken greetings, just nods.

Suddenly a large wooden door in one of the buildings near where they stood was opened by one of the brothers and Paula and her companions stared in horror at what emerged.

Two lines of five girls staggered out. Each line of five had their arms held straight out from their shoulders and thick leather straps wound repeatedly about the arms kept them lashed to a metal bar which ran across all their shoulders. The girls were virtually naked, they had simple plimsol type shoes on but their only clothing was leather and chain harness. Each had a heavy, metal collar round her neck, and threaded through the rings on these was a thick chain which bound them all together. The harness consisted of two chains which hung from the front of each girl's collar. These ran down over her breasts and were threaded through rings at the nipples. From there they ran down between the legs. Paula couldn't see how they were anchored there, but she was soon to find out that each lip of the sex was pierced and ringed and the chains passed through these rings as well. As the two lines of girls passed her Paula could see that the chains were drawn up tight between the buttocks and passed finally through a ring at the back of the thick leather belt each girl wore round her waist. They were then joined and by means of another steel ring were fastened to a leather thong which the brother following the girls was holding. He was thus holding five reins gathered in one hand and in his other hand was a long coach whip. From the metal bar which the girls were supporting on their shoulders four heavy chains hung down and trailed along the ground.

The two men who were driving these teams looked over and saw Brother Davis.

They immediately reined the girls in by pulling at the five straps they each held. This pulled the chains up tight between the girls' legs. There were groans and squeals of pain but a slash of the whips across the naked backs silenced them.

"A good night's work brother?" one of the men called

out.

"We'll have a look at them later," the other added. "A new lot for training's just what you need after a hard day in the fields."

Brother Davis and Sister Lavinia laughed. The men waved and then lashed casually at their teams again. The girls started forward and continued towards the gates of the courtyard which were swung open by two of the white clad girls. Paula and her group watched as the teams, driven by repeated flicks of the whips were driven out and the gates swung shut behind them. They exchanged fearful glances, but then Brother Davis spoke,

"They've been here almost a month now and are nearly ready to become novices. They work in the fields to repay the community for their rescue and redemption." He surveyed their apprehensive faces and grinned again, "You'll be doing the same soon. But now I want you in the Pen."

He jerked his head in the direction of the door from which the teams of girls had emerged and cracked his whip close behind them. Slowly the new captives made their way into the dark.

2.

When Brother Davis had said the Pen, that was exactly what he meant. At the back of the huge room in which they found themselves, and which smelled of horses and leather was a cattle pen. Into this they were herded just as if they were so many cattle. As soon as they were all in, and Paula counted ten of them including herself, Brother Davis opened the gate long enough to select one of them at random. The girl he picked was the one who had been beaten earlier, the rips in her clothes now revealing livid welts. She was led over to a table where a metal collar was fitted to her neck and padlocked on. A leather leash was attached to a D ring at the front and she was dragged out through a door which closed after her and the rest of the party huddled in fearful silence, only able to communicate by terrified looks.

Sister Lavinia stood by the door, smiling at them and toying with her whip.

Paula tried to remain observant. The big room was nothing more or less than a stable. Over on her left there were stalls and four horses were tethered in them.

She had just taken note of this when the screams began from beyond the door through which the first girl had been taken. They seemed to go on for a long time before there was silence. Some of the girls were crying in terror by the time Brother Davis re-appeared and selected the next victim, who struggled this time. The brother took his whip from his belt and delivered three hard lashes to the thinly clothed buttocks of the girl, then she too was collared and led away. Again there was silence for a while before the screams started once more. By the time the third girl had been led away some amongst Paula's group were shaking and moaning into their gags. After the fifth, and again the screams there was a soft trickling sound. Paula looked round and realised that one of the girls, a young looking brunette in a plastic micro skirt had lost all control through sheer terror. Paula looked at her sympathetically as she shivered in shame and fear.

It was excruciating torture, she thought, and undoubtedly designed to be.

When Paula was led out of the pen there were only two pathetic captives left huddling close together. Once her collar was locked on she was led through the door and found herself in a room with a concrete floor and tiled walls. The floor was awash with water and two more of the brothers stood waiting for her with full length plastic aprons on. Paula gazed round fearfully, unable to guess what was coming next.

Brother Davis took off her gag, her manacles and at last freed her hands. Paula's first instinct was to fight her way out but there were three of them and all big men. She abandoned that plan and resigned herself to playing for time.

"Strip." Brother Davis ordered curtly.

Paula looked at him. He was grinning casually and hefting the whip. For a moment she hesitated and the whip lashed out so fast that she never saw it. Instead there was a loud Crack! and a blinding pain ripped across the backs of her thighs. Instinctively her hands went to cover the hurt and she spun round to hide the area he had struck. Immediately there was another Crack! and this time the pain exploded across her stomach. She doubled over and fell against the wall.

Brother Davis came to stand over her.

"Strip you little slut," he said quietly.

Gasping and blinking back tears Paula obeyed.

She tried to ignore the looks of blatant lust on the men's faces as she stripped herself naked in front of them. She had never felt so helpless in her life. These men could do exactly what they liked with her. And she was in no doubt as to what it was they liked. She tried to cover herself with her arms and they laughed.

Leather wrist and ankle restraints were buckled onto her and she was led into the centre of the room. The men went about their work with quiet efficiency now. They raised her arms and clipped the loops on her restraints to a chain which hung down from the ceiling. Each ankle was similarly clipped to a chain. They gave her a chance to see how these chains ran up to pulleys again hung from the ceiling and set some four feet apart, and then down to crank handles in the walls. Brother Davis went to stand against the wall behind her while the other two men went to the handles. Paula's mind rebelled at what she thought might happen. It was impossible. Surely!

"Take her up lads." Brother Davis ordered calmly.

She managed one anguished "No! Please!" and then began to scream as the men turned the handles. Her weight came savagely onto her wrists as her legs were taken out from under her and then raised and spread wide open in front of her. The men wound the handles until Paula's body was parallel with the floor and her head was hanging down helplessly.

Then they turned the hoses on her. There were two of them and both high pressure. Paula shrieked and writhed as a million pinpricks of icy water blasted every square centimetre of her flesh. When at last they turned them off she hung sobbing and exhausted in her chains.

Davis approached her and grasped a handful of hair to pull her head up so that she could look down the length of her body. Between the gleaming mounds of her breasts she saw one of the men standing between her legs with a small steel rod in his hand.

"This'll swill out any filth you've brought in off the street," he said gleefully and inserted it into her vagina. Paula screamed again in revulsion this time as the cold metal thrust up deep inside her. And then she screamed in shock as icy water flooded right into her. He held the rod in and let her writhe for a full minute before he removed it. Then he bent down to look more closely and insert his fingers.

"Hmm, not been on the game too long have you? You're not as slack as most we get.".

He gave her a ringing smack on her rump and without any further comment used his fingers to prise open the closed bud of her anus. Paula groaned in pain and utter humiliation.

"Shouldn't think anyone's been up this. It's tight as a duck's but we'd better make sure."

Once again the hateful little rod invaded her and once again freezing cold water was blasted into her. This time he kept it on until she thought her stomach would burst. She was past screaming now and could only sob and beg them to stop. When at last they did, they let her down and unchained her. She was allowed to stagger over to a gutter which ran along one wall and squat over it while her stomach and sex emptied themselves.

After some minutes she rose shakily to her feet and Davis approached her. He ran his hands slowly over her gleaming breasts, tweaking and twisting the nipples painfully. Paula moaned.

"Open your legs slut," he said.

Lost in her misery she didn't respond in time. She heard a swishing noise and a red hot blaze of pain exploded across the front of her thighs. Once again she screamed and instinctively turned herself away from the pain. But immediately there was another swish and crack and the pain ripped across her buttocks. Paula pressed herself desperately against the cold tiles as four more lashes were laid on. She screamed as each lash sent spears of hot pain searing through her. Brother Davis repeated his command and this time Paula hurriedly turned and obeyed. She gritted her teeth as the man's fingers explored her. He pulled open her labia and thrust his fingers roughly up into her vagina which was only lubricated by the water. She gasped and winced as he invaded her, probing deeply at first and then lingering at the nub of her clitoris, stroking, rubbing and circling it. She had closed her eyes to try and shield herself from the shame but as he continued to work on her she opened them to find him studying her face. He was staring hard at her, calm and dispassionate, as if she was some sort of laboratory animal.

She closed her eyes hurriedly again. Paula's body was a blaze of pain even as she was shivering with cold. But to her dismay, as the stimulation went on patiently, minute after minute, she felt herself begin to respond with a moist warmth deep in the pit of her stomach, she was sure she was becoming wet with juices as the pain and pleasure mingled in ways she had never experienced. At last she couldn't help whimpering and felt that that was the greatest humiliation of all. Brother Davis laughed and withdrew his hand but stared at her thoughtfully. Paula hung her head to avoid his penetrating gaze.

"She's either new on the game or very classy to be on the streets. But yet she does a lousy blow job."

He put one hand under her chin and lifted her face. "You're an odd one alright," he said. Paula panicked for a moment but one of the other men came to her rescue.

"Don't knock it Brother. It'll be a nice change to have a tight little pussy like that to train."

Davis smiled and released her. " True enough. Anyway we've got work to do."

Paula was pushed unceremoniously into the next room where two more of the brothers were waiting. They ordered her against a wall, spreadeagled, and dried her with rough towels taking every opportunity to explore her body as they did so. They passed admiring comments on her breasts, her long thighs and the unusual tightness of her vagina. Once again she found her most secret places being plundered and explored by casual and brutal fingers. But Paula suffered in silence; she was learning.

When they had finished they put her into what they called a training harness. This consisted of a leather strap clipped onto the ring of her collar and running down to her crotch. Mounted on it were two large phalluses and as the men pulled the strap harshly back between her legs the fiirst phallus pushed imperiously into her vagina causing her to gasp with shock as it pushed her lips apart and thrust up into her. The second did the same with her anus. She couldn't help giving a little yelp as the rod penetrated the virgin passage and spread the tender tissues. She had never been penetrated there before today, but this was already the second time. The strap was then pulled up tightly, making her cry out again, and the men laugh. Then the strap was buckled to the back of a thick belt which itself buckled tight around her waist. Lastly she was told to fold her arms behind her and her forearms and wrists were bound together. This pulled her shoulders back and pushed out her breasts invitingly. She was told to sit on one of the plain wooden chairs which stood in two rows and faced a small stage at one end of the room, rather like a small classroom. In an ungainly kind of waddle, which the harness forced on her she went to a seat. Her companions were sitting already and Paula noted that Brother Davis had been making free use of his whip on most of them as well. Although they were ungagged, no-one even thought of talking. The dildos pushed up painfully inside her and she found herself squirming in discomfort, as were several other girls.

At last all ten were present and Brother Davis mounted the stage.

"You are scum." He said simply. "You are not yet ready to be even novices. You will earn that privilege and Father Burton will now address you and tell you why you are here and what is expected of you."

A door at the side of the stage opened and a tall figure in a head-to-toe hooded robe, of the same midnight blue the Sisters wore, entered. Emblazoned on the chest was the red X again. The hood was pulled back and Paula saw a hawk-like face, deeply lined, dark eyed and very impressive. The man was probably in his early fifties she thought, but fit and strong to judge by the confidence with which he held himself.

"I am Father Burton, Master of this monastery of the Church of Ultimate Purification."

Suddenly one of the captives, a tall girl with short black hair interrupted.

"You're a bunch of fucking shits! You can't do this! I know my rights, it's against the law!"

Paula groaned inwardly. She knew the type, the barrack room lawyer. Catch them red handed and they would sit in the station all night and swear that black was white. And they knew their rights, oh yes they knew them alright. But this one was too stupid to see that here they were at the mercy of people who considered they had none at all.

One of the men made a move towards her but Father Burton waved him back and let the girl rant on until she had run out of steam.

"Bring the whole class to the Punishment Wing," he said quietly, and left the stage.

They were lined up in a stone flagged corridor and made to trot. The brothers' whips flicked constantly at their legs. Their breasts bounced and the phalluses shifted inside them. They were driven mercilessly onwards making innumerable right and left turns until at last they stopped, panting for breath outside a heavy wooden door. Paula's large breasts were aching from all the unfettered joggling and bouncing about.

The door was opened by another one of the brothers, and they were ushered into a dungeon. It was stone walled and the only window was small, heavily barred and high up. The walls were covered with racks of whips crops and canes, together with chains and restraints of all kinds. There were hoods and cruel looking steel masks. The ceiling was festooned with chains which hung down from hooks embedded in it. The girls looked round in wide-eyed terror.

As the loud-mouthed girl was separated off and the rest were herded against one wall, they saw that in the centre of the room a strange looking device was already hooked up to two chains. It consisted of a thick metal bar about three feet long attached by several sturdy straps to soft leather boots at each end. The girl was forced, screaming and swearing to the floor where the boots were put on her. They stretched nearly to her knees and were laced up tightly. Her arms were freed and she struck out ineffectually as her harness was calmly removed. Then one of the brothers began to turn a crank handle on one wall and to the onlookers' horror she was lifted by her feet until her head hung some four feet off the ground, her arms hanging helplessly down and her legs spread wide apart. Paula could now appreciate the design of the boots, attached by so many straps to the bar they would distribute the weight so that there was no interruption of the blood supply. She could hang there for a long time.

The girl began to scream in earnest now but no-one paid any attention. Two brothers selected whips furnished with a score of lashes about two feet long and placed themselves in front of and behind their victim who was now writhing frantically.

"Beat her until she attains the silence of submission." Father Burton said calmly.

The girl spat the vilest stream of abuse at him that Paula had ever heard from a female but then the punishment began.

Unhurriedly and keeping to a steady rhythm the Brothers laid on the lashes. Because of the weight of the whips' cords each impact made the girl's body swing helplessly. She grunted at each heavy, smacking impact and tried in vain to twist and shield herself. At first her body only swung a little and for a long time she kept up her tirade. But slowly it faded into screams as the whips cracked down relentlessly leaving welts across her breasts and stomach, back and buttocks. Her body began to swing in larger arcs now. Paula tried to count the lashes but winced and lost track at about thirty when the whips began to lash the opened sex leaving red marks on the insides of the thighs which became more and more livid as the punishment went on. Paula felt her stomach churn at the thought of those lashes slamming into the soft flesh of a female sex, mashing the labia against the delicate skin within and biting up between the buttocks to sting at the secret opening of the anus. At first the girl tried to get her hands up to shield herself but the remorseless beating sapped her energy and soon she was hanging helplessly again. At last the screams became pleas for mercy and then the girl, who was swinging like a pendulum now from one bout of pain to the next was only whimpering, and finally there was silence. One of the men lowered her to the ground where she lay in a motionless heap. A bucket of cold water was thrown over her and she spluttered and stirred.

Hauling her up by her arms and dragging her on her knees, two of the men brought her to Father Burton. He bent down and grabbed a handful of hair, yanking her limp head back until she was staring up at him.

"You have no rights here. And the only law is God's law, before which you stand condemned. Understand? Now be still and obey or you will return here for further correction."

Father Burton smiled grimly as the girl managed a tiny nod. "Display her outside the cells for the rest of the day," he continued to the brothers and they dragged her away.

Now Father Burton turned his attention to the terrified group who had witnessed the savagery of the punishment. He smiled bleakly. "Welcome to the Purification Class."

3

"You are here to be punished and reformed," Father Burton went on. "Or as we prefer, rescued and redeemed. By your vile actions you have reduced men whom God decreed to be your masters, to the status of paying customers. You have taken what God gave you freely and made men pay for it. And the lure of the money involved in your filthy trade has brought lawlessness and sin onto the streets.

"Here you will be purified. You will be returned to your true selves and find again the joy of giving yourselves freely to your masters. And you will find joy in discovering how many ways you can please them. But you will suffer. Because it is only through suffering that true purification and redemption can be gained.

"All over the country our beloved Patriarch is setting up monasteries like this which will purify all those parts of our society which have become corrupt. We are but a small piece of a truly great plan."

Paula watched in horror as a look of reforming zeal came over the Father's face.

"But we will play our part! We will take you, and more like you, and turn you into decent women worthy of serving your men!"

In less than a day Paula had been abducted, chained, abused and beaten. But now she was really frightened. He meant every word he said and her only hope now lay in going so deep undercover that she forgot what she really was. All she could do was survive until help arrived.

"You are the lowest of the low within this monastery," Father Burton went on. "When you have proved your worth - and only when you have proved it - you will be considered for the rank of novice. From there you will begin the long climb towards the rank of sister which is the highest honour, bar only one, to which a woman may aspire. And one day you may have the honour of meeting The Patriarch himself." Father Burton stopped and swept his piercing gaze over his cowering audience. "You will call all men Master from now on, and serve them with your bodies and souls. Take them away Brother Davis."

He turned abruptly on his heel and swept out.

Once again they were formed up in a line and driven back through the corridors, tormented by the whips cracking around their calves and thighs. Sometimes they passed one or two of the girls in white who stood aside and grinned as their sweating, struggling line passed by.

Eventually they reached their cells. Full length iron barred doors fronted a row of tiny rooms on their left. On their right was a pillory. And facing the wall, bent over slightly so that her head and wrists were imprisoned by it, was the girl who had been whipped. Paula and the other girls stared. She was sobbing and her heaving back was covered by zig-zagging welts which ran across her buttocks and thighs as well.

Brother Davis gave them time to take in the sight and let their panting subside then his assistants pushed each of them to stand against a door with their backs to it. He stood before them and in front of the girl in the pillory. He raised a hand and delivered two resounding blows to the quivering buttocks behind him. The fleshy smacks echoed and the girl shrieked and writhed.

"You'll all suffer worse than this before we're done with you. So get used to it. Remember the Father's words, you're here to discover how to truly please those whom God has made your masters."

He landed yet another smack on the tormented girl behind him and grinned at her cry of pain.

"That pleases me. Do you understand?"

There was silence.

"I said, 'Do you understand?'"

There was an uncertain chorus of murmurs, and then the whips of all three brothers went to work. One of them was standing beside Paula and she caught the worst of it. He swung at her naked and thrust-forward breasts, getting in a full blooded lash before she could turn away. It was unlike any pain she had experienced up till then. A fierce trail of white heat shot through her leaving her helplessly gasping for breath and open for a second lash which cracked across her nipples. She screamed and spun round pressing herself against the bars, bruising the soft skin of her breasts again. She heard the whips being plied all up and down the line, each swish and crack being answered by shrieks and screams.

Just as suddenly as it had started; it stopped.

"Turn round," Brother Davis ordered.

Slowly they all did so.

"I asked you a question. I expect a proper answer. I asked if you understood."

This time there was a hesitant chorus of "Yes Master."

Brother Davis nodded grimly.

They were each pushed roughly into their cells and their training harnesses taken off. Once a long loop of chain from a ring in the wall had been padlocked onto their collars, their arms were untied. Paula had to stand beside her hard little bed until all the girls were tethered and then she was allowed to lie down.

She lay for a moment conscious only of her nakedness and how the marks of the whip chafed on the rough blanket under her. The thought that she had been whipped went round and round in her head. It was scarcely credible. Only a few hours ago she had been a competent, independent woman and a police officer. Now she was a chained and naked captive at the mercy of brutal men who had hung her in chains, casually opened the most intimate parts of her body, made her perform oral sex and had whipped her. Her heart skipped a beat at the very thought of that outrage. She heard again how the lashes hissed through the air and how they cracked down on vulnerable female flesh. Her hand traced the welt left by the last lash she had suffered. It ran across her breasts and her nipples still ached and throbbed.

Her thoughts were interrupted by Brother Davis. He opened her door and stepped into the tiny room. He said nothing but simply undressed. It had only been a matter of time, Paula thought, before it came to this. She watched him in silence and saw that he was muscular and lean. In particular she noted the broad shoulders and powerful chest, it was no wonder the whip hurt as much as it did when he swung it. His sex was fully erect already and this time Paula could see it clearly. How on earth had she managed to get him into her mouth at all? The shaft was thick and long, sticking up proudly from the thatch of dark hair at its base. Its head was huge and gleaming, she could almost taste it again just looking at it.

He came to stand over her and looked down thoughtfully. "Let's see if you fuck any better than you suck."

His words jerked Paula back to the very real danger of her position. To be a prostitute in these men's hands was bad enough, to be a spy and at their mercy was unthinkable. She had to forget WPC Cheever, she was Paula the slut, the tart now. She fucked for a living.

She put her hands by her sides and opened her legs. He nodded and then knelt on the bed, astride her. His strong hands reached down and took hold of her breasts.

"Good big tits. I like that," he said, and began to knead them, squeezing them and pulling them hard. Then he switched his attentions to her nipples and Paula gritted her teeth to prevent herself from crying out as he pulled hard at them as well and rolled them between thumb and forefinger. He revived the burning pain of the whip and kept on until at last he made her gasp and moan. Then he slapped them. Paula's eyes opened wide with shock as he did it again, left and then right. The smacks echoed off the stone walls and she cried out again as he slapped for the third time, much harder and she felt the weight of her breast flesh sway across her chest.

Davis grinned as he lowered himself down onto her. "Nice hard nipples too. They'll look good under the whip."

To her dismay she realised that he was right, she could feel the tightness in her breasts now. And then his hand went down to her sex. His fingers roughly parted her lips and he felt his way up into her. She desperately tried to pretend that she was used to this, that men took her body for their pleasure every day. She opened her legs further and he began to toy with her clitoris. He was brutally rough, rubbing at it and flicking it then feeling up into her vagina again. She could feel his breath on her cheek, his weight was crushing her breasts and his hand went on and on playing with her. And at last, just as it had earlier, her body began to respond as though it had been bludgeoned into submission. Paula moaned as she felt herself moisten and a fire start deep in her belly. Davis felt her juices begin to flow over his fingers and he laughed softly. He shifted his position on her and Paula raised her hips to offer herself to his sex. It was what a good professional would do, she told herself and gave a throaty gasp as she felt him push into her and fill her passage. He began to move slowly inside her and she could feel her body try and grip his shaft. Suddenly he withdrew until only the head of his rigid member was inside her. Instinctively she arched her back and reached down to hold his hips and stop him from slipping out.

He laughed again. "I think a few tastes of the whip

have done wonders for you," he whispered. Paula couldn't pretend any more. She was being raped but she didn't care. She just wanted the release which she knew was coming at any moment. He rammed himself back into her, sinking in up to the hilt and making her cry out. He did it again and again. Her arms were wrapped tight around his broad back now and her legs frantically gripped his thighs. Waves of pure sensual joy began to flood over Paula and she urged him on. Brother Davis began to grunt with effort as his pelvis smacked against her. Frantically she snapped her hips up to meet his thrusts and drive him in even deeper. And at last she felt the waves break, sweeping her away, aware only of his cry of ecstasy and his seed spurting into her.

He rolled off her before she had even stopped panting and shaking under him and dressed quickly.

When he stepped out into the corridor he shouted to all of them.

"Get some rest sluts. You're going to need it!" Then he left without even looking at her.

Paula lay dazed and sweating. It was the most devastating orgasm she had ever had and it had been with a brutal man who had insulted her body and hurt her at every turn. Paula closed her eyes in despair. Her first day of captivity wasn't even over yet and already she felt a million miles away from the person she had been.

4.

They were woken by Sister Lavinia running a riding crop along the bars of their cells.

"All of you up. Use the toilets and stand by beds!" she yelled.

Paula found her chain was long enough but realised that as the doors were the full width of the cells there was no privacy. Davis's semen had dried and crusted on her thighs, she longed for a shower. The brothers re-appeared and unlocked the doors while Paula was still sitting. The one who unlocked her door lingered and smiled at her while she wiped herself, knowing that nothing could be hidden from him.

"Brother Davis tells me you're a nice tight little piece. I think I'll try you myself later on, we don't get many come in like that," he said.

As she stood up, shame and fear making her tremble, he entered and bound her forearms behind her back again and released her collar from the chain. But at least there was no training harness. When they all stood outside their cells again and the girl had at last been released from the pillory, Brother Davis told them that the harnesses would be reserved for wearing after a punishment. They would be taken for their evening meal now, he said.

At a walking pace this time they were led to a small room with a plain wooden dining table in the middle. At one end stood Sister Lavinia. At the far end there were steaming pots of food with thick slices of bread beside them and a pile of bowls. The smell was delicious. Paula couldn't remember the last time she had eaten and her mouth watered instantly.

They were lined up along one wall and Paula could see that all the girls were staring hungrily at the food. But Sister Lavinia pulled a bench away from one wall and set it by the table, then she stood beside it and flexed her riding crop. Paula's heart fell. She was sure they weren't going to be allowed to eat just yet. And the Sister's words confirmed her worst fears.

"Before you may eat you will come to me and say, 'I am grateful for my rescue. I submit myself completely to the rules laid down by the Patriarch.' You will then be beaten and allowed to eat."

There was stunned silence as her words sank in. Paula stole glances to her right and left. She saw the others swallowing as fear and hunger fought for control. The choice was stark; either submit or starve, and from what she had seen of the Church she had no doubt that if they didn't submit they wouldn't eat. To her own surprise she stepped forward.

Brother Davis untied her arms and told her to approach Sister Lavinia.

"Mealtime beatings are routine. We leave them to the sisters," he told them all.

Paula did as she was told and faced Sister Lavinia.

"I am grateful for my rescue. I submit myself completely to the rules laid down by the Patriarch."

She was amazed at how easily the outrageous words came to her. But after all, she told herself, she had to survive somehow.

"Bend over the bench," Sister Lavinia told her. She was made to straddle it and then bend down to place her hands on the seat. Paula was acutely aware of how she was exposing herself to the eager gazes of the brothers and could feel the soft lips of her sex pushing back blatantly towards the audience. The crop tapped impatiently at the insides of her thighs and Paula realised she was being asked to display herself even more by opening her legs wider. Would Brother Davis be able to see the remains of his ejaculation still on her skin? She altered her stance and then cried out in shock as the first cut of the crop whistled in. It was a much sharper pain than the whip and she went up on tiptoe and wriggled her hips to try and disperse the intensity of it. The second cut made her draw her breath in with a hiss between clenched teeth and she danced on her toes. The Sister gave her time to settle down before she delivered the third and fourth cuts which left her gasping and blinded with tears, but at least she was able to walk stiffly to the food, help herself and at last, eat.

Paula was amazed at how good the food was, a thick warming stew which put new life into her and made the stinging pain in her buttocks recede a little. As she ate she watched the others gradually succumb. A halting procession of girls approached the bench and bent over. She was amazed at the variety in the size and shape of buttock which was presented and found herself fascinated by the way the soft flesh rippled and the bodies jerked under the stinging cracks of the crop. Some of the girls were plainly overweight and it bit wickedly into the pillows of flesh. At one point she looked away from the scene to find that Brother Davis was staring at her from where he lounged against a wall. He grinned knowingly and she looked down at her plate hurriedly. The next time she looked up she was amazed to see that he was standing beside Sister Lavinia with one hand inside her blouse massaging a breast while one poor girl remained bent over waiting for her beating.

The last girl to give in was the one who had been suspended and whipped earlier. Paula could see her bottom lip trembling as she approached the sister. In a very small voice she said the words and bent over. The other girls went quiet, waiting to see if there would be any allowance made for the livid stripes she already carried. Paula bet there wouldn't be.

The girl was tall and her buttocks stretched into tight curves when she bent over. From where Paula sat she could clearly see the lips of her sex nestling in the hollow at the top of her thighs. With a tightening in her chest she saw the stripes from the earlier whipping running across flesh which was now being exposed for further punishment.

Paula found she had stopped eating and was staring, spellbound at this display of control by their captors. No-one forced her down; they didn't need to. They had subdued and manipulated her so completely that she was volunteering to suffer this time. In silence they all watched as the crop hissed through the air and smacked down regardless. Once again the girl shrieked in agony and after two strokes begged for mercy. Sister Lavinia told her there would be none and delivered the last two lashes just as hard. The girl cried openly as she limped over to the food. Very gingerly she sat down and tried to eat. Watching her Paula was shocked to find herself wondering how much easier her job as a policewoman would have been if she had been able to mete out such treatment. She reckoned the brothers would have no more trouble from her.

When they had all eaten they were formed up in a line and chained together. This time their wrist restraints were simply clipped together behind their backs. But a link of a long chain was clipped to the rings of the restraints worn by the girl at the head of the line and then passed between the legs of the girl behind her, looped through and around the steel rings of her restraints and then through the legs of the girl behind her.. This was repeated all along the line until the chain was finally attached to the last girl. There was a space of four feet between each girl but once they were given the order to march it became very clear that they would all have to stay in step to avoid painful tightenings of the chain. Paula concentrated grimly on the legs of the girl ahead of her and matched her pace carefully. Unfortunately the girl behind her was not as quick a learner as she was and Paula got some agonising jerks on the chain as she got too far behind or stumbled. The chain would tighten, pull her hands back from her body and yank at the length of chain running from the girl ahead of her. That chain in turn would snap up between her sex lips and cause her to wince in pain while having a knock-on effect up the line.

After a painful few minutes they all began to realise the importance of staying in step and the cries of protest and pain became less frequent. Paula had been concentrating so hard that it came as a surprise to find that they had been led out into the courtyard and were now ordered to a halt.

She looked around in amazement. Never had she seen so much naked female flesh. Every girl in the monastery had to be there she thought. They stood in neat rows with one of the brothers in attendance on each row. In the centre of the huge courtyard there now stood a T shaped whipping post and beside it stood Father Burton.

Brother Davis came down their line. "The Church requires healthy minds in healthy bodies," he said. "So we attend to both. When Father Burton gives the signal you will run and you will keep running until I tell you to stop. As you are new arrivals you will run in chains."

Paula groaned. Just walking had been hard enough!

Suddenly there was a shrill blast from a whistle. It was the signal and the three brothers in attendance on their line immediately began plying their whips. Paula was next to last in line and caught several lashes around her calves.

Obediently she lifted her knees and tried to trot in step with the girl ahead of her. This time if any of them made a mistake it resulted in much fiercer jerks on the chain and for several minutes there were cries of pain all up and down the line as they struggled to organise themselves while the whips curled maddeningly around their legs.

At last though they managed to settle into a rhythm

and the crack of the whip came less often. Paula had always worked out two or three times a week apart from swimming and running, and once the chain had stopped cutting up into the tender flesh between her thighs she was able to look around. All the girls were running. They formed an orderly line around the perimeter of the courtyard. The brothers stood on the inside of the line to make sure they ran the whole way round. Paula had never seen so many breasts bouncing so vigorously or so many naked female thighs and buttocks all quivering with effort as the girls pounded the earth grimly while their masters' whips sang and cracked in the air. Sometimes the crack was of leather on skin if one girl was thought to be flagging.

And it was fatigue that now became the main enemy. Some of the girls in Paula's line had obviously never run so far in their lives. By the end of the second circuit she could hear their breath rasping and their pace began to slow. The whips began to torment them again. Their line alone had brothers jogging comfortably alongside them and now they started spurring them on in earnest. Paula could hear her companions gasping and crying, and then the girl behind her fell. There was a massive pull on the chain anchored at her wrists and she had to stop. There was no time to brace herself before the chain to the girl in front tautened violently. Paula screamed in agony as the harsh steel chain bit into the softness of her sex and so did the next girl on and the next, until the whole line was stationary. Roughly the faller was pulled to her feet and taken out of the line. Then the rest of them were whipped up again.

Three more times that was repeated before five circuits had been completed and they were allowed to stop. They stood panting and sweating with their heads hanging. The four girls who had fallen were kneeling by a wall and Brother Davis promised them extra sessions of exercise until they could keep up. The rest of the girls did five more circuits before they too were allowed to stop.

They were given time to get their breaths back before the next ritual took place.

"Form up for punishment!" Father Burton shouted. Immediately the girls all formed into two rows and stood with their legs apart and hands behind their backs. Paula's group were prodded and pushed to the front and made to kneel down. They found they were directly in front of the whipping post. Paula sensed a curious atmosphere around her, half fear and half excitement. Suddenly the door to the Pen was opened and a line of three girls was led out by a sister. They were chained together by their collars. When they stood in front of Father Burton he read in a clear voice from a clipboard in his hand.

"Novice April Anderson. Failure to please a Master sufficiently, second offence. Twenty lashes."

A sound like a cross between a sigh and a groan rose from the watching girls. But one of the brothers only had to turn slightly and it stopped. The girl, a blonde with a slender boyish figure, was unchained and led by a brother to the post. Her arms were raised and spread along the cross bar of the T and her wrists fastened to the chains which hung from it. Her body was pale and vulnerable, the long line of her back curving out gracefully at the waist to her hips and tight little buttocks. Her back was facing the audience and her fair hair hung down it. The brother who had chained her pushed it forward over her shoulders. Then he stood back and flicked out the long whip he held. On the other side of the girl a second brother did the same.

Paula felt that strange surge again that she had felt in the dining room. Here was a helplessly exposed female about to suffer a prolonged flogging but she hadn't struggled or protested in any way. The control these men had was absolute.

She felt again the tightening in her chest as she anticipated the whipping she was about to witness.

"Stand by," Father Burton said to the sister who had led out the victims. Then he turned to the two brothers by the whipping post. "You may begin," he said.

They took it in turns, one laying on a lash from the left, one following it up from the right. As an added refinement which made Paula's pulse race with its sheer cruelty, the victim was made to count the lashes she received.

As with the whipping administered in the dungeon earlier, the men took their time. They set up a steady rhythm which allowed the girl to count the last lash and prepare for the next one.

Swish! Crack!

"One!" The count came in a steady voice but they had all seen how the body had jerked against the post as the whip had curled round her buttocks and bitten into her hip.

Swish! Crack!

"Two!" From the right this time. Again the girl jerked convulsively but counted steadily.

Swish! Smack!

"Three!" There had been a gasp this time before the count. The lash had landed low down on the buttocks and Paula could imagine how it must have snapped round and bitten into the front of her thigh.

The fourth lash moved higher and wrapped round her waist, the tip of the lash must have cut into the soft skin of the lower stomach as it made the girl writhe and twist desperately before counting in an anguished yelp.

Paula couldn't take her eyes off the slim form as its struggles increased under the steady punishment. At times the hips were twisted so far round as the girl tried to spin away from the previous lash that the next one cracked home on ribs and belly.

These were much harsher whips than Paula had seen before and by the seventh lash the girl was heavily marked and screaming continually. The sister moved close in front of her to make sure she was still counting. After the ninth lash she held her hand up.

"No count!" Father Burton announced calmly. "Repeat the stroke!"

Paula knew she should be horrified at this cold cruelty, but found that instead she was horribly fascinated. How much could a girl take? What other refinements could these men come up with to prove their complete mastery over the girls?

The ninth lash was duly repeated. It was delivered low down, where the buttocks joined the thighs. The girl shrieked and managed a count before slumping in her chains.

The sister stepped forward and held something to the girl's face. It must be smelling salts, Paula thought as the girl struggled back to consciousness.

Quite deliberately the punishment continued. Slowly the lashes were applied farther and farther up the girl's back which arched in agony as she tried to press herself against the upright post of the T, her body making futile attempts to escape the pain.

The fifteenth lash must have cracked around her ribs far enough up for the braided leather to have curled across her breast. She arched and twisted in silent anguish before slumping once again. And again she was revived to suffer the last six lashes, capable now only of hoarse yells at each crack of the whip, exhausted writhings and whispered counts.

When at last it was over, Paula swallowed, suddenly aware that she had been so riveted to the scene in front of her that she had hardly breathed and her heart was hammering. The girl crawled away from the post on all fours and was ignored. Paula's eyes followed her though, unable to tear themselves from the sight of the dark lines snaking almost right round the body. It was as if the whip had been searching for the intimate places where previously Paula might only have thought of a lover reaching. In some of the places though, the harsh caresses of the whip had split her skin. Paula watched her until she collapsed by the wall and a bucket of water was thrown over her. The water cascaded off, tinged pink from where she had bled.

In the meantime the second girl had taken her place at the whipping post. She was condemned to only ten lashes for some trivial misdemeanour and took them stolidly enough. She was a more heavily built girl and only the final three lashes brought cries from her.

The first two victims had been novices, but the third was an initiate. They were the more senior girls and allowed the white dresses which Paula had seen that morning. She stood accused of failing to obey one of the sisters properly. Father Burton sentenced her to fifteen lashes. But as she was senior, he decreed that she was to be turned round at the post.

A murmur went round the watching girls. Paula glanced about her and saw an unmistakable look of excitement on the faces behind her. Maybe they were just glad it wasn't them out there, she thought, but she knew her own reactions went deeper than that.

The girl was tied with her back to the post, her arms pulled painfully back and out which left her breasts and the full expanse of her belly terribly exposed to the whips. But she faced her coming torture with a bold, almost challenging expression. In fact Paula could almost have sworn that she smiled at one of the men before the first lash cracked across the bush of hair at her pubis and she stiffened as if an electric shock had gone through her. She counted the strokes of her punishment in a clear voice despite her gasps and screams.

As they watched the heavy cords of the whips bite into and then fall away from her breasts, it seemed incredible that she held onto consciousness until the tenth lash despite her body's frantic attempts to twist away from each blast of pain. Again the smelling salts brought her round and she made it through without passing out again. But like the first girl she collapsed when she was taken down and had to crawl away to be doused in water.

When the punishments were over, Paula felt as if she had been through an emotional wringer. She was horrified, excited and exhausted all at the same time.

The last thing she saw as they were marched back indoors was the whipping post being put away. The three girls who had been flogged at it were now struggling to lift the upright out of the hole into which it had been sunk, and carry it away to its storage place.

As someone who believed in authority and order, Paula couldn't help feeling admiration for how thoroughly the Church of Ultimate Purification set about its work.

5.

Paula's group stood in front of their cells. For the first time both their wrists and ankles were free, although the collars and restraints stayed on. But no thought of anything other than the release of exhausted sleep was on their minds as they listened to Brother Davis.

He told them that they would remain naked until they attained the rank of novice, at which time they would be allowed to wear a simple brown shift. They would have no name until then either, they would wear the number of their cell instead, which would be clipped to their collars on an inscribed disc. One of the brothers passed along the line attaching them. Paula's number was three, she could feel no outrage at this further humiliation only a resigned acceptance of the Church's remorseless programme of suppression.

She did however groan when he told them that numbers one, two and three, were required in the house before they would be allowed to sleep. Numbly she watched as the other girls were put in their cells and chained for the night, then the three who had been picked were marched off with two of the brothers keeping watch. There was the small relief of having the simple liberty to move her hands now, and she tried to look around her as they went. She thought they passed the door of the Punishment Wing but the maze of passages and the number of turns they made soon became too much to remember. At last they arrived in front of a closed door and were halted. The door was opened by one of the sisters. She was a tall, dark haired woman and as Paula looked at her she was surprised to see that the plunging neckline of her blouse which revealed the smooth skin of her cleavage also revealed the stripes of a whipping. But the woman herself carried a whip. Clearly the heirarchy of the monastery was complicated and Paula found her tiredness dropping away to be replaced by curiosity.

The brothers left them and the woman took over, leading them through carpeted passages which were lined with items of antique furniture and pictures.

She took them up a huge staircase and then stopped in front of another door.

"You will all be called on to serve in the Lounge regularly," she told them. "We women do not merely pay lip service. . . " she smiled at her own joke, "to the teachings of the Church. Here you will be tested on everything you will be taught. Here you will serve your masters."

She opened the door and Paula saw that here indeed were the masters and here was the future they had in store for her.

The room was luxuriously appointed. The carpet was a deep crimson, large leather armchairs were grouped around tables and the walls were covered in bookshelves. At the far end was a kind of bar, from which some of the initiates were serving wine. The brothers, some thirty of them Paula thought were sitting and relaxing. Some were playing cards, some smoked and some were fondling the girls. Dotted amongst the men were the sisters, who appeared to be treated as equals. In the centre of the floor stood two girls. As they were naked, Paula had no way of gauging their rank but she gaped at them. They stood back to back with their legs spread wide apart and their anklets chained to eyebolts the floor. Their forearms were folded and bound together behind their backs, with the addad refinement that a leather strap had been looped tight in their hair and pulled taut before being tied off to the bonds on their arms. Their heads were thus forced back onto each other's shoulder and they had no choice but to stare at the ceiling. Paula took all this in and let her gaze move down over the rings at their nipples until she saw their sexes and then she shuddered. Each lip of the sex was pierced by a ring and each ring had a taut chain attached which ran down to the wide spread ankles where it was clipped onto the restraints. The labia were wrenched wide open and stretched. In a motionless tableau the two girls stood, helplessly offering up their breasts and sexes to whoever wanted to casually enjoy them.

The sister gave them a moment to look around then chivvied them over to the bar. Here she gave them small aprons which barely covered their own sexes and really only served to tempt hands to lift them and explore, as Paula found out. A silver tray with delicate chains attached to the bottom was fastened to each girl's right wrist and they were simply ordered to serve.

As soon as Paula's tray was attached she saw a man beckon her over. Her heart sank, it was the brother who had said he would have her himself. Fortunately he was fully engaged with one of the initiates for the moment. She was curled in his lap, her white dress hiked up over her naked hips. As Paula approached she saw that one of his hands was exploring deep in her sex. The girl's arms were wrapped around his neck and her tongue flicked teasingly at face and neck. He told Paula to fetch him wine and she returned to the bar, pouring him a glass and then placing it carefully on her tray to carry back. When she returned Brother Davis had joined him and as soon as Paula bent over to place the glass on the table, she felt his hand run over her buttocks and then slide between her thighs. She felt her blood begin to pound as she recalled how arrogantly he had taken her earlier and then remembered herself just in time to open her legs wider for his foraging fingers.

"She's a classy bitch alright," Davis said as his fingers parted her lips and began to find their way up into her. "She's got a bit to learn with her mouth though."

His companion laughed. "Then let her see how it should be done," he said.

He took his hand out of the girl on his lap, who moaned as he did so. "On your knees and give this one a lesson," he ordered. With no hesitation she slid down in front of him and began to undo his trousers. He smiled up at Paula and held out his fingers which glistened from the juices of the girl who was now beginning to run her tongue slowly up and down the shaft of his erection.

"Clean them," he told her. Paula felt Davis's eyes on her and knew the whip wasn't far away. She bent over and took the fingers into her mouth, running her tongue around them and getting her first taste of another girl's arousal. It was pungent and musky, not unpleasant she was surprised to find and certainly better than another beating.

They made her stay and watch while the initiate took a long time swirling her tongue around the tip of the brother's member, dipping her head every now and then to let him find the depths of her throat and then returning to patient licks and kisses until fiinally he pushed his pelvis forward and grabbed a handful of her hair. All the time Brother Davis kept his hand working at Paula, ignoring her clitoris but pushing his hand into her vagina and then withdrawing. She found at last that she could no longer resist the inevitable excitement deep in her belly and felt herself begin to moisten. She was helpless, a captive; there was nothing she could do about it so nothing was her fault. They were the only law here and she had to accept it.

Through half closed eyes she saw Davis's companion begin to buck and thrust into the girl's mouth and Paula knew that she herself was moaning even as he cried out and spurted himself into her throat and Davis's hand allowed her nowhere to hide her pleasure.

For what seemed like hours Paula and her two companions were kept busy, scurrying back and forth. She lost count of the hands which stroked her buttocks and pushed casually into her sex, not caring whether they excited her or not, only interested in the pleasure it gave them. And under so many anonymous hands, she herself became anonymous. She was simply a body to be used, and she submitted quietly when one of the brothers who had been fondling her ordered her to kneel in front of one of the chairs. She offered him her buttocks and opened her legs immediately, recognising him as one of the men who had administered the punishments. The leather of the chair was cool and smooth under her body as she pressed her breasts down onto it. The brother who wanted her had been idly rummaging his fingers inside her for some minutes and his member now slipped easily into her wet vagina. The constant handling of her breasts and sex had left Paula in an almost permanent state of arousal, and now at last her impatient channel was filled and she felt it eagerly gripping the shaft as it pushed into her and began to steadily ream her out. Bright shafts of pure pleasure lanced through her every time it rammed in, never had she experienced anything so intense. But then never had she been so aroused for so long, so constantly and arrogantly handled, so frightened and so abused. The fires in her belly grew and she gasped in delight when she heard his body slap against hers and his member seemed to penetrate to the neck of her womb. Urgently, she moved her hips against his thrusts and ground hard against him when he pressed in. She was just as helpless impaled on his sex as if she had been tied for his whip. And that thought made her moan as his thrusts became harder and faster. It was her second rape and she was building towards a devastating climax, surges of primal joy making her cry out as she juddered and writhed under the assault of the sex which was piercing her so ruthlessly.

Suddenly her hair was grabbed and her head pulled painfully far back. She found herself staring up at Davis who regarded her coolly as she undulated and writhed, finally crying out joyfully as she felt her climax break over her and the man's seed flood into her. Davis didn't let her go until the man had withdrawn and she moaned again as he left her empty. He nodded thoughtfully. "You're a whore alright. I wasn't sure for a while, but you're a whore right enough," he said and let her head fall back.

Dazed from her orgasm and petrified to learn how close she had been to disaster she got to her feet and resumed her duties. She felt the semen begin to trickle down her thighs as she served more wine to a table where one of the sisters was sitting. She got a ringing smack on her buttocks from her.

"Wipe yourself you slut. Why d'you think you've got an apron?" she said.

Without even thinking about it, Paula opened her legs in the middle of the room and did as she was told, pushing the cloth back between her thighs and wiping it along the groove of her sex, pressing it in hard to soak up the sticky emission. She was acting the part of a complete whore and doing it well, she told herself. She lost count from then on of how many men took her. But was grateful they all wanted her sex rather than her mouth.

Each of the men drove her to an orgasm, and the harder they drove her the more she came. Totally beyond caring for anything except the next brutal assault from hands or cocks she tottered from table to table, burning and sore. But time and again she knelt, straddled a lap or bent over a table. She heard the amused comments as she moaned and sighed out her climaxes. The tiny apron became sticky and crusted with semen as she wiped herself with it after each man had finished. And when it seemed that she would surely collapse from exhaustion, the games began. The two girls held imprisoned in the centre of the room having been ignored all night now became the centre of attention. Paula watched as two of the initiates were singled out. Each initiate knelt in front of a girl and at a signal from one of the men began to lick at the wrenched open sexes before them. The object was to see which initiate could get her girl to climax first. They played the best of three, laughing as the wretched prisoners moaned and writhed futilely in their restraints while the tongues of the kneeling girls flicked and probed, licked and rasped. Paula had never seen a woman having sex with another woman, but she was so tired she couldn't be shocked, just glad of the rest it gave her aching body. But as each of the prisoners came to a shuddering climax, then relaxed back into their chains while the relentless assault of the tongues continued, Paula was amazed to find her own sex quivering and spasming in sympathy with the ones being so expertly teased into repeated orgasms.

After one of the girls had stretched rigid, shuddered and screamed at the third orgasm the game was over. And now Paula and her companions became the centre of attention, and while the brothers and sisters cheered and laughed they were ridden round the room. Freed of their trays they crawled on all fours while various brothers rode on their backs and spurred them on with their heels kicking at the girls' thighs. They rode them until they collapsed, their hands and knees burning from the carpet. One of the sisters stood over them as they lay huddled and gasping on the floor and plied her crop a few times but although they stirred and moaned they couldn't go on. Paula let the pain rip across her bottom and thighs. It was worth it just to lie down.

Reluctantly the game was abandoned and they were left to lie where they had collapsed. At long last Paula heard people begin to drift away and a man's shoe prodded her in the ribs. He told them to get up and slowly they staggered to their feet. The girls in the centre of the room had been taken down and had gone. The brother who had made them get up now took them back to their cells. In the corridor outside the Lounge, Paula saw several of the brothers entering what must have been their rooms. Some of them were taking sisters with them but the initiates had gone. Staggering with weariness they made the long walk back.

Once in their cells their wrists were locked to their collars and their collars chained to the wall.

Paula slept immediately.

6.

Breakfast the next morning followed the same pattern as the previous night's supper. Sister Lavinia stood ready to hear their submission, administer the crop and then let them eat. This time there was no hesitation. All the girls accepted that there was no help for it. Paula was fifth in line for the beating and hardly noticed the regular swish and crack of the crop as it worked its way towards her. It still hurt every bit as much though, she thought ruefully as she eased her buttocks onto the bench to eat. Out of the corner of her eye she watched the men enjoying the spectacle of the bent over girls receiving their ration. At least tonight it would be three other girls serving in the Lounge where all the day's pent up arousal seemed to be allowed free rein.

She stopped eating suddenly when she realised that there had been a pang of regret at that thought. Between her legs her sex still throbbed. She had never been fucked so much. Or so hard.

WPC Cheever would have been ashamed, humiliated and furious. But she wasn't here, Paula the whore; Number Three, was. And her feelings were less clear.

She was so deep in thought that she jumped when the door crashed open and Brother Davis with four other brothers entered. That made eight brothers in the room. What was going on?

"On your feet my sluts and line up!" he said cheerfully. "Today you're going to be ringed!"

Some of the girls already sported nipple rings in one nipple, one or two had belly buttons pierced, but only Paula and the two girls who had served with her the previous night knew where these rings were going to be placed. They exchanged despairing glances. Paula's heart thudded with terror, she had never even had her ears pierced. The thought of escape was ludicrous, there were too many men, too many whips. She had no choice.

Her legs trembling she stood and went over to the wall, waiting with her back to it. The brothers formed them up as they had before, with loops of chain running between their legs and locking to their wrists behind them.

In fearful silence they walked between their guards. They went past the Punishment Wing then turned and went into the courtyard. They were marched across it, other girls going about their work turned and looked at them, grinning knowingly. At last they were brought to a halt in a corridor of the building opposite the one which housed them. A door was unlocked and they were led in. It was cold and bare but at least Paula could see no implements of torture and discipline, just metal rings set high in the walls. One by one they were taken out of line and stood with their backs against the cold stone. Their wrists were released and refastened in front of them, then their arms were raised and fastened to the rings by short lengths of chain. Finally a gag consisting of a simple strip of leather was pushed between their teeth and rammed as far back as it would go, then it was tied tightly at the backs of their heads.

Eventually all ten of them stood round the room, helpless and silent. The fact that their arms were pulled straight up above them made their breasts jut out and several of the men took advantage of that fact to stroke and tease them. Somehow Paula wasn't surprised when Brother Davis came over to her and began to knead and squeeze her breasts. He pulled harshly at the nipples and she let out a muffled cry.

"They'll look much nicer in a few minutes, believe me," he told her. She looked into his eyes which met her terrified gaze steadily. "You'll make a good servant of the Church." He cupped one breast and stroked it one last time before leaving her. Her fear was such that her nipples hadn't responded to his touch.

There was no need for a guard once they were safely chained and gagged so the girls were left on their own. But about twenty minutes later two of the men came back. They took down the girl next to the door and led her out. Paula counted four more till it was her turn.

She thought about how the girls in the Lounge had been tied last night, their rings pulling their sexes wide open. She was willing to bet that that wasn't the only way the brothers could find to tie and display a girl once she was ringed.

One by one they were taken out. Some who thought they would only have their other nipple pierced went quietly, others tried to struggle. The girl next to Paula, who had been in the Lounge put up as much of a fight as she could but was dragged away easily enough.

Paula too tried to fight but her legs were kicked out from under her and she was simply dragged by her arms, while her feet scrabbled for purchase behind her.

She was taken into the next room and saw the long table with its legs bolted to the floor. Her struggles redoubled until Davis stepped over. He grabbed a handful of her hair and pulling her head back delivered a ringing slap which stunned her into submission. The men lifted her easily up onto the table, pushed her down onto her back and began tying her. First her arms, with her wrists still bound were pulled back over her head and strapped firmly to the wood. This made her back arch and pushed her breasts up. Next a wide leather belt mounted at its ends on the table itself was buckled tightly around her waist and finally her legs were wrenched wide apart and her ankles strapped down as well.

One of the brothers calmly whistling between his teeth began to examine her. He ran his hands over the prominent mounds of her breasts and pulled at the nipples, stretching the pink flesh away from the tawny areolae. He glanced down at her when she moaned into her gag.

"Big tits always look good when they're ringed," he said, pulling the right nipple taut.

Paula had been rolling her head from side to side in a frantic denial of what she knew was about to happen but when she felt the touch of a cold liquid she couldn't help craning her head up to see him just finishing wiping disinfectant over her. He moved with such quiet efficiency that she hardly saw the long, almost needle-thin blade of a wickedly pointed knife suddenly appear in one hand and before she knew what was happening the point of the long blade had pushed through the tender flesh of the nipple he was holding with his other. She saw the steel pass clean through before a sharp pain made her moan again and she let her head fall back. There was a curious, cold feeling and a soft click. When she looked again, her right nipple had a gold ring right through it. He dabbed at a few spots of blood and then just as efficiently pushed the thin blade through her left nipple. Again she felt that oddly intrusive coldness as the metal of the ring followed the blade through her wounded flesh and then there was the soft click as the internal lock was sprung. Both her breasts were now pierced and he moved down to examine her crotch.

Paula screwed her eyes tight shut. But through the throbbing at her breasts she felt him pull at her labia, opening them, spreading them and then running the knife through each of them.

She shrieked into her gag and wrenched at the straps which tied her as she was pierced for the first time. She couldn't move but the pain of trying to distracted her from the much worse one at her belly. Again she writhed and screamed as the lancing pain shot through her body for the second time, and then there was that cold feeling as the metal was pushed through the wound and finally two very definite clicks as the rings were locked.

She was released and taken, walking wide legged to avoid aggravating the pain in her loins, to yet another room. It was a long one with three wooden bars running the whole length of it. The five girls ahead of Paula were already mounted on these but she was too drained by fear and shock to struggle as she too was mounted.

They turned her so that her back was towards the bars. The one nearest the floor passed behind her ankles and they were shackled to it, once again well apart. Then they made her lean back so that the second bar passed behind her waist. Then she was pushed even further back, so that she was staring at the ceiling and she felt the third behind her shoulders. Her wrists were released so that her arms could be pulled out, one hand nearly touching that of her neighbour, and then using the rings in the restraints, they strapped them to the bar. She was spread out and bowed painfully backwards as the third bar was set so much farther back than the lower two. The tension in her arms was terrible, her whole body seemed to throb and ache but they were just left to suffer. From time to time Paula heard the others moaning as well.

One at a time the rest of the group joined them until all ten were mounted in a row. Even in her discomfort, Paula could appreciate what a pretty display they made. Ten naked girls, all ten sexes spread wide open, all their breasts offered up helplessly from their bent back bodies.

There was no support for her head so as the hours passed she alternated between letting it hang down and staring up at the ceiling, with craning it painfully up so that she could squint down and see the gold gleaming where it was irrevocably embedded in her body. When all ten girls had been pierced and mounted, Father Burton came to address them.

"Today will be a day of Contemplation," he told them.

Contemplation days, they were to discover, were something they would come to dread.

"For the rest of the day you will stay here," he smiled at the chorus of muffled groans which greeted this announcement. "You will think of the chaos of sin and wickedness in which you lived your previous lives and how you now have discipline and authority to guide your steps along the paths of righteousness. You will think of the rings which now mark you as the property of the Church of Ultimate Purification and consider how you can best serve the Church to repay it for your redemption, and how utterly you are now bound by its rules." He paused for a moment and smiled. "At this stage of your purification you will probably harbour thoughts of rebellion and possibly even escape. Forget them. In time I promise you that you will come to thank us and you will not want to leave."

Paula listened in disbelief. All her thoughts about the way her body had reacted to her submission of the previous night, had gone. There was only outrage at the way she had been mutilated. WPC Cheever was back. She had to get out. Somehow she had to get out. And when she did they would pay for what they had done to her.

But the day wore on and on and no numbness came to alleviate the discomfort of their bondage. It simply got worse until Paula lost all her anger and sank under the pain which slowly but inexorably climbed up and up to become agony. All the girls cried and moaned but no relief came.

Occasionally one of the brothers would enter and work his way down the line, turning the rings so they wouldn't stick to the wounds, then he would leave them again and their despair deepened every time. The demands of their bodies couldn't be entirely denied and as the hours wore on, more and more frequently Paula heard the sound of trickling liquid as one or other of them gave up the fight and let go. Even Paula herself did at last. She cried with humiliation as she did so.

Truly they had reduced her to nothing now, she thought. No dignity, no choices, just an anonymous instrument for the pleasure of men; decorated to their taste and tortured at their whim.

At last she came to realise that even if by some miracle she did escape, it would do her no good. She could never again be who she had been. She would always carry the knowledge that these men had made her enjoy being raped by them, had made her bend over and be beaten without even having to hold her down. And even if she ever got rid of these rings, she would always know that she had carried them and in the privacy of her mind had harboured a secret admiration for the way the church enforced its discipline.

There was no going back. The only reality was this agony, and the men who had inflicted it and could stop it. They had the power, they had the control.

And before they were released, that control was demonstrated.

Brother Davis and nine others entered. They untied the gags and then stood back. There were several minutes of gasps and cries of relief as stiff facial muscles were worked again.

"You will now beg us to release you," he said.

Without a second thought Paula joined the chorus. "Please Master! Please untie me!"

"In a minute," he replied smiling thinly. The men now approached them and turned the rings once more, but then they set about calmly feeling deep into each girl's vagina. Paula couldn't believe it as the fingers probed inside her and the heel of the hand began to stroke and rub at the clitoris.

"Please Master!" she wailed, "let me go!"

No hint of expression passed over the man's face he simply went on patiently pushing his fingers up her, withdrawing them and then playing with her pleasure bud. Paula wept with the pain and frustration but gradually, incredibly, in the midst of the pain she felt her belly begin to feel hot and moist. At her breasts she felt the tightness and throb of her perforated nipples erecting. She knew her clitoris would be taut and full, pushing up from its hood of soft flesh, begging shamelessly for more. The man must have felt the juices begin to lubricate her because his movements became faster. Paula moaned in absolute humiliation, she was practically crucified and still her body was being made to feel excitement. But she couldn't deny her own sensations, and to judge by the increased writhings and cries on either side of her, she wasn't alone. Slowly, just as the pain of the long day had escalated into agony, now the enforced pleasure began to escalate into ecstasy. The man's fingers were now sliding easily into her. It felt like his whole hand was going up and her channel was gripping it eagerly. Trying to pull him further in.

With a cry of despair Paula submitted to the madness of being taken to an orgasm at exactly the same time as she was suffering the worst pain she had ever endured. Her stomach spasmed and her hips bucked to meet the relentless probing of the hand deep in her sex, she let her head fall back and her body take her over completely. She was beyond thought, her sex lips quivered and spasmed in their turn, ripples ran through her belly again and there was a voice shouting hoarsely. "Yes! For God's sake go on! Yes!" It was hers.

Despite its almost impossible position her body arched even further and she shook in every limb as a blinding storm of sensual overload sent her into frantic spasms for one more devastating time. And then it was over. The man's hand withdrew and left her lips quivering in the aftermath of the orgasm and her stomach muscles still knotting. Only then did he untie her.

As each girl was freed she fell to her knees, sobbing and gasping, confused and dazed. Slowly they began to massage feeling back into cramped limbs as the aftershocks died away. The astonishment of the orgasm and the pleasure of release was so great that even their rings were forgotten.

Brother Davis spoke again. "Today the Church of Ultimate Purification has taught you that those who God put in mastery over you have the absolute authority to bestow pain or pleasure on you. We will bestow or inflict whichever pleases us, and whichever will best train you. You have also learned that the worst thing that can happen to you is for your masters to leave you."

"Yes Master!" came an immediate and fervent chorus, as ten memories recalled the long horrors of the day.

Paula realised that in her exhausted state there was only one emotion now; gratitude that the men on whom they depended so completely had come back for them. Yes, let it be pain or pleasure Master but don't leave me again.

Brother Davis surveyed the floor under the bars. "You will be taken for your evening meal and before you are exercised afterwards, you will return and scrub this floor clean. Do you understand?"

Again there was an unhesitating chorus. "Yes Master!"

At the command to stand Paula and the others climbed stiffly up and waited to be chained again. She was so grateful to be free of the bars that the prospect of a chain, even one running between her legs didn't seem too bad. So she greeted the news that tonight they would be allowed to walk freely, with nothing but joy and further gratitude.

In an obedient line they walked back to their dining room where Sister Lavinia waited for them.

As the line shuffled towards her and her crop, Paula didn't really notice how they all put so much more feeling into the words they spoke before bending over the bench. All she could think of was food, and a little pain was a small price to pay. Although her beating still made her dance up onto tiptoes and her eyes flood with tears, it seemed almost petty compared with what they had been through.

There was still no talking allowed but for the first time the girls met each others' eyes. They were all looking at each others' rings and secretive glances and smiles were exchanged. They had something in common now.

After the meal they were marched back to the room in which they had been imprisoned and set to work on hands and knees, scrubbing the stone floor till their knees were red and the brother who stood over them was satisfied.

Then they ran. And this time they ran free of chains. Paula found herself intoxicated with the sense of liberation it gave her after all the bondage. And she was aware of how her rings swung from her nipples. Between her thighs she felt the occasional tug from the rings there. But it was such a small discomfort, easily outweighed by the feeling of comradeship she got from running alongside naked girls who had been through what she had. And there was an undeniable glow in her belly when she glanced at the strong young men who wielded such total control with such careless ease.

In their cells, when they wearily trooped back they found a small tub of cream on the tiny sinks in which they washed. They were told that they should rub the cream onto any traces of beatings at the end of each day and it would help disperse bruising. Paula rubbed it onto her bottom with complete peace of mind, smiling as she heard three more girls being sent to the Lounge. And when she lay down to have her wrists fastened to her collar and the brother leaned close down to her to padlock the chain from the wall to her neck, she breathed in the male scent of him. He turned her nipple rings once more and didn't need to tell her to open her legs for him to do the same with her labia.

Paula's last thoughts before sleep were that WPC Cheever had gone for good. Today she had been changed. She was Number Three until it pleased her masters to return her name.

7.

Two nights later Paula was back in the Lounge.

She was naked apart from the tiny apron and the tray chained to her wrist. She was bending down to carefully place four glasses of wine on the table for the brothers seated round it. One of them was idly working his fingers inside her while another was stroking her breasts which swayed as she bent and moved. He was running his fingers over the nipples, just catching them enough to tweak them between thumb and forefinger, then pulling playfully at the rings which hung from them. She could feel the tightness as the nipples swelled and stood out while deep in her belly she could feel the hand steadily churning her juices until her eager sex made hungry sucking noises, her hand was trembling as she tried to put the glasses down.

"This one's coming on well. Mind you she was a good one to start with," one of the men said.

"She fucks willingly enough, but Brother Davis says she isn't so good with her mouth."

The attractions of her long thighs and the unusual tightness of her hole had meant that no-one, apart from Brother Davis had gone in her mouth.

Another of the men hailed Brother Davis across the room and asked if he knew whether she was any better with her mouth now. Paula blushed and bowed her head. She heard Davis shout back that as far as he knew no-one had tried her. The men were genuinely shocked. One of them made her kneel down and they took a long look at her mouth, admiring the generous lips.

"We've got no-one on display tonight," the one who had had his hand inside her said. "Why don't we get one of the sisters to ginger her up a bit and then see to it."

There was general agreement and one of the sisters was called over. It was Lavinia.

"Take this one into the Games Room Sister and show her what to expect if she doesn't perform up to standard."

Sister Lavinia smiled grimly at Paula. "It'll be a pleasure Brother Gibson," she replied and told Paula to follow her. She went obediently but with her heart pounding. It was the familiar surge of fear and excitement. Whenever she thought she had seen the ultimate in how casually cruel a man could be towards a girl who was at his mercy, these men topped it with yet another breathtaking display of callousness. She had become used to her body being talked about as if it was merely an object, but now they weren't even bothered enough to beat her themselves. And she was sure a beating was what she was in for to judge by their words.

Sister Lavinia led her along the corridor outside the Lounge. It was lined with doors which Paula thought gave onto the brothers' rooms, but Sister Lavinia stopped outside one of the doors, opened it and gestured Paula in.

The room she found herself in was huge. Again it was expensively furnished and in the opposite wall was a large bay window which looked over the grounds at the front of the house. Over on her left she saw a billiard table and over on her right, with no real surprise, she saw an arrangement of bars and posts.

"This is where they whip us for pleasure rather than instruction Number Three," Sister Lavinia said, standing close behind her. Paula turned in surprise at her use of the word 'us'.

"Oh yes," Lavinia went on, " we are all women after all, and therefore we all submit to the men in accordance with the teachings of the Patriarch himself. I count myself fortunate to have been given many a good thrashing in here, and been the better for it. In fact I don't think you'll find a pleasanter room in which to enjoy one." She laughed at the astonishment on Paula's face. "My dear little girl, you'll understand in time. Now get rid of that apron and then you can undress me."

With trembling fingers Paula took off the apron and detached the tray. She had been on the end of almost continual flicks from the whip and a few real lashes, and of course there were the regular four strokes at meal times, but so far she had managed to stay clear of serious punishment. And as for undressing another woman!

"Get a move on girl!" Sister Lavinia told her impatiently.

Slowly Paula reached out to undo the top button of her blouse. The low neckline meant that this was where her large breasts pulled most strongly at the material. Paula felt the tension relax as the button came undone. She undid the three others and then pulled the blouse free of the skirt's waistband. Sister Lavinia took over and shrugged it free of her shoulders. She had superb breasts, Paula had to admit, large, full and firm. Their tips were a dusky pink and the ringed nipples stood out hard and engorged from them.

"Kneel," she told Paula curtly. Paula knelt and undid the the two buttons at the waistband. As the skirt dropped she saw the bush of curly blonde hair at her delta and the gold of the rings through her sex lips. "That's better," she said, stepping out of the skirt, "I always work better without clothes to restrict movement. Now let's get you ready."

Mesmerised by the swaying of the generous hips and smooth buttocks, Paula followed her over to the enormous marble fireplace. Around the perimeter of the hearth ran a wooden bar at waist height. She was told to bend over and stretch her arms out so that the bar passed under the length of her arms and across the top of her chest. Paula obeyed and her wrists were strapped down, then Sister Lavinia dragged her ankles well apart and using short chains anchored to bolts in the floor fastened her restraints. Paula felt a cool hand pass over her labia and toy with her rings.

"We'll give those a taste of the whip tonight. If you haven't learned to enjoy a beating yet, that should ensure you perform well in the Lounge." Paula shuddered at her words and looking to her left saw the woman open a large cupboard and select a whip. It wasn't one of the long ones she had seen used at the whipping post, it was like the ones she had seen used on the very first morning, in the Punishment Wing. The lashes were about eighteen inches long and the leather of each was knotted at irregular intervals.

Paula braced herself as Lavinia came to stand behind her. "You have full permission to scream as much as you like," she said pleasantly, and then struck.

She ignored the taut curves of Paula's buttocks and went instead for the area where they joined her thighs, and in particular the hollow at the top of the thighs from which Paula's lips pouted. The pain was exquisite as the lashes followed every contour of her body and the knots bit into the tender flesh of the labia. To Paula it felt as if a bolt of lightning had shot directly up into her belly. Her breath exploded from her lungs, her eyes bulged and she couldn't even start screaming before the second lash smacked in. Then she screamed, a high keening scream which she hardly recognised as coming from her. Her throat tightened as the pain caught at it. Of their own accord her stomach muscles bunched and spasmed in a desperate attempt to tuck her exposed sex back, away from the next lash. Dimly she heard a hissing in the air and then the third lash smacked home, again the whip curling lovingly into every hollow and over every curve of her body before falling away. The shaft of agony which struck up into her this time left her body only one avenue of escape. Her knees buckled and she fell onto them. This left her kneeling, gasping and shrieking at the bar. Her legs were still splayed open though, thanks to the chains at her ankles. For a moment there was no fourth lash and Paula had just begun to dare hope that three was all she was getting when she heard the whip hiss through the air again.

She would have gladly taken the lashes which followed across her shoulders and back. But Sister Lavinia had no intentions of letting her off that lightly.

She wielded the whip in vicious uppercut strokes from then on. And the lashes cut right along the length of Paula's labia, seeking their way between them and up into the soft tissue around the clitoris. Starbursts of brilliant agony exploded behind her eyelids as the leather strips slammed into it, licked at it and curled upwards to flick at her belly. She bucked her hips in a silent frenzy of disbelieving pain and wrenched at her wrist restraints when the fourth lash came. At the fifth and sixth lashes she simply put her head back and howled. All sense of herself was obliterated, she was just a blaze of agony from her crotch to her throat and she went on howling even when the whipping stopped.

When her bonds were released she collapsed into a

foetal position, clutching her hands around her aching and throbbing sex.

Sister Lavinia gave her only a few seconds and then hauled her up by her hair. Through pain racked eyes Paula stared up at her.

"Now, I'm going to see every man who wants to go into your mouth tonight enjoy a good long suck. And I'm going to see every drop of sperm they empty into you taken down and kept down. Aren't I?"

Paula could only nod. She knew now what she would get if anyone wasn't satisfied.

A few minutes later Paula, followed by the now demurely dressed Sister Lavinia went back into the Lounge. Paula had been given time to dry her eyes and recover a little, although she still walked stiffly. Dangling at her side the sister still held the whip and Paula was very well aware of its presence.

There were some amused comments from the brothers about the livid welts around her belly, and she saw one or two of the initiates smiling mockingly at her tear stained face. But two of the brothers who had so casually condemned her to the whipping, took hold of her and tied her in the middle of the room. She was made to kneel up and short chains, again attached to bolts set in the floor were locked behind her knees which were spread wide apart. Her wrists were raised to shoulder height, stretched out to either side and fastened to chains hanging from the ceiling. It was an identical posture to the one in which she had just been flogged. And as if any further threat were needed, Sister Lavinia and her whip stood in front of her while she was tied.

Brother Gibson was the first to present himself. Paula watched as first the gleaming head and then the thick shaft of his sex came free from his trousers, jutting stiffly towards her mouth. Without a second thought this time Paula opened her mouth and let her lips trail around the head as it pushed in, her tongue rubbing at the slit and feeling for the sensitive place beneath it. A place she had learned to avoid when having reluctantly taken previous boyfriends into her mouth, it usually meant they would come before she could get them out. Now however the prospect of hot sperm splashing against the back of her throat was one to be relished compared with the alternatives.

The brother placed his hands on either side of her head and began to guide her back and forth. When he pushed in deep she concentrated on relaxing her throat and letting him get as far in as he could go. When he withdrew, her tongue pursued him, licking and swirling. The salty male taste didn't seem so bad now, and when he emerged entirely from her, he didn't need to tell her to run her lips down the long ridge on the underside of the shaft. And when she had gone as far down as his clothing would let her, she rubbed her cheek against the soft skin stretched over the steel hard shaft. Urgently he pulled her head back and thrust in again, this time he didn't wait for any subtle caresses but went right for the back of her throat, he pushed hard and Paula tried desperately not to choke but then he withdrew a little way and she felt his shaft swell and the pulses begin. She braced herself for the next thrust and began to swallow as he rammed in and his fluid splattered deep into her throat.

She heard him give a gutteral moan and kept swallowing, amazed that she could ever have found the pungent, animal taste so unappealing. With one or two last shuddering spasms he spent himself and inquisitively Paula let her tongue continue to explore the rapidly shrinking member, lapping at the slit from which the fluid had spurted and cleaning up the last of his emission.

At last he pulled out of her and she heard him laugh huskily, "Amazing what a few touches of the whip can accomplish Brother Davis."

Her immediate emotion was one of relief. He had enjoyed her and the threat of the whip had receded a little. But also there was some pride. The sight of her helpless body had made him stiffen and the passionate work of her mouth had brought his pleasure to a climax.

She was given no time for thought though. Almost immediately another rigid sex was pushing at her lips and demanding her attention. It was shorter and thicker than Brother Gibson's, making her stretch her lips to their widest to let the huge head have free access. When this one came there was so much semen, and he stuffed her so full that however fast she swallowed some of it trickled out onto her chin. When he withdrew, Paula panicked for a moment. Would spilling any mean the whip again? She relaxed when he ran his fingers around her mouth to wipe it off and then let her lick them clean.

Time and again the brothers presented themselves to test the quality of her performance and gradually she sank into a kind of trance. Her imprisoned arms ached, her body hurt from the whip and from kneeling up, her knees burned, but she kept licking and sucking and kissing. Her mouth was no longer hers, it was simply another passage into a female body which could serve to give pleasure to men. And she took pride and pleasure herself in the number of times she brought them to a climax, listening for their cries of joy as the thick seed pumped into her willing and open throat.

Eventually she was left alone, the taste and scent of men filling her, and the pain of her bondage tormenting her. She must have passed out because suddenly a hand was tapping her cheek and groggily she opened her eyes. Brother Davis stood over her and the room was empty. He released her arms and she cried out in pain as they were allowed to fall to her sides. He rubbed her shoulders to help the circulation back and when she had flexed them until they stopped hurting he spoke quietly to her.

"Well my little whore. Now you can use your hands as well."

She needed no further bidding but simply reached forward and felt the long bulge of his erection at his crotch. Slowly she set about freeing it and at last it reared up before her. This time she closed both her hands round the shaft and drew it towards her mouth eagerly, teasing him with her tongue for a long time before letting her lips close softly around him. Her hands reached round his hips and pulled him forward as her mouth ran down and down the length of his shaft and then up again. She explored him with her hands, reaching into his clothes to stroke the tight scrotum and cup it gently when finally she surrendered to his urgent thrusts. She let him move her head to meet them, not caring that he was ramming the back of her throat, just waiting for that precious moment when he would swell even more inside her and then begin his release. He gave a gasp at last and she was rewarded once more by the hot jets flooding into her. He held her head tightly to him for a long time as his hips pumped at her and his sex jerked wildly in her mouth. But at last he was spent and regretfully Paula cleaned him up before he withdrew.

"If you respond to the whip like that. I'll have to give you a real thrashing one day," he said.

8.

For the next month a relentless routine was established. The day began with their declaration of submission to Sister Lavinia. The four strokes of the crop were followed by breakfast. After breakfast they would be marched into the house itself for prayers. These were conducted by Father Burton in a kind of crypt under the house. The girls would kneel and pray for forgiveness for their sins against those whom God had meant to be their masters. And within a few days Paula had forgotten that she had no sins of that type to confess and did so anyway. After prayers on most days they would be led to the Pen and there they would be harnessed like the girls they had seen on their first morning. Paula soon got used to the cold feel of the chains being fed through her nipple rings and labia rings. She took longer to get accustomed to having her arms tied at full stretch to the metal bar which ran across their shoulders. But she was beginning to get accustomed to having no choice, and once harnessed they were driven naked out to the fields.

The heavy chains which hung from the bar they were tied to were then attached to ploughs and harrows, and the day's work began.

Paula suspected that there were two aims, the first was to make them fit and to work off the dissolute lifestyles they had led. That was not so much of a problem for her, but some of her companions suffered terribly, ending the day hardly able to stand and the others on the team having to work all the harder. The second aim she thought, was to keep them so exhausted that they accepted the discipline quietly and any memories of their previous lives faded quickly.

The days in the fields were long and arduous. They staggered through the heavy soil pulling the machinery behind them and all the time the whip played on their shoulders and backs. At night they rubbed on the cream only to present the whip with nearly a blank canvas the next morning. And on that the brothers would once again inscribe their criss crossing patterns of weals.

On those days they didn't return till late afternoon. At about midday they were given a brief rest when their driver would feed them with fruit which they ate from his hand standing in their harness. And then they worked on until they were driven back and were allowed a few minutes to shower before prayers again. Then they had the evening meal, preceded by the inevitable beating before being exercised in the courtyard.

On some evenings there were punishments at the T shaped whipping post. They learned that these were punishments that Father Burton wished everyone to witness. There were many others administered in the Punishment Wing, frequently they were led past it and heard the swish and smack of a whip, or the agonised groans of a girl undergoing some painful bondage or suspension.

On days when they weren't working in the fields they were taken on runs. Paula enjoyed these. The brothers would mount their horses and ride alongside the girls as they ran across country. The monastery estate was vast and they never saw another person, nor did Paula ever get any clue as to where they were. She didn't really care any more, there was just a residual curiosity.

In that previous life which she now hardly remembered she had run for the police athletics club and she would easily outpace her companions and often she would run almost alone. When she got ahead it was usually Brother Davis who rode up and accompanied her.

She found that she loved the feel of running naked, the cold air on her body, her muscles moving smoothly under skin that glowed with health. And beside her the steady pounding of the horse's hooves with Brother Davis spurring her on to greater efforts. He was a superb horseman able to lean easily down out of the saddle to flick his crop at her tight buttocks as they shuddered temptingly with each long stride she took.

Paula came to accept quite calmly that she could run much faster with flashes of pain from a whip striping her bottom to spur her on; and welcomed the aid to her performance.

She became aware as the days passed that pain and pleasure were mingling inextricably for her. The pain of a beating with the crop had come to mean the welcome taste of hot food was not far away, and the pain became an acceptable part of hunger and appetite appeased. The blazing sting of the lashes wasn't any less, it was just that it didn't register so much as something unpleasant. Similarly the backbreaking work in the fields was making her tougher and fitter than she had ever been, and it was the whip which drove her to that increased toughness. She was stronger and faster than she had been and it was Brother Davis's relentless wielding of whip and crop which was achieving that.

In the evenings, in the few minutes they had before they were chained for the night, she would look down at the muscular contours of her body with real pride, the stomach and thighs firm and strong but still sheathed in smooth womanly curves.

Father Burton told them that this first month, the month of purification, was when their slates would be wiped clean. After this they would begin the long climb towards their new status within the Church.

And certainly Paula found that she was changing.

The distinctions between punishment and reward were blurring as well as those between pain and pleasure.

She was beginning to react to them as parts of the same thing, different sides of the same coin. And all of them were dispensed by the Masters, acting for the Church of Ultimate Purification which was the creation of the Patriarch.

9.

The weeks passed until it was only a matter of days before the month of purification would be over and Paula's group would become novices.

Even though the group was forbidden to talk at any time, except to answer a direct question or at the order of a brother or one of the sisters, Paula could feel their excitement and shared it. They knew that the novices didn't work in the fields and that they were allowed to wear clothes. It was only a simple shift which would barely cover their modesty but that seemed now like a luxury beyond their wildest dreams. And then at last they would become initiates and be allowed the short white dresses. . . and shoes! She had seen how at prayers the short skirts could be flicked up when sitting or kneeling to reveal tantalising glimpses of what was on offer for the brothers. She had seen the flirtatious glances directed at the men from under the lashes of respectfully lowered eyes.

Of course the brothers could take what they wanted at any time, but Paula found the prospect of inviting them to take it, deeply thrilling. Being naked and available was all very well, but to be just clothed enough to have something to reveal made Paula feel very hot and moist.

Paula could also see similar attitudes developing in

her companions. Some of them seemed to positively invite the whip. Hardly a day went by without one or other girl being put in the pillory outside the cells and given a sound thrashing while the others looked on. Inevitably the squirming of the body under punishment inflamed the brother inflicting it and he would have her as soon as the girl was well striped. But Paula noted with growing incredulity that as the days went past the girls' wrigglings were becoming less those of pain than of pleasure. Instead of backs bowing away from the lash they began to arch so as to offer themselves up more openly. And now the sex of whichever brother took the girl would slide easily into her body when the punishment was complete. Sometimes Paula glanced along the line of watching girls and caught that same look of excitement she had noted that very first night when they had seen the whipping post used. But although girls who were sent to the Punishment Wing often returned dischevelled and marked, yet obviously secretly proud and happy; they all feared the whipping post. Two of them had received thirty lash sentences during the month and the whipping was so heavy that it was clear to all that there could be no pleasure to be had there.

    She was reflecting on this while they were being run one afternoon. They were far out on the estate, the brothers on their horses guiding them through woods and across moorland they had never seen before. She was thinking that the Church was maybe the strict heirarchy she had always wanted. Like the police force it had levels of seniority, it had uniforms and it had rules. She knew exactly where she stood and she liked that. She responded to discipline and order, wasn't that why she had joined the police in the first place? Although that discipline now seemed a poor thing compared to the ruthless discipline of the Church.

    She thought with some pride of the fact that she had never been put in the pillory outside their cells and had never had to wear the awful training harness after a punishment. In fact she had never been punished. Since the day they had been ringed she had submitted gladly to all the rules and after the whipping Sister Lavinia had administered in the Games Room she had made sure her sex and her mouth were always ready and willing to serve. Paula couldn't help feeling a little smug about the fact that she seemed to be picked to serve in the Lounge more often than any of the others. And although she couldn't ask, and he certainly wouldn't say, she had a feeling that Brother Davis was proud of her. Often when one of the men finished with her and she stood up to wipe herself, she would see him keeping an eye on her from across the room. Once they became novices however, he would no longer be in charge of them. And Paula felt a tingle of excitement at the thought that then he might take her himself a bit more often.

Her reflections were interrupted by the sound of a horse's hooves catching her up. She looked around and realised that she had got a long way ahead of the group. Unusually Brother Harris was in charge today instead of Brother Davis. He was a thickset, dark man with a quick temper and a hard whip hand. To her surprise he didn't keep pace with her but pulled in front and reined in. She stopped and looked up at him.

"We're going to see just how fast you can really run Number Three. Hold your hands out."

She obeyed automatically but was puzzled by his uncharacteristic good humour. He was grinning as he dismounted and approached her. Using a long rein he tied her wrist restraints together and then tied the other end to the pommel of his saddle. Paula looked on in dismay but didn't dare say anything.

He remounted without even looking at her and put his heels to his horse. At first it was just a walk. Then it was a trot and finally it was a canter. Paula ran as she had never run before but the fact that her arms were tied in front of her made it doubly difficult to keep up. Brother Harris looked back and laughed as he pulled his horse away from the route the other girls were taking, the way back to the monastery.

Through sweat blurred vision Paula saw that they were going even farther out into the estate than they had been before. Already her breath was rasping in her burning lungs and her legs pumped desperately. And still he pulled her farther away from the monastery.

At last, inevitably, she couldn't keep it up and fell headlong with a despairing wail. Her arms were wrenched cruelly as she pitched forward, hit the ground and was dragged along over grass and mud until Brother Harris reined in. She lay still, panting and gasping while he dismounted and came back to her. Her nipples were aching from having been dragged violently across the ground and the whole of her breast flesh felt bruised.

Suddenly a line of white hot pain exploded across her shoulders and there was a dry Crack! as if a pistol had been fired. Paula's body reacted with an involuntary arching of the back and she saw him reeling in the long horsewhip, preparing to lash her again. It was the heaviest whip she had ever experienced, the pain and the weight of the blow had left her breathless. She had become well used to the crop but grimly she realised that she was in for a totally new kind of flogging. She got her arms under her and began to rise but another lash cracked down and this time the whip curled round her ribs and bit into the soft flesh at the side of her breast where it hung beneath her. She cried out and flattened herself against the ground again in an instinctive attempt to shield herself. But the next lash had her desperately rolling away and trying to rise again. Brother Harris had moved round to stand at her head, and it was laid down her back, parallel to the spine and buried itself deep in the crack between her buttocks. The long braided cord snaked into the secret crevices of her body and tore into the soft flesh of her sex lips. It made her shriek and frantically try to get her legs under her. But Harris gave her no chance to rise on her own. He pounced on her and deliberately hooked his fingers into her nipple rings to haul her up. She screamed again as the tender pink nipples were wrenched away from her body and she shot to her feet faster than she believed possible. He kept pulling up though, so that she had to dance up onto tiptoe to try and stop the pain. Only then did he speak.

"There's only a few days left Number Three to make quite sure that you know you are nothing except what we allow you to be."

" Master!" Paula cried desperately, "I know I am nothing! Really I do!"

"Father Burton wants to make absolutely sure."

He released his agonising grip on her and returned to his horse, urging it back into a trot. Paula staggered after him, trying hopelessly to galvanise her aching legs into action again.

The next time she fell, he dragged her for much longer before he stopped. Paula knew what was coming this time but had only got up as far as knees and elbows before he whipped her again. And again he went for her breasts to start with, they swayed invitingly beneath her body, Paula knew, but there was no help for it. She had to get up. But two lashes in quick succession which made them judder had her helplessly folding her arms under her to protect them. Too late she realised that this left her haunches raised and once again the whip cracked down between her legs. Instantly her anus and the entrance at her belly were engulfed in fire. She curled herself into a ball and squeezed her thighs tight shut but still the whip found its way between her buttocks and she stretched out in agony. But Harris obviously knew just how much to inflict and coiling the whip he hauled her up by her hair this time. Pain and exhaustion made her slow to focus her eyes on his face. He left her for a few minutes. She was shaking and crying and it took some time before she was ready to face any more. Once she had got her breath back, she tried begging him for mercy, but he just smiled and put his heels to his horse again.

Father Burton and Brother Davis stood at the window of the Father's office and looked down into the courtyard. Paula's group were being herded in at the end of their run. The naked girls either collapsing or standing bent over with hands on knees while they recovered enough to be led away to the showers.

Brother Davis's brow creased. "There's only nine Father."

"I know," Father Burton replied and then paused for a second. "Brother, you have done your usual fine job with the new intake, but I am concerned about Number Three. I have watched her carefully, and from the very first she has held herself differently from the usual sluts. While the Church has been running this programme I have come to know how sullen and defiant they can be to start with. And how they slouch until they are trained not to. But this one is different."

"I know what you mean Father. She has pride."

"Exactly. And whoever heard of a street whore with pride? But what's worse is that she still has it. And as you know, they must be stripped of all traces of their previous selves before the Church can construct their new characters. This is what the Patriarch teaches us."

"She is very obedient Father."

"Hmm. Have you ever before seen a slut go through her purification without at least one thorough chastisement?

Have you ever known one avoid being displayed in the pillory, or never having had to wear the training harness?"

"I think Father. . . . .I think she takes pride in her obedience."

"That cannot be tolerated. I have given orders that she will have a special regime between now and the end of the month. She is to be pushed to her limits."

"She can take it Father. In her own way she's as hot a little slut as any of them."

"She'll have to be Brother. I have been told that the Patriarch himself is to visit us soon. And I will have nothing go amiss."

"No Father."

At that moment Brother Harris rode in beneath them. The horse was walking now. At the end of the leading rein Paula was being dragged full length through the dirt. She was streaked with mud and grass stains but even through the dirt the livid welts left by Brother Harris's whip could clearly be seen.

Father Burton smiled bleakly, " It has begun."

Paula had crawled on hands and knees to the shower and let the water cascade over her. Brother Harris watched her silently and all too soon made her dry herself and go to prayers with the others. For the first time in weeks taking the four strokes of the crop before supper was a major ordeal. The horsewhip had been applied, she realised, with just this in mind. Sister Lavinia made her spread her legs a little wider so that the tender skin on the insides of her buttocks which bore the marks of that earlier beating, could get the full force of the cuts. She yelped and cried at each lash, wriggling so much that Sister threatened her with extra ones if she didn't keep still.

She wasn't exercised with the others. Instead she

was put in the pillory and left there until all the others were chained for the night. She just couldn't understand what she was being punished for. Tears of self pity stung her eyes as she shifted uncomfortably, the wood clamping her neck and wrists was tight around her collar and restraints. Her striped back and buttocks felt horribly exposed and at least two of the brothers had taken the opportunity to deliver stinging smacks as they passed. If she had broken any rules she would have expected punishment and accepted it as necessary. But she had always tried to be obedient. Her thoughts ran on and on, but got her nowhere.

At long last she was allowed out. But she was shoved sraight into her cell and chained tightly for the night before she had had a chance to answer the call of nature. She tugged hopelessly at her chain but it had been deliberately shortened by over a foot. There was no way she could reach her toilet.

The result was inevitable and the brother who woke her the next morning made sure everyone knew. Paula wanted to dig herself a hole and pull it in after her as he yelled insults at her and told the whole group what she had done. She was given an extra stroke of the crop before breakfast and could see the smirks on her companions' faces. It was worse than anything she had ever known. Even the day of Contemplation after they had been ringed hadn't been so awful. At least all of them had been tortured and humiliated together. Now she was being singled out for no apparent reason and she felt terribly isolated. She was made to scrub the floor of her cell while the others were harnessed for the fields, but Brother Harris left her in no doubt that she would wish she had been able to go with them. She was to have another Contemplation Day, on her own.

She was marched to the Punishment Wing and waiting for her was Brother Davis. For some reason the most horrible moment of all was when Brother Harris told him how she had wet the floor of her cell in the night. She could feel her face flaming bright red as she looked down at the floor.

However when he took charge of her he seemed businesslike and not spiteful or gloating. Her heart swelled with gratitude towards him as he led her to where she was to be imprisoned for the day and she tried her hardest to obey his orders instantly. She was taken to a large room this time, in the middle of which two thick wooden posts stood. They were set about four feet apart and to the bases of these her ankles were first attached. After them her wrists were fastened to her ankles so that she was bent over in the classic position for punishment aimed at the buttocks. But Davis was far from finished. He went to where a whole range of chains were hung and picked four fine ones with clips on the ends. Paula couldn't restrain a groan when he fastened two of them to her labia rings and the other two to her nipple rings.

"I didn't tell you to make any comment. I'll punish you for it in a moment."

He yanked down hard on the chains to her breasts and Paula had to bite her lip to prevent any sound escaping. He too was obviously bent on punishing her for whatever reason. The chains were clipped to her ankle restraints at such a tension that her breasts were extended into curiously pointed shapes. Apart from the pain, she was terrified of the metal rings being pulled with agonising slowness through the flesh and tearing free. He did the same with her labia rings, pulling until there was a burning ache deep in her sex.

"Don't worry. They won't tear," he told her. He went back to where he had got the chains from and returned with a ball gag. It wrenched her mouth wide open and blocked it to the point of making her panic, but she found that if she kept calm she could breathe just freely enough. She knew she was facing a whole day tied in this posture and didn't think it could get any worse but as a finishing touch Brother Davis passed a steel bar behind her head. It slotted into holes in the posts and passed through the ring at the back of her collar, pulling her head up so that she had to look ahead of her. Then he squatted down in front of her and looked her in the eye.

"You are nothing. Do you understand that Number Three?"

She tried to nod.

"It doesn't matter in the slightest to me or any of your masters whether we make you scream with pain or pleasure. We will whip you for any reason we like. And we will go on doing it until you learn that in the eyes of the Church of Ultimate Purification you are nothing."

She tried again to nod her understanding.

"Over the next few days we will see. And if we think you haven't learned that, then you will go back to the beginning and do the whole month again."

She tried frantically to shake her head.

"Oh yes you will," he said. "And the first thing I will do is flay every square inch of skin off your back." He stood up and she was left to stare straight ahead of her, aghast at his words. But still he hadn't finished. He unslung the whip he carried from his belt and showed it to her. It was a simple, single leather lash but the handle was in the shape of a very large phallus.

"Now I'm going to punish you. And then I'll leave this for whoever wants to use it on you."

He went behind her and gave her six lashes. Her buttocks were already badly marked from Brother Harris's whipping and Sister Lavinia's crop, but he didn't let that bother him. Her eyes bulged and she made hopeless muffled whimpers into her gag as he set to work.

Her position meant that her buttocks were drawn

very tight and her sex was blatantly exposed. The whip cracked across its lips which were drawn open by the rings and it stung maddeningly at the pink flesh of the inner lips. He didn't let the lash wrap round her hips but played it full and accurately right on her bottom. Each stroke landed heavily on the already crimson skin where the crop had left its narrow ridges. She would have howled the house down if she could, but even that relief was denied her. And any movement whatever was impossible, she couldn't even wriggle, she just had to absorb each burst of pain and wait for it to build, lash by lash until her whole body was ablaze. When he had finished he simply shoved the whiphandle deep into her vagina and left the lash to trail down between her legs. Then with a final admonition to think about his words he left her.

The pain of having the phallus rammed violently into her dry channel at first eclipsed the fires raging across her bottom, but as it dulled the pains merged and became indistinguishable. The whole area of her loins throbbed and hurt. And to make it worse she was acutely aware of how lewdly she was exposed to anyone coming into the room. She was bent right over, obviously well whipped and the lash hanging down from her wrenched open sex announced quite plainly that she was there for more if anyone wanted to administer it.

Time passed with agonising slowness, and in the silence she distracted herself from the discomfort by trying to understand why they were doing this to her. Once again they had humiliated her beyond anything she could have imagined. But why? She had submitted to them, she had been beaten and she had taken it. She had been raped again and again and she had opened herself obediently. There had even been some perverse pleasure in the arrogant way the sexes of her masters had plunged into her wide open mouth and sex. Once again tears of self pity sprang into her eyes when she remembered how she had been so proud of her obedience, of taking so many men in her mouth that night in the Lounge. At that she felt the first stirrings of warmth in her belly and the discomfort in her vagina eased as it lubricated around the leather shaft which was stuffing it.

Her thoughts were rudely broken into by the door crashing open, and Brother Gibson entered with one of the initiates. They ignored her totally and she watched as the girl shed the little dress which Paula so coveted, peeled down the thong back knickers and stepped out of her shoes. She was a shapely brunette with high, well rounded breasts. When she was naked she adopted the position which Paula had seen adopted by all the senior girls when in the presence of a master. She parted her legs, put her hands behind her back and looked down.

"Father Burton has decreed that as you are to go out into the world to continue our work in a few days," Brother Gibson told her, "you are to spend today in contemplation of all you have learned here. Above all you will think of your absolute obedience to the laws laid down by the Church."

"Yes Brother. I will do so gladly," the girl replied.

Paula watched in fascination as the girl was mounted for her period of contemplation. Her labia rings were clipped like Paula's but the chains were run up to her nipples and clipped to the rings there. Further chains were clipped to her nipples but left hanging for the moment. The girl held out her wrists without having to be told and even smiled at Brother Gibson as he clipped her restraints to heavy chains which hung from pulleys in the ceiling. The brother went over to a crank handle set in the wall and turned it until the girl was hauled up by her wrists so that her feet dangled two feet off the floor. She let out a gasp as her weight came onto her arms and stretched her body so that the chains from her sex to her breasts became taut. But as Paula watched the brother now clipped the chains from her breasts onto her wrist restraints, pulling them up and increasing the tension from her labia. As the girl was hanging directly in front of Paula, she could see how the lips were being yanked brutally upwards and apart so that she could see the pink gash of her sex.

Brother Gibson pushed a small platform under the gilr's feet and watched as she scrabbled for it and found relief from her suspension by being able to stand on tiptoe. But to her horror Paula had seen that the top of the platform was covered in metal spikes. Once again she felt that strange admiration for the Church's ability to refine and prolong torment. The girl could relieve the pain in her arms, breasts and belly by standing; but only until the spikes threatened to puncture the skin under her toes. Then she would have to let herself swing again until the pain became too bad and she would have to swap it for the slow pain in her feet. And as the day wore on, Paula could see that she would have to swap more often and eventually she would probably have to let the spikes drive into her. Then each pain would be as bad as the other.

The brother came to stand just to one side of the girl and began to stroke his fingers along the tender flesh between her open lips. Paula's mouth went dry as she watched them rub and circle the little bud of her clitoris, making it swell and engorge despite the girl's plight. In only a few minutes she heard the girl groan and sigh. The flesh of her sex was now glistening with juice and the hand of her tormentor went on working at it. Eventually she gave a despairing gasp and let herself swing. Immediately she opened her legs and Paula saw Brother Gibson's hand probe into her hole. Her own vagina responded as she watched his fingers disappear into the girl and then withdraw, shiny and slick. She could even catch the musky scent of the girl's arousal as she swung by her arms and tried to grip her thighs around his questing hand. He laughed softly and pulled the hand away. The girl moaned desolately.

"Not yet my girl. Not for a long time yet." He ran his hand over the smooth swell of her hips and round behind to her buttocks. "You can have the whip later. I promise."

Then he turned to Paula. "But this one needs it now I think." He removed her gag and held the fingers which had probed into the other girl in front of Paula's mouth and she didn't need telling. He wouldn't put them into her mouth though, he made her lick at them, curling her tongue round them one at a time until he was satisfied and replaced the gag. The pungent taste of arousal and the cruelty she had witnessed had set waves of heat spreading throughout Paula and she could hardly feel the shaft of the whiphandle, so open had her channel become. Brother Gibson moved behind her and pulled it out making her cry out in shock.

"Well now, that's better," he said, "nicely lubricated. The sight of discipline's getting you good and hot. A real slave at last maybe. And that's what we need Number Three, slaves for the Church."

And then he whipped her. This time the lashes were directed at the tops of her thighs. The pain in her sex as the whip slammed across her lips which were not only pulled open now but peeled apart and engorged by excitement, made her try to bounce up and down on her imprisoned feet. It was the only movement she could make in response to the flashes of agony. Each remorseless Smack! echoed round the room just a split second before her agonised but muffled screams and sent wave after wave of bright pain lancing through her. Paula could tell by the way he took his time between each lash that he was enjoying every second of his power to whip the helpless sex in front of him.

And at last it all became clear to her. He didn't care about her pain. All he was doing was taking his pleasure. He could fuck her or flog her as much as he liked. Beyond being a body which gave him those options; she was simply nothing.

She was here to be a slave. A slave to the teachings of this Church, which put men in Mastery over her. A slave could have no pride in her slavery. She could have no feelings except those she was allowed to have. If she was punished, it didn't matter that there was no reason. She was helpless in the face of whatever they wanted to do to her.

Smack! Yet another lash whipped across her lips and as she understood at last the depths of the submission required of her, a surge of arousal swept up inside her. The day of her ringing had only taught her a part of what she needed to understand. Pleasure and pain were the masters' to bestow, she had understood that. But now she knew she had to abandon herself entirely. She only existed at all in order to have them bestowed on her.

Smack! Another lash and with the pain, another wave of heat.

Yes! She thought, it doesn't matter! I don't matter! Whip me brother, whip me as much as you like. I am nothing except what you make me. .

Smack! And this time she tried to push herself up to meet the pain and expose herself more eagerly. But now the pain was triggering the most powerful waves of sensual pleasure she had ever experienced. And they fed on her knowledge of her own willingness to open herself to anything which was required of her.

Smack! Another surge of exquisitely mixed pain and pleasure made her wrench at her shackles and she longed to be able to tell Brother Gibson all she now understood.

Smack! Paula found herself becoming almost dizzy with delight at her own submission and realised that she was going to come. Her sex was responding more eagerly to this pain than it had ever done to any other stimulation.

The whipping stopped and Paula groaned into her gag. She could feel the swollen and livid lips of her sex quivering in anticipation of an orgasm more strange and more devastating than she had ever had before. She had to experience it! But instead she felt the brother's fingers find their way into her soaking entrance, she moaned in despair as he ignored her clitoris and withdrew from her. Another lesson. She would only be allowed to come when they wanted her to. And the pleasure of that realisation itself only heightened the urgency in her belly.

Brother Gibson wiped his fingers dismissively on her back, replaced the whiphandle in her vagina checked her bonds were still good and tight, and then he left and Paula's torture was complete. She was almost fainting with the need for something or someone to move in her channel, to stimulate her the way only a male shaft could. But although impaled on a phallus, she couldn't move.

10.

From time to time during that agonising day, one or other of the brothers would look in on the tortured girls. Paula had to endure in silence. Although her vagina felt full it was desperate for the release of an orgasm. And added to the almost physical ache in her sex, there was the very real pain of her bondage.

The initiate who suffered with her at least had no gag and could moan as the see saw of pains grew slowly worse.

At last Brothers Harris and Gibson entered.

Brother Harris attended to Paula. And it was a very

different Paula now. He wrenched the whip out of her and commented to his companion that it looked as though the slut was truly tamed to judge by how she had juiced all over the handle. But then, to Paula's relief he began her final whipping. It was a savage one and she was grateful for it.

He removed her gag before he began and she was able to ease the ache in her stiff jaw muscles.

"I'm going to give you a real thrashing now," he said. "And we'll see if you've learned your lesson. How many lashes shall I give you Number Three?"

"Master. I will be glad to take as many as you please to give me." She replied without hesitation.

"Good answer. I think we'll just see how many you can take."

Once again he played the whip over the tender flesh of her lips where they pushed back towards him from between her thighs. She could feel now how swollen and open they were but only wished she was free to expose them even more for him. She was eager for the stinging bite of the leather lash, knowing it would finally unleash the storms of pleasure which were dammed up inside her.

At first there was only the excitement of the echoing Smack! ricocheting around the room and the bitter pain knifing through her, but after only three hard lashes she felt herself transported by the pain and the cruelty. She loved being able to gasp and cry at each blow now, knowing it would increase his pleasure in whipping her. The fires in her belly began to glow with white heat. She felt floods of sweet juices release inside her and yelled all the more as the blows became harder. He must be able to see how juicy I am, she thought. I'm pulled wide open and I must be running with the stuff.

It was a real thrashing by now. The whip rained lashes down on her and she was past caring. He didn't wait for the effects of each one to register, and she could picture his face alive with the joy of beating her. Faster and faster the lashes came and wilder and wilder became the swirling chaos of joy in her whole being. Until finally an explosion of colour, sensation and emotion went off somewhere deep in her belly. She shrieked and went rigid in her bonds while her vagina went into helpless spasms. And at last the whip changed direction, cracking down vertically and slicing along the open slit of her sex to push her over the edge and into unconsciousness.

When she came round, at first all she could hear was the whip still being plied. A girl was screaming and it must be her she thought. But then she realised she was lying on the floor and the most delicious sense of fulfillment pervaded her aching body. She knew now that she loved the burning traces her masters' whips left on her. She opened her eyes and saw the initiate being whipped.

Brother Gibson had kicked away the platform and the girl was swinging freely as she writhed and screamed. Paula watched transfixed as the screams became moans and her body's gyrations at the end of its chain became more languid and sensual. And at last each lash was greeted with a breathless cry of pleasure and Paula saw her sex gleaming with the nectar of her arousal. When the lash began to curl round her taut breasts the cries begame more urgent and finally they reached a climax which sent ripples spasming through the whole length of her tortured body. And only when the girl hung motionless did they take her down to lie sobbing and gasping at the feet of her masters.

Brother Harris attached a lead to Paula's collar and led her back to the cells on all fours. She no longer cared. The humiliation meant nothing to her any more. In fact she would be grateful if they gave her permission to enjoy it.

There was nothing they couldn't do.

The rest of her group were having supper, he told her when she was back in her cell. There was food by her bed but before she ate that. . . he didn't finish his sentence but simply undid his trousers.

Paula wasn't surprised. She knew by the heat in her bottom and thighs just how much of a thrashing she had taken and how much he would have enjoyed giving it to her. It was only fair, she thought, as she knelt up and began to lick carefully up along the ridge of his shaft. As she let the shining purple head caress her cheek and felt the hardness of his erection in her hand, Paula knew that she would feel no pride now when he emptied himself into her, just the satisfaction of having had a master pay her enough attention to enjoy her. And she owed him a debt of gratitude, he had taken the time to give her a really good thrashing.

Very carefully she let her lips and tongue tease and stroke his member. She tried to blot out any pleasure she felt and concentrate solely on his. At last she felt him grip her head and give a gutteral moan. She rubbed her tongue quickly against the sensitive spot on the underside of the head and then held him tightly as he bucked against her grunting with the effort of ramming himself into her. Eagerly she swallowed the warm fluid jetting into her throat and relished the taste of maleness. It was the taste of the Master who would use her at his pleasure and into whose absolute power she now gave herself. She went on licking at him long after he had finished pumping himself into her, working at the shrinking sex to make quite sure it was clean. The image of Sister Lavinia kneeling in front of the policeman the night she was captured, came back to her. Now she understood why she had taken so long about cleaning him.

And of course she understood what Sister Lavinia had told her in the Games Room. Of course she would welcome a thrashing now, and enjoy it.

"Good. I think you're going to be alright Number Three." Harris said as Paula regretfully allowed his sex to slip free of her lips. "But you will be required in the Games Room soon. You may eat now and then wait."

He left her and Paula calmly ate her food, then sat on her bed and awaited whatever would come her way.

Four of the brothers came for her.

They unlocked her cell and entered. Suddenly four big men in her tiny cell made Paula feel very small. It was an exciting feeling. They crowded round and towered above her. She tried to adopt the position she had seen the initiate take, earlier in the day. But one of them gave her the order to turn right round. She did so slowly and parted her hands to allow them to see the devastation her repeated whippings had brought to her backside. A cool, strong pair of hands fondled her buttocks.

"She takes a good bit of punishment. Mind you she looks strong enough."

One of the men moved round to stand in front of her. He reached down and felt the long muscles of her thighs. "These could take you for a good ride brothers!" he said. Paula kept her gaze averted downwards and accepted all the comments as nothing but compliments paid to a mechanism which was suited to their purposes. She watched the man's hands move up her thighs and grasp the rings at her sex. He pulled at them, opening her as she had been most of the day. "I think I'll try in here first, and then see what the rest of her's like."

He moved away behind her and another man took his place. This one was interested in her breasts. He took them in his hands and held them as if to weigh them, then rolled his hands round them and pulled at her nipples. With a shock Paula recognised him as the brother who had pierced her there. She couldn't help a little gasp at the sharp pain. At once she was sure she would be punished but there was only laughter. "Come on then brothers, let's get started," the one who had pierced her said.

They pulled her arms round behind her back and took her wrists up to between her shoulder blades before fastening them, and then pulled a short chain tight between the back of her collar and her wrists. This made her arch her back and display her breasts. But with her head pulled back it made walking difficult. She stumbled several times on the way into the house and up the stairs to the Games Room. She heard noise and laughter coming from the Lounge as they turned into the last corridor and then into the Games Room itself.

She was steered towards a corner beside the fireplace at which she had been whipped before. She was made to stand facing the wall and her legs were roughly kicked apart. Paula waited patiently, gazing at the wall in front of her. She was delighting herself with the thought that she didn't exist for them as a person, simply as a body.

The brothers continued to talk for a while and exchange comments about that body until finally she heard footsteps approach her. They came close enough for her to feel the pressure of a man's naked body against her back. Her imprisoned hands were pressed against his chest. She couldn't suppress a sharp intake of excited breath. Were all the men naked?

On the occasional nights when she hadn't fallen straight into exhausted sleep she had stirred in her bed and felt herself moisten at the memory of Brother Davis's firm muscular body pressing down onto her that very first day.

Her hands were released and she was allowed to turn around. All four of them were indeed naked. Two lounged on a large sofa and one stood against the billiard table. In a quick glance before looking down again Paula registered the ridged stomachs, the broad shoulders and strong thighs. She felt a tightness at her breasts as her nipples began to engorge and her belly turned to molten liquid. She was left in the middle of the room for a moment while the brother who had freed her went to the cupboard from which Sister Lavinia had selected her whip. But when he returned he wasn't holding a whip. Instead he held the largest dildo Paula had ever seen or could have imagined. It was sheathed in leather which had been worn smooth. But it was the sheer size which riveted her gaze. Its massive head was even equipped with a representation of the slit which a real phallus would have and she could see how the veins on the shaft had been carved under the leather sheath, but surely no vagina could accommodate that monster. He thrust it at her. "Masturbate with this." He told her.

She took hold of it with a suddenly shaky hand, her fingers couldn't come anywhere close to encompassing the shaft. The brother joined his companions and Paula felt their eyes on her.

A straightforward whipping wouldn't have bothered her in the slightest but she simply didn't know whether it was possible for her to do what she had been ordered to do. But she knew that once again she was being tested.

She gazed down at the shiny hemisphere of the huge head and felt her vagina begin to dry and contract. Paula risked one more glance at the brothers and noted that their sexes were beginning to wake and throb towards erection, and she noticed too the corded muscles of their arms which wielded the whips so powerfully. Those whips which had taught her so much about herself and which now took her farther than she had ever believed possible. But now she had to inflict on herself more than she believed she could take.

Standing alone, she opened her legs wider and

began.

11.

The thought of how shamelessly she was exposing herself to the impassive gazes of her masters came to her rescue. As she looked down her body she saw her nipples begin to harden again and slowly the fires in her belly began to smoulder once more.

Paula held the phallus in one hand and reached for her crotch with the other. As she bent her head forward to look down between her breasts, her hair fell in curtains around her face. Irritably she flicked it back and bent again, this time pushing her pelvis forward as she settled her legs even wider apart.

In her far off and long abandoned previous life she had only ever masturbated a few times. Boyfriends had not usually been scarce, and on those few occasions she had played with herself in the dark privacy of her bed. But now she put the fingers of her free hand between her lips and parted them as wide as she could before beginning to stroke her clitoris. She took her time, swirling her finger tips around it and then letting them trail over it lightly. She felt how it nestled in its protective folds of soft flesh and teased it into thrusting up and then again pulled herself as wide open as she could for her audience. She knew she was wet and wanted the men to see how her sex flesh was responding. Now she rubbed her hand hard down over the firm little nub, making herself gasp as a jolt of delicious pleasure ran tingling through her. Then she dragged the fingers up over it again and tilted her hips as she splayed her lips wide once more to show off the glistening moisture which was starting to flow from her sex and dampen her pubes.

She found herself longing to see if her labia were really as full and open as they felt to her. They felt even more soft and compliant as she let her thoughts turn to how they had been whipped over the last day. With a moan she put her head back and reached even farther under herself to put a finger into her hole and begin to work it, stirring the floods of her musky nectar. She reached again and put three fingers in but groaned in frustration that she couldn't get them farther up. Her channel was quivering with eagerness to grip a thrusting shaft. But she wouldn't let it; not yet.

Although she was completely absorbed and now desperate to test her body with the enormous phallus she held, a part of her still wanted to display her arousal yet more blatantly. She brought her head forward, not caring about her hair swirling in dischevelled waves around her face and craned her neck down as far as she could. Her hips bucked of their own accord as she pressed her hand brutally hard to her frantically erect pleasure bud. The ripple of joy which ran through her made her legs tremble and she groaned again as she slowly brought her hand back along the crease between her lips until her fingers emerged, soaking and shining with the juice which flooded her.

Through half closed eyes she saw four throbbing erections jutting towards her and wanted to feel all of them find their release in her body in any way they chose. She hardly noticed her hands join to grip the enormous shaft and bring it to her entrance. But once it was there she pushed up and let out a cry of astonished delight as she felt herself open wider than she had ever done before. But even then there was a moment's pure agony which only sent fresh torrents of arousal crashing through her as the head stretched and tested her to the limit. And then it was in.

Paula's legs felt as though they would give way before the explosion of pleasure which engulfed her as the shaft pushed up and pressed against every millimetre of tissue in her channel, and still there was more to get in. She moved her hands down and pushed again, and again her body took it in. It felt as if it would spear into her very stomach but one last time she reached down and pushed, bucking her hips to draw it in and let it do its worst. She felt the walls of her vagina eagerly gripping the monstrous intruder and with a grimace of ecstasy she began to move it with her hands now only holding the leather scrotum, so completely had she taken it in. It only took a few thrusts, the hungry sucking noises her sex made as she withdrew it and then pushed it back up bore witness to her approaching climax. All at once she couldn't hold the slow rhythm and began urgent little stabs upwards right at its fullest penetration. From a long way off she heard her own voice crying out at each thrust and felt her vagina go into wild spasms while every muscle in her stomach writhed and rippled. She felt herself stagger helplessly and then at last a billow of utter joy brought her crashing to the floor and she curled around the shaft which impaled her while her body shook and twisted under the wave after wave of orgasm which ripped through her. For a long time afterwards echoes and aftershocks ran through her and she was helpless to do anything other than lie in an exhausted huddle, still with the phallus deep inside her.

It felt as if an entire part of her body was being sucked out when a hand reached between her legs and pulled it out of her. She cried out in shock and rolled onto her back, only to find the brother who had put her rings in lowering himself onto her. He had no need to do anything other than push himself straight into her. Although she had contracted sharply when he had emptied her, she was so moist and had been stretched so far that he slid in and was thrusting up before she fully knew what was happening. Her display had obviously met with their approval because he was in a hurry for his release. Paula lifted her hips to meet each thrust and groaned in pure luxurious pleasure as she felt her channel once again grip eagerly at a shaft and jolts of stimulation began to run through her. She flung her arms round his broad back and pulled him down onto her, urging him on to ream her out harder. It was against the rules for her to speak but she was past caring now. His thrusts became faster and she arched her back as his pelvis slammed into her and she felt him begin to pump. The feel of the hot sperm flooding so deep inside her triggered another devastating orgasm which kept her bowed up off the floor and she matched him cry for cry as he pounded the last of his strength into her.

She was given no time to recover. As soon as he rolled off her, she was hauled to her feet and half carried over to the sofa. The brother who was supporting her had his arms under her shoulders and his hands were already gripping her breasts and pulling hard enough at her nipples for the pain to clear her head a little. It was just enough for her to see what was required next. One of the brothers lay full length in front of her, his sex rearing up stiffly.

Paula knelt quickly above him and reached down between her legs to grip his shaft and steer it straight into her gaping entrance. He grasped her hips and began his thrusts immediately, just as urgent as his predecessor. She rode him easily, her body finding the rhythm instinctively. At times only the head of his member was in her and she could feel her lips fluttering desperately to try and grip him. Then she was grinding herself down against him as he pushed up and she made mewing noises of joy as she felt him spear up into her depths. Vaguely she was aware of his hands reaching up and cupping her breasts so she pressed forward and leaned her whole weight against them. He trapped her nipples between his fingers and squeezed. With her own hands she pressed his, urging him to squeeze harder and arching her back to offer them up better.

But suddenly there was a hand in her hair and her head was turned to the side. Right in her face was another rigid sex imperiously demanding her body. She reached out with one hand and put it behind the man, feeling the hard muscle of his buttock and pulling him towards her. Her mouth opened and she felt the long shaft push in for her throat.

Paula fell into a sort of delirium. She was being fucked at both ends and her body was already in a kind of overdrive. Effortlessly it matched the rhythms of the two sexes. In a daze Paula felt her body urge them on, her vagina sucking at the shaft which filled it, her mouth licking and sucking as well. Finally the man under her shifted his grip back to her hips and began to buck faster and faster. At the same time she heard the man who was using her mouth give a hoarse shout and then they were both pumping. Desperately afraid she would faint from sheer joy Paula hung on to the buttocks of the man who was now filling her mouth with hot salty fluid. She tried to moan as yet another orgasm exploded inside her and this time her whole body seemed to be a firework going off in silent bursts of light and heat, but she spluttered on the sperm being pumped into her mouth while down below yet more sperm seemed to be spurting up to meet it. A sudden cataclysmic shaft of sensual short cicuit transfixed her as the man beneath arched his back in one final spurt and she went into spasm once more while still trying to swallow and cry out at the same time.

She slid sideways down onto the floor as the man who had been in her mouth withdrew. She lay trying to get her breathing back under control, swallowing and gasping by turns. She could feel sperm on her cheeks and chin from where she had spluttered and choked at the moment of her climax. She wiped at her face and licked her fingers, reluctant to waste any of the precious fluid. If she was punished for spilling it in the first place, she wouldn't be surprised and the prospect of further whipping no longer frightened her. From between her legs she could feel sticky trails begin to find their way out of her body. Her blood pounded through her veins and she felt as if there was no strength left in her limbs. She couldn't even stir or groan when she felt powerful hands under her shoulders and she was lifted groggily to her feet.

Blearily she focused her eyes on the face of the fourth brother. He smiled at her.

"Now it's my turn."

He took her over to the billiards table and bent her over it. She was grateful for the support it gave her under her torso. She wasn't sure her legs would take her weight. Every now and then she could feel a ripple run through her muscles as the recent earthquakes in her body still rumbled faintly. Her sex stung and burned her where it had been so violently treated over the last twenty four hours but never had she felt so completely used. And this left a warm feeling in her belly. She had been a creature of pure sexuality.

She rested her cheek on the baize of the table's surface and ignored the slight tickling it caused at the tips of her breasts. Whatever was coming next she wanted it, and she concentrated on relaxing so as to be ready.

The door opened behind her. It must have been a girl bringing a tray in from the Lounge because she heard drinks being poured and then the door closed again. The fourth brother came to stand behind her. He had positioned her with her legs wide open and now began to explore her with his hand. She was still slick with her own fluids as well as those of the other two men who had taken her there. His hand ran slowly up her slit, just touching her throbbing clitoris before moving up again and gently pushing into her hole. Although it was tender, she was so slick that his fingers slid in and she stirred and sighed in pleasure as they felt their way up into her. She was disappointed when he withdrew them but waited patiently for further probings. When they came however she couldn't help herself from starting violently. His fingers began to force themselves into her back passage.

When he felt her jerk in surprise he put his other hand on her back to hold her down. Paula bit her lip but subsided. She had never been taken in the rear before and she fretted that she wouldn't be big enough. If it hurt she didn't care, just so long as she could take this Master there, if that was what he wanted of her.

He calmly delved back into her sex and Paula felt herself begin to tighten around his fingers as her anxiety deepened. He felt her contract round his fingers and laughed. "I'd heard that it looked like no-one had been up that way. Not many sluts we get in here that haven't been well used in the arse. Still, better late than never."

His hand returned to her anus and he poked his lubricated fingers into her. It was a strange feeling but Paula bore down to try and help him in. "Good girl." He said.

Then she yelped as he prised her open with the fingers of two hands. But as soon as she felt the head of his penis touch the mouth of the tight little passage she settled her legs even wider and tried to relax. However, the feeling that her flesh was being torn as he began to push made her grimace. The rending pain made her hiss between her gritted teeth. It grew worse and worse until she was sure he would never get in. But at last it peaked and was eclipsed by the relief of feeling him probing up into her stomach and beginning to stimulate the membranes which separated that passage from her vagina by pressing them towards the front vaginal wall.

Paula was delighted. Now every passage that could be open to a man was open. And she loved how the shaft of the sex seemed to touch every sensitive cell of this virgin passage as it pushed apart the tight lining. She was sighing and groaning by the time he had fully penetrated and began to withdraw. Her head jerked up in dismay as she felt him begin to do so but a breathtaking feeling of pleasure flooded through her as he emptied her tight little tunnel until only the tip of his erection was inside her. She raised herself onto tiptoes and pushed back so as not to lose him and felt her sphincter close on him, then gave a throaty cry of utter abandon as he thrust in again. But this time he reached round in front of her belly and she felt his fingers begin to toy with her clitoris just as he reached his full extent inside her. She began to shake her head in denial of just how high she was going to be taken this time. "Oh God!" She heard herself wail as he began to slowly empty her passage again while still rubbing at her furiously erect bud.

All the time he withdrew she heard herself make a strange moaning growl as entirely new pleasure centres burst into life and flooded her exhausted system with sensation. When he was held only by her sphincter once more, he stopped.

"What shall I do with you Number Three?" he asked.
"Fuck me Master!" she replied with no hestitation.
"And shall I whip you afterwards?"
Her hips were swaying desperately against him now

and she tried to remember the words.

"Yes Master! Please whip me if you like, but for pity's sake fuck me."

Quite suddenly he rammed himself all the way in and pressed his hand hard against her clitoris at the same time. She screamed. And then screamed again, every time he rammed in so hard that he slapped his hips against her. Even the peaks of ecstasy she had scaled so far that evening were revealed as being only stepping stones towards other peaks. She cried, she begged for mercy, her hands scrabbled at the baize but the tidal wave of pleasure just went on and on building. He was going to kill her if he didn't come soon she thought hazily. Time after time she felt the piston of his sex ram up into the tight cylinder of her arse and send electric shocks to every nerve in her body and meanwhile his hand worked brutally hard at her clitoris until she could hardly breathe under the constant barrage. And when her orgasm came it sent her arching up off the table as each muscle seemed to lock against its neighbour to keep her rigid while white hot paths of light blazed through her brain. But at last she felt him come and heard his final roar as he rammed her one last time then withdrew from her.

She slumped forward and darkness closed over her.

When she came to, she found she had collapsed to the floor again. Slowly she hauled herself up into a sitting position and looked around her. The brothers were dressed again. She looked longingly at their uniforms of black trousers and white T shirts with the red X on them. Now she knew what was under those clothes she wanted them all over again. She looked boldly at their faces, knowing it would probably get her punished but wanting them to know how grateful she was to them for having taken their pleasure with her. She froze in terror though when she saw Father Burton sitting quietly in an armchair over by the fireplace.

Hastily she looked down again.

She heard him rise from his seat and approach her. The hem of his dark blue robe and his shoes appeared in her field of vision. In a panic she wondered if she should kneel up or fling herself down at his feet. But it didn't seem to matter, they were talking about her and as usual ignoring her.

"Well?" She heard the Father ask. "What is the verdict?"

"She's good material Father," one of the brothers replied. "Very obedient and eager to please."

"If she had any pride left, I think it's been beaten out of her." One of the others put in. "But she'll need some trainig to rein herself in. She comes as often as it pleases her to."

"That can be attended to. But you think we've got a little whore who can be trained to serve?" The Father asked again.

Paula was trembling. This was the culmination of the testing.

"I think," it was the voice of the brother who had taken her last and most devastatingly, "I think that whatever she may have been before, she is certainly a hot little slave now who is ready to give pleasure to any man she is told to."

Oh yes, Paula thought. All I want is to be told.

"Good. And of course it is our duty to direct her submissiveness in the ways of the Church. So we'll let her be tested for a novice and see what we can make of her. Now did she incur any punishments tonight?"

"She spoke out of turn twice and was willing to accept a beating just so long as I fucked her Father." The brother who had taken her last spoke again. There was general laughter which even Father Burton joined in with. He bent down and lifted her chin so that she looked up into his intense dark eyes. He looked at her for a long time and she felt he was looking right down into the depths of her soul where he could see how desperately she now wanted to be nothing.

"I think she understands." He said finally, letting her go. "I will stay to see her beaten."

"We thought the strap would do nicely Father."

Paula heard Father Burton resume his seat while one of the brothers went to the cupboard again. She kept her eyes glued to the carpet until the brother came to stand right in front of her, a three foot, supple looking leather strap hanging from one hand.

"Kneel up and then put your head down on the floor." She did as she was told and knew what a sight she must be presenting to Father Burton. Her haunches stuck up into the air and between them the lips of her poor abused sex pouted towards him. He would probably be able to see how they were still full and open. In fact listening to the men discuss her had set her off again. And of course she was crusted with sperm from three men. As she moved she could feel it pulling at her skin, it must be caking her buttocks and inner thighs very obviously she thought. But then quite calmly she found herself thinking that they were bound to whip her there so the strap would probably get rid of it.

She pressed her forehead to the floor in front of the brother with the strap and folded her arms above her head. But that wasn't good enough. He wanted them stretched wide apart. She obeyed and realised that this was a posture of complete submission in front of a man. And to add to the arousal which that thought set off, he placed a foot on the back of her neck.

"Give her four Brother." Father Burton spoke.

The brother repeated her sentence to her adding, "and you'll count them."

Paula wished she could see herself. From where the brother was standing over her with the strap how tempting a target she must make. Her hips swelling out from her waist and the cleft of her buttocks giving him a perfect line to aim at in order to send the belt smacking down between her parted legs. She knew the pain would be excruciating and looked forward to suffering it in front of them to prove her submission.

She felt the brother's weight shift on her neck as he raised the belt.

It made a loud swooshing noise in the air over her back and exploded all along the crease of her anus and that of her sex.

"Aagh!. . . . " She thought she had been ready but the weight of the leather and its width caught her totally by surprise. It didn't single out any one part like a lash of a whip. It blasted the whole area. "One!" She managed to shriek.

Smack! " Oh God!. . . Two!" She had to fight against the desire to shut her legs tight together. The second stroke had even reached right through and dug into the hair at her pubis.

Smack! "Aaah!. . . Please! Three!" She didn't know what she was begging for. Her fingers scrabbled at the carpet and her hips waggled desperately.

"Oh No!. . . I can't . . "

Smack! "Aaah! God! Four! Please no more!" She cried and moaned under the brother's foot. She was too tender and sore to repeat the orgasm of earlier, under the whip. But she balanced perfectly between the pleasure of abasing herself so utterly and the agony of the whipping. As soon as it stopped she wished it hadn't.

The brother kept his foot on her neck while she writhed under it and Father Burton approached.

"I do not approve of profanity during a whipping. Bear that in mind next time Number Three."

"I'm sorry Master!" Suddenly she was ashamed of the fuss she had made. Hadn't these men taught her only today that this was her destiny, to be fucked or flogged and it didn't matter which.

"I.... I can take more if you want." She stammered.

There was silence for a second. The foot came off her neck and Father Burton squatted down to lift her chin again. He stared intently at her once more. Paula struggled to blink back tears and meet his eyes.

"Your enthusiasm does you credit. But I think you've taken enough for one day." He stood up, "however, there will be other days and perhaps I will take you up on that offer then."

He turned and swept out.

Paula was hauled to her feet and helped back to her cell.

12.

She fought her way up from sleep which was so deep it was practically unconsciousness. Her eyes blinked open and slowly she began to recall the momentous events of the previous day. And as she did so a comfortable warmth of well-being spread through her whole body. She knew exactly who and what she was now. And who she had really been all her life.

'A hot little slave, ready to serve any man she is told to.' That was what they had said she was last night. And how right they were.

Paula realised that she had kicked off her thin blanket in the night and now lay with her legs splayed, the cool air playing soothingly around her inner thighs, her sex and her anus. They still throbbed dully and she clung to that feeling as a further badge of her slavery. She had been whipped to an orgasm. She had masturbated openly in front of four of her masters who had then fucked her almost into oblivion and buggered her the rest of the way. And finally they had whipped her again while she knelt in complete submission at their feet.

But best of all she was going to become a novice and have the chance to go on serving the masters.

She stirred and stretched while a delicious tingle ran through her at these thoughts.

Brother Davis came to unchain her. He said nothing and she searched his face in vain for any expression. But as she climbed slowly to her feet and began to try and ease some of her stiffness, he told her that Father Burton had excused her from her breakfast beating and would allow her to work at the monastery for the morning. At the door of her cell he turned and gave her just the slightest of nods before leaving.

Paula's heart sang. What greater sign of approval could a slave hope for.

She applied another copious layer of cream to her bottom and her inner thighs, working it gently into the livid areas where individual weals had crossed each other to produce whole patches of soreness. Lastly she smoothed it along her labia and felt its healing coolness on her tender membranes. They would soon be ready for use again.

At breakfast it felt very strange and lonely to be seated on her own while her companions queued up to be beaten. She had a 'master's eye view' of obediently displayed buttocks being striped for the first time that day by the crop. The other girls glared at her as they straightened up and came to get their food. Paula longed to remind them that only yesterday she had taken an extra stroke and been publicly humiliated. Besides, the real truth was that she would rather have been taking her usual ration with them. She hadn't liked being singled out yesterday and she liked it even less today. She knew that she belonged with them now and only wanted the same treatment they got. But the rule of silence was absolute.

While the rest of the group was harnessed for the fields, Paula was set to scrubbing down the table they ate at and carrying the empty bowls and leftovers to the kitchens. Sister Lavinia stood over her all the time and went with her.

It was the first time Paula had been into the house except to be taken to the Lounge. It was a hive of activity. Gaggles of initiates were hurrying in and out of rooms talking excitedly amongst themselves. As soon as they saw Sister Lavinia though, they quietened and went past with respectfully downcast eyes. And of course the brothers spread a wave of silence in front of them wherever they went.

In the kitchens, and under the watchful eye of Brother Gibson there were novices working at cleaning up from breakfast and preparing the lunch. Here there was only such conversation allowed as was needed for work, but even so there was an air of excitement which Paula could almost taste. Her own heart pounded at the thought that in only a few hours from now she would be allowed to work here. But what was everyone else's excitement about? For the second time that day she found the rule of silence a real trial.

As she followed Sister Lavinia back towards her own familiar part of the monastery, Paula decided to accept whatever punishment it took, but she was going to have to ask what was going on. As it turned out though she didn't have to.

When they reached a quiet corridor, Sister Lavinia stopped and turned.

"Alright. I can see you're bursting to ask. I'll give you two extra strokes tonight for being inquisitive and I'll tell you." She looked at Paula and smiled.

"Yes Sister. Thank you Sister." Paula replied meekly.

"A new batch of sluts arrives tomorrow. Brother Davis and I will be collecting them tonight. But apart from that, the current novices will become initiates. However the real excitement is because every few months the initiates themselves have to move on, and they will be doing so in only a couple of days' time."

"Where do they move on to?" Paula forgot herself, "Sister... I mean."

Sister Lavinia laughed. "When you become a novice my pretty little Number Three. You become available for use by us Sisters." She reached out and ran a hand slowly down over one of Paula's breasts, letting it linger at the nipple before tweaking it playfully. Paula shivered with pleasure. "And then I think I'll punish you for that." She went on, "some of the initiates move on to monasteries where they may be needed to serve, some go out into the world to serve the Church there. The rest are sold."

Paula gaped at her and she laughed again, "Don't look so shocked. The Church needs money to carry on its work and they are a very valuable resource. The Patriarch teaches us that though we must reform the world, we still have to live in it. And they will still serve in a way."

"But. . . " Paula began.

"Enough now. As a novice you will see the sale, so be still and wait."

Paula spent the afternoon back with her group, harnessed to a harrow and pulling her weight gladly. She took her extra two strokes of the crop at the evening meal and was grateful for having after all been excused the morning beating. Although a day's rest and the cream had helped, she still writhed and swayed her hips under the lashes as they bit into the bruises left by the repeated whippings of the previous day. By the time she had taken the usual four she was gritting her teeth and sweating. For some reason the pleasure she had so recently found in her beatings deserted her. Although she was as glad as ever to proclaim her submission and bend over obediently, the fiery stinging didn't trigger the responses at her belly and remained merely satisfying rather than exciting.

However, after the fourth lash Sister Lavinia leaned over her and grasped one of her breasts which was swaying under her as she fidgeted on her toes to absorb the stinging. Paula felt the cool hand close on her flesh and looked down to see it pull at the weight of it and then roll the nipple. She continued to stimulate it until it began to harden. Paula watched as it filled and stood out then sucked her breath in sharply when she saw and felt one of the Sister's fingers hook itself into her ring.

"Remember what I said this morning. After tomorrow, I can have you whenever I want. Now you're going to dance prettily for me aren't you?"

"Yes Sister." Paula whispered, her eyes fixed on the finger in her nipple ring. Sister Lavinia began to pull downwards, slowly but persisently. Paula whimpered as the tension increased and pain began to radiate out from the delicate flesh.

"Dance nicely now, or I'll flay you every chance I get."

Paula grimaced. "Yes Sister! I promise!"

The Sister let her go and stood up. She laid the crop along a line she had already traced in the smooth skin of Paula's buttocks and moved it a little. Paula flinched, knowing that she was going to overlay the next lash and wanted her to know it. Her breast throbbed and suddenly she felt her belly begin to burn. Between her spread buttocks she knew her lips would be engorging and starting to peel open. That was all it took. A little considered cruelty and she would lap up whatever abuse was heaped on her.

She felt the crop lifted away and waited for the swishing sound it made as it descended. She heard it in time to lift herself up to meet it and gasp as the pain exploded redly. If only it was one of the brothers, she thought. But her body was responding anyway, she felt her lips quiver as Sister Lavinia laid the crop across the tops of her thighs for the last stroke and pressed it in so that the leather shaft caressed her labia. Paula's breath hissed between her teeth as she steadied herself. She felt the pressure release as the crop was lifted again and then it sliced back down. Again Paula went up on her toes to meet it and embrace the burst of hot pain. She felt her juices start to flow in earnest but it was too late. She would just have to wait.

Slowly she stood up and rubbed her bottom, letting the other woman see her fingers trail languidly across the parallel lines scored in the soft pillows of her buttocks, and turned to smile over her shoulder. Sister Lavinia returned her smile briefly and then curtly ordered her to take her place at table.

They were woken as usual the next day but after breakfast were taken to the showers. To their amazement they found there was shampoo as well as soap. In addition they were given extra time by the brothers who watched them and Paula spent it lathering her long black hair and luxuriating in the hot water flowing into her face. Today there was plenty of time to enjoy the way her skin gleamed wetly and to work the soap properly into every crevice. She looked about her at similarly gleaming bodies, several of them with legs straddled and hands working gently between them. The brothers allowed them this exhibitionism. There would be no work in the fields today. Never again, if they behaved themselves.

They were given the usual towels to dry themselves but for today there was an extra one, and when they returned to their cells they found hair dryers had been plugged in along their corridor. There were simple chairs beside them and they helped each other in turn to blow-dry and brush their hair. Paula felt better for this simple luxury than she would have believed it possible to feel. If only there was a mirror!

But she found the faces of her companions went some way to providing one. The miserable band of scruffy sluts which had arrived here was gone. In its place was a group of lean and fit girls who looked at one another with real pride. They wore rings at their breasts and sexes, all of them carried the marks of the whip and the crop; they were slaves now. But as they carefully made the most of their hair Paula knew they were all more aware of their femininity than they had ever been in their lives.

They were also aware of their guards' eyes on them

and Paula found herself, along with the rest indulging in this uniquely female ritual. She tossed her mane of hair, fluffed it with her hands and reached up to brush it so that her breasts rose and swayed invitingly. Like the others, she did it far more than was strictly necessary.

Although there was complete silence, there was complete understanding. If the guards had chosen to take them into their cells and beat them or take them, they knew they would all have submitted gratefully. They were purified at last.

13.

They were lined up outside their cells for the last time. But for the first time in weeks they were chained together as they had been in their early days, with a chain running between their legs and fastening to their wrist restraints behind them.

"You're going before Father Burton, and you'll have to prove to him that you're purified and ready to serve the Church, so you'll come before him in chains. If you let us down, then pray to God for help. Now move!" The brother in charge cracked his whip around the legs of the girl leading and suddenly the mood of excitement turned to one of apprehension.

They were turned to face their right and told to walk. It took a little practice and a few painful jerks of the chain before they got back into the swing of keeping in step. Paula couldn't help feeling a slight pang as they left their cell corridor for the last time. She had been reborn here, and reborn as someone she would never have dreamed that she really was.

They marched through corridors which were now familiar, past their dining room and the Punishment Wing but then they were turned to their left and taken into the courtyard. And here they saw Brother Davis and Sister Lavinia returning from a mission to pick up the next intake of girls off the street. There was the white van which Paula had almost forgotten, its doors were open and the girls were being taken out.

The van must have been farther afield this time because it had returned much later in the morning than it had when they had arrived. Paula's group was told to halt and they were allowed to see the huddled line of bewildered girls, gagged and cuffed, just as they themselves had been, take their first look around them. Paula exchanged knowing grins with her companions, she knew they were thinking the same as her; that they would love to be on hand to watch this lot get their first taste of real discipline and hear them squeal.

They were allowed to watch until Brother Davis had herded them to the Pen and then they were taken on into the house itself. They entered by a large, imposing door through which they had never been before and found themselves at the back of the main hall

Normally they either went down from here to the small chapel for prayers or, in the evening they were taken upstairs to the Lounge. But today they were taken down a long passage on the ground floor and at last ushered into a huge drawing room with a stone vaulted ceiling. Here they were halted once again. They were unchained from each other but their hands were kept locked together behind them. Their guards had them kneel down and shuffle on their knees until they were face to face with the wall on the left of the room.

Paula could smell the faintly musty odour of old stone as her face touched it and felt its cold strike into her breasts as they too made contact. In front of, and slightly above each girl was an iron ring from which hung two slender chains and Paula noted that each chain had an alligator clip at each end.

They were told to part their thighs and one of the brothers began to run another chain along the line. It was anchored to a further ring set at one end of the line and at the height of their loins. He set about passing it through both of the rings which hung from each girl's labia. He took his time and repaid them for their flirtatiousness earlier. He let his fingers stray as he reached round each of them and parted their lips to stroke and flick at each clitoris until he had made it erect and eager for more. Then he moved on leaving the girl to moan quietly and contemplate an arousal for which there was no fulfillment.

He took a sadistic delight in taking Paula higher than the others. He reached further round under her belly and pushed his fingers up into her as well as rubbing at her helplessly swelling clitoris. He kept on until she was good and moist, her face pressed against the stone and her eyes closed to concentrate on what pleasure she could get from this teasing.

Sudddenly she felt him put his lips close to her ear and whisper. "You're reckoned to be the hottest one we've got my lovely. So don't go thinking it's all over once you're a novice." He pulled the chain tight between her rings and moved on.

She managed to stifle the groan of disappointment which welled up in her throat as he pulled his fingers out of her and thought instead about the implied threat in his words. She didn't expect it to be 'all over' once she was a novice. She would have been desolate if she thought it was. If she had been allowed to speak she would have told him that she welcomed any further challenge.

When the chain had been fed along the line their hips were pulled tight against the wall. But then the same brother came back and clipped the short chains which hung in front of them to their nipple rings. As each chain had a clip at both ends he was able to adjust them, by looping one end over the ring and then fastening the clip to the right link, to ensure that each girl's breasts were pulled up and held fast. Paula now found that she had to turn her head to one side to press it as close as she could to the wall, and even then there was a constant and uncomfortable tug on her nipples.

The men stood back and admired the view. And Paula could imagine that ten naked females, legs apart, kneeling submissively and held by their slave rings must have made a fine one. However, as always there was a finishing touch to be added. A metal bar was passed behind all of them and this was fed through the rings on their wrist restraints. Once in place it was lifted a little and pulled back to be slotted into two posts which were mounted in the floor at either end of the line. There was a chorus of agonised groans as all the girls felt their arms painfully wrenched up behind them and held by the bar. It also had the effect of making them press their faces even harder against the unyielding stone to try and alleviate the discomfort.

"Very pretty," the brother in charge said finally. "If you ladies wouldn't mind waiting here a while, someone will be along shortly. Or maybe not so shortly." He laughed and they heard the men leave, closing the door behind them.

There was silence apart from the occasional whimper. Paula was sure that all the men had left and there was a terrible temptation to talk in whispers and try to guess what was in store for them. But until they were novices, any talking was forbidden. It must be a kind of test she decided. Obviously her companions had decided the same because the silence continued unbroken for what seemed like hours. The pressure on their shoulders, the ache in their backs and the pull on their breasts became worse and worse. The groans and cries became nearly constant. But still no-one dared speak.

At last they heard a door open again and footsteps approach. A shadow loomed over them and Paula could see that it was Father Burton.

"Well done." He said simply. "Release their arms and we will proceed with the rest of the tests."

With sighs of relief they felt the bar lifted down and then pulled out from between their wrists. They had passed the first test.

Two girls from the end of the line on Paula's right were released. Their wrists were also freed and they stood up and began to rub their shoulders and flex their arms. The brother who had whispered to Paula was now in attendance and he allowed them a few moments before taking them through a door which Father Burton had passed through while they were being released. The rest of them were left alone, but they were too pleased at having passed the first test to jeopardise everything by talking now.

Paula and the girl on her left were the third pair to be taken. They went through the door and found themselves in a sumptuous office. The carpet was deep and their bare feet sank deliciously into it. At the far end of the room, under a large window was a desk, and behind this sat Father Burton. He beckoned them over and the brother who was standing behind them, put a hand in the small of their backs and pushed.

They approached nervously and stood uncertainly before him.

"First you will repeat the vows that Brother Davis has taught you." Father Burton told them abruptly.

Haltingly to begin with they started repeating the vows which had been hammered into them after morning prayers, day after day. "I vow to serve the Church of Ultimate Purification with my body and my soul. I vow obedience to the rules laid down by the Patriarch and I vow obedience to all who act in his name.. . ." They vowed to repay the church for their redemption by working in any way they could to its betterment. Above all they acknowledged that they were subservient to their masters and that complete obedience was the most important way in which they could serve.

When they had finished Father Burton said he was satisfied that they had learned their words adequately and that aspects of their vows would be tested in due course. For the moment they would be taught the correct way to make them.

"Now you have the chance to begin to serve, you must learn that more will be expected of you. You will have seen and maybe begun to learn that when you stand in front of me or any other person who the church has put in authority over you, you will stand with your legs apart, your hands behind your backs and you will look down. Failure to do this from now will be a punishable offence. Do it."

They did as they were told, and were then informed that Sister Lavinia and Sister Helen would be attending to their deportment in future. "The way a woman holds herself, the way she stands and moves is every bit as important in pleasing her master as any other of her actions." Father Burton told them.

He went on to tell them that on the command 'drop' they were to get onto all fours immediately. On the command 'kneel' they were to kneel back on their haunches, part their thighs and again place their hands behind their backs. Finally they were told that if the command 'Open' was given them, they were to stand with their legs wide open and their hands clasped behind their heads with their elbows pulled back level with their shoulders. As soon as they adopted this position Paula realised that the command meant exactly what it said. They would be open to anyone to examine any part of their bodies.

They were tested on these commands until Father Burton was satisfied and then in the respectful stance they had been taught they repeated their vows. They had hardly finished when there was a knock at the door. Telling Paula and her companion to remain as they were the brother opened the door and one of the initiates came in. She held a sheaf of papers and went straight to Father Burton, and stood beside his chair. "They require your signature Father." She explained.

He spread the papers and began to scan them. Paula managed to raise her eyes enough to watch and was amazed to see that quite casually the hand which wasn't busy went straight between the girl's legs. She was standing in the same posture Paula was and she saw how easy it was for him to get up under the short dress. His long fingers stroked at the insides of her firm thighs for a moment before going farther up. She saw the girl's body make a subtle shift and she guessed she was accommodating the fingers in her sex. When he had finished the paperwork he looked up and told the girl to drop, then he waved Paula and her companion away. The brother guided them to a door on the other side of the desk, and as they left Paula caught a glimpse of Father Burton swivelling his chair to face the girl. However she had no time to wonder what she would be commanded to do for the Father because in the next room Brother Davis was waiting for them.

He was dressed in a full robe like the Father and it bore the same red X, but his was brown. He stood beside an arrangement of metal bars fixed into wooden posts. In his hand he held a long cane.

"You have two more tests to pass. Here your willingness to suffer pain for the Church will be tested. In addition your obedience will again be tested."

Paula listened in dismay as the nature of the test was outlined. Each of them would take two strokes at a time while they were bent over the bars. The one who wasn't being caned would be made to stand just behind the one who was. In that way she would be able to see exactly what punishment was coming her way. They would not be tied, they would not be told how many strokes they were to receive and each order to bend over would only be given once. Paula glanced at her companion and saw her swallow nervously.

"This beating is given solely for your instruction in total obedience. It is neither for your punishment nor my pleasure. Number Three, I will start with you. Bend over."

Paula braced herself, but the idea of refusing never even entered her head. She bent over the first bar which was at waist height and then reached forward for the second bar. This was set slightly higher and far enough away from the first to make her stretch forward. She didn't need to be told to open her legs. She spread her grip on the second bar to brace herself better. Although she wasn't having to bend right over and grasp her ankles, she was well stretched and knew her buttocks were nicely taut.

Brother Davis gave her no warning. There was the briefest of whirring noises behind her and a Thwack! immediately after. Paula had thought that she had experienced everything that could be inflicted on her. She had been on the receiving end of the crop, the horsewhip and a variety of lesser whips and straps. And as she had settled herself she had thought that a caning couldn't be all that much worse; if at all.

But the very first stroke drove the breath out of her and left her gulping stupidly, her eyes staring ahead of her in disbelief. As she drew in her breath again the second stroke landed and she shrieked with all her might. So concentratedly did the thin shaft deliver its pain that for a second there was a delay and then the full force of it arrived. And went on growing. Even as Paula dazedly straightened up she was swallowing and gulping for air as pain raged through her body.

She tottered away from the bars but stopped on Brother Davis's command. The other girl, looking very pale was lowering herself now. She had seen what just two lashes had done to Paula. But Paula was now to watch, and know what was going to be unleashed on her in just a few seconds. She wiped a tear from her eye and obediently fastened her gaze on the tight curves of the buttocks in front of her.

She bit her lip and winced as the cane whipped in with wicked relish, seeming to bury itself in the soft skin. Paula saw ripples run through the flesh and immediately a far more livid line than the crop left was traced across her bottom. The girl jerked and gave a breathless sob before the second lash came in and she too shrieked.

In a haze of terror Paula could once again only marvel at the Church's ability to concoct exquisite tortures. To take six and get it over with was one thing, but to have an unknown number of strokes delivered so slowly, and to see how she herself would look as she suffered was quite another. But it was this very ability to create slaves and then make them submit, time and again to worse and worse tortures that made Paula embrace her slavery.

She didn't wait for the command to bend over. However reluctant her body was, she knew she didn't want to do anything else.

Thwack! Once again there was that second's numbness before the line of fire blazed fully, but this time she managed to clench her teeth over the scream that rose in her throat.

Thwack! There was no restraining the scream this time. It blasted out of her and she felt herself wriggling frantically to try and diffuse the full agony.

She couldn't help clasping her hands over the four incandescent lines on her bottom as she watched the other girl scream and writhe her way through another two.

Wiping away the tears which the savage stinging was forcing from her eyes she came forward for her next two and stole a glance at brother Davis as she did. He was casually flexing the cane and waiting for her with no particular expression on his face. "Bend over." He told her with complete authority in his voice. And once again that feeling she loved, the feeling of being helpless, of being nothing came over her. It didn't lessen the pain of the fifth and sixth strokes but it turned it into the breathtaking excitement she was becoming familiar with whenever she was whipped. And the fact that it was Brother Davis helped her moisten and melt even as she screamed in delicious pain and jigged up and down frantically to try and absorb the savage heat. She hoped he could see how wet and open her shamelessly exposed lips were before she stood up.

When the caning had started she had nurtured some hope that six would be all they were going to get. But now she didn't care, it was nothing to do with her. She was simply there to have inflicted on her anything they chose to inflict, this thought made her want to plunge her hand straight between her legs and masturbate while she watched the other girl being beaten. Controlling that urge wasn't helped by seeing how seductively the girl's hips swayed and how the buttock flesh trembled at each lash, and like Paula her lips were so open the glistening pink flesh within was clearly visible. In fact it even came as a relief to be ordered to go down again when the other girl had had her six. And this time Paula didn't hurry, she settled her grip firmly on the bar, shook her hair back proudly and arched her back so that her buttocks were better offered for beating.

Brother Davis saved the best for last and sadistically laid the last two lashes across the tops of their thighs. This time the pain was so acute as the thin whippy shaft cracked across her sex lips that Paula thought she would faint from the exquisite blend of absolute agony and piercing joy. It seemed as if fires were being lit right inside her and she arched her back even more and froze in a kind of spasm that imitated orgasm but was only its precursor on this occasion.

Thwack! The last lash came and Paula heard herself let out an animal wail as the pain climbed to regions where it went beyond a physical sensation and became her whole being, every nerve ending in her body seemed to burst into flame and she came with an intensity that left her bucking and twitching on the bars for several minutes before she could stand. Brother Davis gave her the merest hint of a smile as she straightened up and turned around. Paula's heart sang.

But still she danced on her toes and rubbed at the ridges of fire while the last two lashes were delivered to the other girl. She too arched, froze and screamed at the end when the pain and her willing submission to it carried her to a blinding climax. And then it was over.

The girls looked at each other, both rubbing and both jigging but neither with a trace of self pity for having suffered for no reason other than that they had been told to. And they were both filled with the same pride and pleasure. Brother Davis smiled openly for the first time ever.

"There are bowls of cold water and flannels in the corner. You can use them before your final test," he said.

The relief was delicious and they took it in turns to dab the flannels gently on each others welts. Paula was filled with admiration for her companion's slender hips and tight buttocks, she herself was more fully built. She knelt behind her and spent a long time pressing the cloth to the livid lines. And when she stood back she had to admit that the marks suited her. She would please any man looking like that. And as she bent forward to allow the girl to do the same for her she saw the brother who had brought them in shift his stance a little to accommodate the straining bulge in his trousers. She would have loved to have been ordered to her knees in front of him. But they had other ideas.

14.

In a passage at the back of the house, which was far less grand than where they had been, they were stopped outside two doors. The brother who had taken them from the caning room addressed them.

"In each of these rooms is a man. They are men the Church will redeem in due course and by methods which needn't concern you. All you need know is that you are required to please them. They can do whatever they want with you for the next hour. They have been in prison for some years and have only been released today. Do you understand?"

It was only their relentless training which allowed them to stammer out, "Yes Master," as his words sank in.

The brother nodded, opened a door and shoved Paula in. Before she could recover, she heard a key turn in the lock.

Again her training came to the rescue and she adopted the respectful stance she had been taught.

But her thoughts whirled.

An ex-con? She was supposed to submit to someone she might have helped put away in the first place? She was caught in a bizarre role reversal. The ex-cop becoming the prisoner of the ex-con.

What would a man who had been in prison do to her? And he could do anything he liked. She was aware that she was sweating with fear, but one thought came to mind and calmed her. She wasn't really serving this man at all. She was serving the Church. She was nothing except what the Church wanted her to be.

They were testing her and she wanted to be tested. That was all that need concern her, obey and serve. She looked up a little and her courage nearly failed her.

She was in a bedroom. There was a four poster bed in the middle. Over against the far wall was a dressing table and beside it was a doorway to an ensuite bathroom. She took all this in at a glance but then focused on the man who was lying on the bed.

He was gross, squat and heavily built. He was stripped to the waist and his stomach rose in a pallid mound covered in hair. As she looked at him he rose on one elbow and returned her stare. She noted that despite the fat his chest was broad and powerful, but his face was a network of scars. He took a long pull on the cigarette he was smoking before grinding it out in the ashtray beside his bed and then he sat up, swinging his legs off the side of the bed.

"Fucking hell." His voice was gravelly and as coarse as his features. "So my luck's changed at last eh? Five years inside then the day I get out some kid tells me he's got a job for me. And I get a woman I can do anything I want to; and I don't need to pay for her." He grinned at her, displaying a mouthful of rotten teeth. "That's not a bad deal."

He rose and approached her. She could smell the stale sweat on him.

By submitting to this animal she really would be nothing, nothing but a slave to the Church. And in spite of her fear a small tingle of excitement ran through her at the thought of her coming degradation.

The man reached out and grasped one of her breasts in a huge hand. "Good tits; not too big, just right." He moved round behind her and let out a low whistle. "Someone's already had a good go at you haven't they?"

"Yes Master." It was hardly more than a whisper.

"And they tell me you enjoy it."

"Yes Master."

"Well you're going to get a lot more of it. Ever had your tits whipped?"

"Yes Master."

"Good. But we'll come to that later." He moved back round to stand in front of her and she could see one hand massaging the front of his trousers. "Right now I just need a fuck."

She was ordered over to the bed and told to kneel down. He came to stand in front of her and she didn't neeed to be told to finish undressing him. As she slid his grubby underpants down his sex jutted out at her. It wasn't above average length but the shaft and the bulbous head were broader than anything she had encountered.

"Lick it." He told her. Obediently she moved her

head down to where it speared up from the tangle of black hair and began to run her tongue up the shaft. He tasted acrid and she could get the sharp smell of urine mingled with the smell of sweat. She closed her eyes when she got to the enormous purple head and let her tongue trail across it. There was some pre ejaculate at his slit and she lapped at it, preferring the musky taste of his excitement to his other tastes. When she ducked her head to lick at the tight scrotum and his smell became almost overpowering, she felt her belly begin to heat and melt at the thought of how complete her submission was. When he fucked her, she thought, he would find her entrance moist and open to him. Undoubtedly that would spur him on to whip her afterwards, but that was what she was here for and the brothers would be pleased with her.

Once she had run her tongue slowly up the ridge on the underside of his shaft, he pulled her head away abruptly. "On the bed!" His voice was thick with urgency.

Paula climbed onto the bed and lay back, spreading her legs wide open. He knelt in between them and stared hungrily at the rings in her lips.

"A real little slave aren't we?"

"Yes Master." She couldn't disguise the eagerness in her voice. She had her own reasons for wanting him to ream her out, but that didn't matter.

He tugged the rings apart and she gasped at his roughness but revelled in it too. She could feel how the lips were full and open, and he couldn't fail to see. She heard him give a throaty laugh and gasped again as she felt his fingers plunge into her and she lifted her hips to urge him on. But he fingered her only long enough to feel the juice in her channel and then he lowered himself onto her. His weight crushed her and she groaned a little, but then she felt her lips pushed wide open by the thrusting member and lifted her legs to wrap them round his hips and open herself still farther. His need was so urgent that he rammed straight in and began pumping his pelvis against her immediately. She held onto his back and felt herself respond to him. He was only concerned to get his release inside her and his use of her body simply as a receptacle for his sperm, made Paula squirm and moan with pleasure.

His climax came quickly, his back arched and he gave a roar of relief. And Paula was so delighted at her own submissiveness that despite his speed she felt her vagina grip him and spasm as well. She gripped her hands in his greasy hair and cried out in her turn as he shot jet after jet of his seed deep into her.

He rolled off her almost immediately and stood beside the bed. She could see the light of vicious excitement in his eyes. His sex was shrinking but it was shiny and slick now.

"Lick it again, and suck it this time you whore."

She knelt down and did as he told her. Even though he had shrunk after his ejaculation, she still had to open her mouth wide to get him in. She sucked and licked at him to get rid of the sperm which clung to him and very soon she felt him harden again. But he didn't want her to bring him to a climax in her mouth and as soon as she started moving her head up and down, he pulled her away.

"Oh no you don't," he said leering knowingly at her. "You reckon a blow job's going to make me all nice and lovey dovey. No chance. They've left me a choice of whips and I intend to use them."

He hauled her to her feet by her hair and pulled her to the foot of the bed. As soon as he ordered her to stand with her back to the bed, Paula realised he intended to carry out his threat of whipping her breasts. As she held her arms out for him to clip her restraints to the chains which hung from the posts, she could feel her heart pounding. She was thrilled at the idea of being whipped as a slave, but terrified of the cruelty she saw in his eyes. He kicked her legs apart, fastened them and then went to the dressing table where a variety of implements had been left for his pleasure and her pain. She watched him apprehensively as he fingered them all and then returned with a single cord whip. The handle and the lash itself were braided, the lash was about two feet long and had a wicked metal sheath at its tip.

"We'll start with this and see how those lovely tits can dance."

He stood to one side of her so that each stroke would land full across both breasts. At the very first one Paula felt the breath knocked out of her as it slammed home. The metal tip bit into the flesh under her left arm and she felt the weight of her breasts shudder and sway. Helplessly she watched him lift his powerful arm back to deliver a second lash. She closed her eyes before it landed and bright lines of pain seared across the insides of her eyelids as it smacked across both nipples. She cried out and tried to twist away. A third lash cracked down and her scream followed the fleshy smack instantly. The pain made her open her eyes wide and as she gasped for breath before the next one she saw the look of almost delirious excitement in the man's eyes.

She felt more truly helpless than ever before. He could, and probably would whip her till she bled and there was nothing she could do about it. It simply didn't matter what he did to her. Between her wide spread legs she felt herself respond. And as another lash cracked in, this time delivered with a slight upswing so that it caught the undersides of her breasts and she felt them ripple, she also felt a rush of the most intense excitement she had ever felt. Even greater than her recent excitement at being caned. This time there was the thrill of the unknown as well. Instinctively she tried to twist away again but then pushed herself forward against her bonds to urge him on to do his worst. He lashed at her stomach next and she let out a breathless sob as once again the air was knocked out of her. Her stomach muscles clenched automatically but she felt her hips buck suggestively as well. The man spotted it and lashed her across her pelvis, the metal tip gouging a mark on her hip. This time Paula felt the juices churn in her sex and her hips bucked and undulated of their own accord once more. The man stopped and moved in front of her. She looked at him through half closed eyes as she took advantage of the pause to get her breath. She could feel sweat starting out on her body from the pain. And at her crotch she could feel his sperm trickling out of her mixed with her own juices. He was looking at her in disbelief.

"You're really loving this aren't you?" He asked.

"Yes Master." Paula heard hersellf gasp, and then groaned in pure pleasure when she felt his hand cup her soaking sex. He parted the soft and glistening lips to push his fingers up into her and swirl the flooding nectar of her excitement. She let her head fall forward to look down the striped front of her body and see where his hand reached into her. The sight racked up her arousal one more notch and as she sweated and panted her sex made hungry sucking noises while his fingers worked at her.

"How many can you take I wonder?" He asked quietly.

Paula closed her eyes the better to feel her gathering excitement. "As many as you want me to Master," she heard herself reply. Abruptly he withdrew his hand and she almost wailed in frustration, she had felt the first quivers of her approaching orgasm begin. But then he hit her. He brought his open hand up, hard, between her spread legs and it smacked wetly into her engorged lips. She cried out in shock. He did it again, and again she cried out but more throatily this time. This cruelty was making her come even faster. She tilted her hips forward for the next one but he stepped back and before she could beg him, he started in with the whip again. This time he curled it around her right thigh. His aim was devastating. It bit into the soft skin right up by her slit and the metal tip stung the bottom of her buttock.

Her head snapped back at the impact and the first wave of her orgasm crashed across her in a storm of livid pain and pleasure. She heard herself scream and her body bucked and writhed, desperate to feel his shaft spear up into her and drive her to total fulfillment. But he moved to her other side and repeated the same lash with the same accuracy. It drove her rigid agaist her chains and she arched for a second quivering and spasming, her sex frantically rippling and flooding its juices out between her gaping lips. Then the storm passed and she hung limply in her chains, her head lolling against one shoulder and her breath rasping in her throat.

Dimly she felt him release her and could only collapse onto all fours until her head cleared. Her breasts, stomach and sex pounded with the aftermath of the whipping. But he gave her no time. He was still stiffly erect and again used her hair to haul her up and this time he threw her onto the bed. She sprawled face down and felt him lift her hips from behind. As eagerly as her dazed state allowed she gathered her legs up under her to raise her haunches for him. She buried her head in the bedclothes and pushed her bottom up to show him her sex, but all he did was wipe his hand briefly along the crack and use the juice to lubricate the closed bud of her back entrance. She moaned in anticipation and reached round behind her to pull her buttocks apart for him.

And as his fingers pushed into her and wrenched her open she bore down to help the head of his member drive into her. Again he was in a hurry and as soon as he felt the narrow channel grip his shaft he thrust in as deep as he could. Her body shuddered and rocked under the repeated blows as he pulled back and then rammed in again, his hips slapping against her. Paula was still dizzy from the massive orgasm she had had under the whip. And she had just begun to respond to the penetration deep into her stomach when felt him grab the fronts of her thighs and pull her against him. She felt his member pulsing as he held her pinned to him and it shot yet more sperm into her, then he released her again. She groaned in frustration as he slid out of her and she rolled onto her side to see what he would want next.

For a moment Paula thought he might have finished with her. He knelt with the folds of his stomach hanging over his loins and he was panting. But then he sat back and grinned.

"Now lick again," he said, "and all of it this time."

She knew immediately what he meant. His legs were open and the nearly flaccid sex dangled between them. She turned herself and crawled towards him.

She began by licking and kissing his inner thighs, running her tongue nearly up to his scrotum but stopping just short and starting again. Moving from right to left and back again, she tasted his sour sweat soaked skin. Whenever she came closest to his groin she got the sharp smell of urine again, mixed with the musk of his emissions and his overall aroma of unwashed body.

Gratitude flooded over her each time this happened, he was giving her the opportunity to abase herself utterly and she waited patiently for the order she knew would come. At last he lay back with a sigh of contentment. "You know what I want." He said simply.

"Yes Master," she replied and moved closer to him to allow her mouth to explore further. She caressed his scrotum first. To start with it was wrinkled and slack but as her tongue lapped obediently around his balls and toyed gently with them, she felt it start to tighten and saw his member begin to straighten and fill, jerking erect once more. But he didn't want her there, not yet. She ducked her head and ran her tongue along the ridge behind the scrotum which led to his anus. His smell filled her nostrils now. Her lips and tongue encountered the matted hair which coated the insides of his buttocks. She probed between them, using her hands to lift and open his legs to get her head further under him. She shifted closer again and then her questing tongue flicked out once more and at last found the puckered opening of his anus. She heard him moan and she licked eagerly at the salty, earthy tasting entrance. Lost in a delirium of submission she pushed again and felt the entrance open to her tongue and she pushed it in to the dark passage. Her own excitement mounted as he arched his back and moaned again. She paused for a second to lick her lips and lubricate her tongue better, then pushed it up deep into his anus again, twisting her head round to get as much penetration as she could. Her tongue was aching now and saliva was running down her face but then she felt his hand in her hair and he pulled her off.

"Get me a fag," he said breathlessly. She was kneeling back between his legs and panting herself, she could feel her sex lips quivering with arousal as she looked at his throbbing erection. His command puzzled her and she looked at him blankly.

"Get me a fag and light it you daft bitch." He sat up and swung a hand back as if to slap her. She slipped hurriedly off the bed and found the cigarettes. Fumbling in her haste she extracted one and lit it, coughing on the acrid smoke.

"Give it here," he told her, "and then get back to work." She gave it to him and climbed back onto the bed. "You'll find out what I want with this in due course." He waved the cigarette, "but now I want you there." He pointed at his erection.

Still dazzled and thrilled by her degradation, Paula bent down to take him into her mouth. She felt an extra surge of warmth in her belly as she did so. What did he have in store?

She kept her bottom raised in the air as she sucked at him to give herself a better angle to work from. It let her slide her mouth well down his shaft and she could taste an exciting mixture of sperm, her own juices and her own anal musk, from where he had buggered her. To have that shaft which had speared into her sex and her backside finally erupt in her mouth was going to make her come herself, she was sure. She could feel the heat in her sex and wondered if she could get one hand down there to masturbate with while he spurted into her mouth. But then she found out what he intended to do with the cigarette.

"Keep your arse up good and high," he told her. She was right down on him and feeling him at the back of her throat, but now he sat up over her and she had to turn her head sideways to get him in because of his stomach. But she kept on working at him, there was the salty taste of his seed at his slit. He would come soon, but before he did he reached over her and she felt the heat of the cigarette in the cleft of her buttocks. It stung and burned at the tender skin on the inner sides of them. She wriggled her hips desperately and gave a muffled shriek of protest around her gag of flesh. He lifted it away slightly and she felt one hand reach further down to the crack of her sex. The other pushed her head firmly down. He was going to burn her! She thought he had done everything to her but now, while he came in her mouth he was going to burn her! A wild excitement raged through her, and she moved her head urgently on him. And as she felt his member swell and the pulses begin to run through it, she settled herself so that her legs were farther open and the tender lips of her sex offered up to this new torment. He began to spurt into her mouth and she heard him gasp just before a lightning bolt of pain lanced through her as he ground the burning cigarette into the very crack between her lips. She was so moist that it just had time to send one stupendous burst of pain through her before it was extinguished. But it was enough to tip her over the edge. She writhed and tried to cry out as she came but choked on his fluid as it pumped into her. His hand held her head down and she spluttered helplessly while her stomach and sex rippled and shook as every nerve in her body seemed to overload at the same time.

When he finally let her go she curled up, coughing, gasping and nursing her sex with both hands. It hurt terribly now the orgasm had passed and she rocked herself and groaned.

He got off the bed and dressed calmly. Then without a word or a backward glance he went to the door and knocked. It opened almost immediately and then he was gone.

15.

In the minutes which followed, Paula slowly sat up and took stock. The pain at her sex had subsided to an angry kind of tingling and she opened her legs wide to have a look. Bending over herself she opened her labia and even found that she used her rings for ease. There was some redness but nothing which looked too bad. She noted how closely the lines of the whip lay to her lips and felt a surge of warmth at the memory of the pain. She shook her head in amused despair at her own depravity.

For once no-one seemed to be in a hurry to make her go anywhere or do anything so she walked into the bathroom to find some cold water for the burn. She found a flannel and after wetting it she held it pressed between her thighs. She also found a bottle of mouthwash. But her main discovery was a mirror. It was a small one mounted over the basin but Paula was able to look at herself for the first time in weeks. She found her face was thinner, but if anything that made her better looking she felt. Her hair was a mess and she raked it back with her fingers. She looked at herself again. It wasn't the face of a victim she decided. She may have been whipped, buggered and now even burned; she may have been ordered to lick and kiss every orifice of that awful man, and had obeyed. But her face was that of a woman who has explored every inch of her own sensuality. Her cheeks were flushed and her lips still soft and full. She smiled at her reflection - proud and wanton, then shook her hair out and allowed the tip of her tongue to appear teasingly between her lips.

"Bring on the next test brothers," she told her reflection. But just then she heard the bedroom door open and suddenly all her confidence vanished and she hurried back.

It was Brother Davis.

"Open." He ordered her, and she snapped into position. She shivered as he ran his fingers over the welts on her breasts and stomach but he ignored her and bent to look at her thighs. He traced the marks where the lash had curled round her and finally let his hand run along her labia. She winced as it passed over her burn mark.

"What did he do there?" Brother Davis asked.

"Burned me with a cigarette Master."

"Were you good and moist at the time?"

"Yes Master."

"Then you'll be fine soon enough." He straightened up and tilted her chin to look into her eyes. "He said you were very good after a whipping."

"Thank you Master."

For the second time he smiled openly. "How you do love the whip Number Three." He said.

She smiled back shyly. "Yes Master."

He became serious again."You all did well. There are ten criminals on their way to a monastery now, quite willingly. They may have been in prison but they're all the type to re-offend. But once we've got them. . . " he gave an ironic smile, "they won't. Of course we could have abducted them but it's so much easier if we use these little honeypots." He tapped her sex lightly. "Then they walk into the trap of their own accord."

He turned away and told Paula to follow him. She obeyed, but her thoughts were in turmoil. Her past life had made a most unwelcome intrusion. Honeypot.

She had come full circle. So where did she go from here?

The other girls were waiting in the corridor and when they were all assembled, they were marched off to their new quarters.

They were now to be housed on the first floor of a wing of the house itself. And outside the door of their room, Father Burton was waiting for them. He had a large book open in front of him and before they entered the room they were asked their names and he recorded them. She was no longer Number Three; she was Paula again. There was one more ritual to be observed, their metal collars were unlocked and removed. All of them flexed and rubbed their necks as the weight and constriction were removed. They were all fitted instead with soft leather collars which buckled on. Almost literally lightheaded Paula entered her new quarters.

They were to live in a long room with all ten beds standing along one wall. Opposite them were wash basins, and above those was one long mirror. At the far end of the room were toilets and showers, all of them open but no-one cared. It was a room, not a cell. The beds were arranged in pairs with five foot high wooden partitions between each pair. Paula wasn't surprised to see from the rings and chains that they would be imprisoned at night, but felt comfortable with that. She wasn't sure she wanted to sleep in freedom anymore.

But best of all they were allowed to talk. At last they found out each others' names and as they crowded in front of the mirror they caught up on weeks of forbidden chat. Mainly it was that day's events which occupied them however. The mirror was big enough to reflect them all from head to waist and they compared the marks of the various whips which had been used on them, turning and twisting to look at breasts, backs and buttocks. It was the first time that Paula or any of them had seen their own bodies so clearly in the aftermath of a beating. They were all fascinated and Paula could see that same pride which shone in her own eyes, reflected in nine other pairs. There were jars of the same cream they had used in the cells and they all helped one another rub it into their cuts and bruises. The girl who had caused trouble on their first day and whose name was Caroline, now helped Paula by attending to the marks of the cane on her buttocks, and she returned the favour by helping her reach weals which stretched across her shoulders and down her back.

It was only later that night, just before she fell asleep, when Paula realised that only a few weeks before, she and these girls would have been on opposite sides of the law. They had despised and hated each other. But now they were her companions and she had stronger links with them than with anyone else in the world. They were links that had been forged in pain and which now held them together in the pride of total submission.

Sister Helen, a slender brunette who moved with the grace of a dancer came in and gave them their clothes. The shifts may have been simple but they were well enough cut to fit each girl's figure snugly and they fell on them with cries of delight. Paula found the sensation of cloth against her skin very strange for some time but also found herself looking forward to having something to remove before the next man required the use of her body.

Later they were taken to the main dining room. It was a huge panelled room with a long top table at which the brothers and sisters ate. Then there were shorter tables set at right angles for the novices and initiates. The sister on duty stood at one end of the serving counter. Paula learned that they would no longer have to repeat their submission out loud but they would still be beaten. However a tawse rather than a crop was used.

When it was her turn Paula laid her upper body down on the table, as she had seen the others do and hitched up the short dress to bare her buttocks. The tawse made a satisfying smack as it landed on her and she felt a wide swathe of heat spread over her cheek, mingled with a sharper stinging. Each girl got two on each cheek. Back in their room the girls found that it left wide red patches with white stripes like finger marks within them. But it was less severe than the crop and left the buttocks clear to take a lot more if required.

While she ate Paula watched the initiates take their beatings and envied the elegance with which they were able to do it. The short, slightly flared skirts of their dresses were very easily flicked up as each girl bent over. And she noticed how their heeled shoes emphasised the length of their legs curving up gracefully into the swell of their taut buttocks. She watched entranced as the tawse slapped down and sent little ripples running through the flesh.

The sight gave her the answer to her earlier uncertainty about what the future held for her now she had come full cirlce.

She wanted to be an initiate. She wanted to wear that uniform.

16.

Within a few days those girls who had completed their training as initiates were dispatched. Some were taken by brothers from other monasteries. Some, but only a few, were taken to the headquarters of the Church. It was rumoured in whispers that these would go into the outside world to work for the Patriarch on special assignments, and they were especially envied as they would meet the Patriarch himself.

The rest were sold off.

On the day of the sale, the novices were taken out to a large barn on the estate. Inside, a raised stage had been built at one end. Down one wall were tables laden with food and drink for the guests. Paula's group had been working in the kitchens preparing the food for two days now. At the back of the barn was where they would be. A complicated scaffolding arrangement of thin steel poles had been erected. At the centre of the arrangement were ten X shaped crosses which were supported and braced by the other poles. As Paula took in the fact that the X shaped frames had chains attached to the four arms of the X, she guessed that they were to be mounted on them.

She was right. Each girl was attached by her restraints to a cross, which left her spreadeagled so that her legs and arms were stretched wide open exactly imitating the X of the Chuch's symbol. The poles themselves were quite slender, so as not to interfere with any examination of their bodies which anyone might care to make. Once were they all mounted in a long line Father Burton addressed them.

"You are not for sale today. You are here to encourage the bidding on those who are, and to encourage anyone who is unsuccessful in purchasing a girl to return the next time. Although you will not be gagged, as some might wish to inspect your mouths, the rule of silence will apply. And it will be absolute." He told them.

They were left to wait for an hour or two before the guests arrived. Paula had wondered who the guests would be. Who would the Church allow to see its slaves? Now she found out. A large crowd of men and women entered. Three of the brothers stationed themselves along Paula's line, to enforce the rule of silence she presumed. At first the guests ignored them and concentrated instead on the food and the drink. But after a while a steady stream of both men and women approached them. Paula was surprised by the number of women.

The men all had an aura of power and wealth about them. Many were obviously foreign and one or two wore Arabic robes. Some of them had women with them, simpering little tarts Paula thought contemptuously, and wondered how they would scream and writhe under the whip of a real Master. A few of the women were obviously slaves themselves and wore collars with leads attached and which their masters held. The remainder were very different. They were hard faced, but exquisitely dressed and coiffured, and they were obviously here on business. Traffickers, Paula thought, looking for slaves to sell on. They discussed all the girls quite openly, comparing the sizes of their breasts and looking for good muscle tone to withstand the rigours of slavery. Paula was so used to being talked about in her own hearing that the only thing which irritated her was one man who said he thought she could take twenty or so lashes quite easily. She had to bite her lip to prevent herself from telling him that she could take a lot more than that.

Paula found that she attracted quite a lot of attention. Male hands were run up the long muscular curves of her thighs. Her breasts were squeezed and weighed. Her sex was dug into by countless hands and fingers rummaged inside her until she had to bite her lip again to stop herself from moaning. She knew her own body well enough to know that the more outrageously it was treated the more it would respond, and sure enough when fingers were removed from her vagina they came out glistening with her juice.

"Very responsive. And a good build to take a lot of punishment," she heard one dark skinned man say. Now there was a man who knew a good slave when he saw one, she thought. "Could be raced too," he went on. His companion who looked American agreed and reached round to grasp and sqeeze her buttocks. "Yeah, nice ass as well. Bet that bounces real good when it's whipped." He pushed a finger roughly up into her anus and Paula tried to accommodate him but had no real way of moving. "Nice tight little channel there. If she's not beaten to shit by next time, I wouldn't mind bidding." He too tried her sex and pronounced it very interesting and then they passed on to the next girl, wiping Paula's juices off their fingers on her stomach.

For the first time she was fingered by a woman. A blonde holding a glass of wine in one elegantly manicured hand had been watching Paula for some time and at last approached her now. She was handsome, but Paula could sense the toughness in her. She was alone and for some time just caressed Paula's breasts while looking keenly into her face. Paula remained silent despite the way her breasts felt taut and full, the nipples standing out proud and hard. But when the woman pulled and twisted them hard between thumb and forefinger, she moaned against her clenched teeth. The woman gave a cruel little chuckle and shifted her attention down below. Paula couldn't help a little shiver as she felt a female hand for the first time stroke her clitoris. All the men had gone straight for her hole, but this woman knew better. She spent a long time patiently fondling the little nub which was erect in the first place but was soon throbbing with excitement. Paula desperately shut her eyes and tried to choke back the moans which were being forced relentlessly up her throat. She could feel her lips quivering and she wanted the woman's hand to reach up inside her now. But she stopped suddenly and Paula blinked in surprise. The woman looked at her coolly and then spoke with a Scandinavian accent.

"If you make any noise, they will whip you?"

Paula nodded.

"If you were mine I would show you how a woman should really be whipped. Before I sold you of course." She smiled and touched her fingers to Paula's mouth before passing on. Paula licked her lips and got the taste of her arousal from them. It was a poor substitute for the orgasm she had been on the brink of. But when she thought that one day she could really be sold to a woman like that, she felt her sex lips dry and her vagina contract immediately. She was sure that an owner like that would escalate cruelty to new and unimaginable heights.

For another hour or so all the girls were fingered and explored but at last the auction began. There were five being sold. One of the brothers stood to one side of the stage and acted as auctioneer. He told the guests that each girl had been trained in obedience, deportment, dancing and general household service, as well as, of course, in all the arts appropriate to a slave girl.

Each girl was led onto stage by a brother who held a lead which was attached to the rings at her belly. At the very front of the stage she adopted the 'open' position and let the guests get a good look at her, then she was made to turn around slowly while maintaining the position until she faced her audience again, and the bidding began.

Paula was amazed at the amounts of money which were bid. Most of them fetched around a million pounds but one especially attractive blonde went to an Arab for nearly two million.

That night Paula was put on display in the Lounge. She and a girl called Linda, the small girl who had been whipped beside the van on their first niight of captivity, were called for. The brother who came for them made them strip and then clipped their wrists together high up between their shoulderblades, by attaching their restraints to their collars with a short chain. He clipped their leashes to the rings at their bellies, just like the girls who had been sold earlier that day. And Paula found it very exciting to be led through the house in such a way. She felt utterly enslaved and wished only that there were more people to see her.

On many occasions she had seen girls displayed and knew that the brothers took great delight in devising excruciating positions for them. Right at the start of her enslavement to the Church she had been terrified at the thought of what it would be like to be displayed, but now her heart was hammering with anticipation of what they would put her through.

She wasn't disappointed. The room was empty when they reached it except for another one of the brothers and without a word to the girls the two men set to work. They stood them back to back and chained their ankles to the floor well apart, then they released their wrists from behind their backs and clipped them together in front of them before raising them high above their heads by means of a chain hanging from the ceiling. The chains from which they hung were adjusted so that they were able to stand on tiptoe with a little bit of leeway to lower and raise themselves. Even so Paula could feel immediately that the strain on their legs and thighs was going to be extreme indeed by the end of the evening.

But as usual the brothers had other refinements in mind. Chains were clipped to their labia rings and fed up through their nipple rings before being attached directly to the ring in the ceiling from which the main chain hung. These were adjusted so that there was less slack in them than in the chain which held their wrists. Paula could see what that meant straightaway. If they lowered themselves to take the strain off their legs, then the chains through their rings would pull painfully up at the labia. And as if that weren't enough to ensure an amusing display of tortured female flesh, they produced the finishing touch and both Paula and her companion groaned aloud when they saw it. A small transformer was placed on the floor in between them, by twisting their heads they could see the wire trailing from it to the mains. Four thin wires came from the front of it and two were connected to each of two tripods which were positioned between each girl's legs. On top of the tripods were phallus shaped rods sheathed in leather, and halfway down the shafts Paula could see the glint of metal contacts. To make matters even worse the brothers adjusted the heights of the pillars so that the rods just nudged at the entrance to their vaginas. If the girls accepted the pain of the rings pulling at their lips, they could sink a little way onto the rods, but if they went too far then the moist tissue of their vaginas would make contact with the metal terminals on the shafts which would deliver a shock.

All the elaborate preparations had only just been finished when the rest of the brothers arrived, accompanied by the initiates and the new girls who would be serving. One of the brothers who had arranged their display went casually over to the wall and turned the current on. Immediately Paula felt the phallus begin to writhe lewdly and vibrate between her lips.

That evening alway stayed in Paula's memory as one of the longest of her life. Her legs ached and the idea of what an arousing display she must make, produced an excitement which the constant vibrating at her sex only encouraged. She could feel her lips quivering with desire to grip the shaft and sink onto it. All around her she could see girls being put to use. Hands were run up thighs and fingers probed under the short white dresses, the new girls were frequently on their knees sucking at stiffly erect members.

Every now and then one of the men would stop by Paula and her companion to fondle their stretched taut breasts and worsen the torment of their arousal. And the worse the torment; the more Paula could feel her juices flow. Her belly felt as if it was full of molten lava.

She let her head fall back and groaned, dimly she heard laughter at her distress and that cruelty pushed her beyond her rational capability. Her body took over and her trembling legs eased her down onto the maddening shaft. The pain in her labia as the rings were pulled up was consumed by the relief in her leg muscles and she surrendered to the tireless stimulation of the rod which now pushed into her. At last her channel had something to grip and she could feel it contract eagerly around it. She sighed in pleasure and began to move up and down on it in short, careful movements, but the surges of arousal which now ripped through her after so long a delay made her abandon all caution.

She was sure she could reach a climax if she could just keep her movements under control for a few moments more. But it was hopeless, as the waves of joy built and built she lost any control and ignoring her rings pulling her sex lips up cruelly hard, she sank herself onto the shaft. The jolt which followed felt as though a sledge hammer had been wielded right inside her. She screamed and her body leaped upwards to stretch rigid and shake uncontrollably for a second. When Paula could look around her again and take stock, she found she was as high up on tiptoe as she could reach, her legs vibrating with strain. But still the hateful rod was writhing and vibrating ceaselessly at her entrance. Behind her Paula heard an agonised shriek from Linda as she too let herself sink too far.

"One all!" she heard a voice cry.

"I'll bet the black haired one scores the most. She

can't get enough at the best of times!" another voice shouted.

Bets were laid and every time one or other of them succumbed to the lure of trying to ease their pain and allow the rod to bring them to an orgasm, they would fail miserably. They would scream and jerk rigid in their chains while applause and boos would break out round the room.

Twice during that interminable evening the current had to be turned off and Paula had to be revived by smelling salts. She existed in a blur of frustrated arousal and pain, punctuated by peaks of agony every time she sank too low. But at last they were taken down when Linda could no longer support herself at all, and every time she was revived collapsed onto the dildo immediately and shuddered into unconsciousness. Paula curled up in a ball on the floor and ignored all that went on around her while her hands nursed her sex. .

It was Sister Lavinia who roused her eventually from her exhausted torpor and took her to her room, leading her by a leash clipped to her belly again.

Paula had never yet seen the private quarters of either the brothers or sisters, although some of the group had, but the reports didn't do justice to the reality.

The carpet was deep and soft, and the bed linen on the huge four poster more expensive and finer than anything Paula had ever been able to contemplate for herself in her previous life. Inevitably the carved posts of the bed were equipped with chains but it was the carvings themselves which caught Paula's eye. She stared at them. Each post was carved in the shape of a naked woman with her hands raised above her head and tied, and each woman's posture perfectly captured different reactions to different stages of being whipped. The ones which formed the posts at the foot of the bed were arching their backs away from an invisible whip and trying to look over their shoulders at where the next lash was coming from. One of them was twisting to look over her left shoulder and one was twisting to the right. At the head of the bed the two women were depicted as having had their beatings and their heads hung down between their raised arms, their backs to the room. As Paula looked closely she could see that the artist had carved lines across their bodies which were picked out in darker stain and formed lifelike representations of the weals left by the whip. The bodies of the women were skilfully carved in every detail, the curves of their breasts and buttocks looked as though they would be warm and alive to the touch. The faces of the two who were still being whipped had expressions which Paula recognised instantly. The heady mixture of pain, pleasure and passion which swept over her every time she herself was whipped.

Sister Lavinia gave her plenty of time to stare. "They are lovely aren't they? The Church rewards its faithful servants well Paula. Don't forget that." She said at last.

"No Sister." Paula replied dutifully.

She remained standing in the centre of the room while Sister Lavinia helped herself to a drink from a low table set by a luxurious armchair beside the fireplace. She sat and drank slowly, ignoring Paula for the moment.

"I promised you a whipping when I was allowed to have you." She said at last. "And after tonight I think you've earned one. Besides I think you should be allowed to come quite freely before you start the next phase of your training."

Sister Lavinia finished her drink unhurriedly before rising and approaching Paula. She was led over to the other side of the bedroom and shown where she was to be whipped. It was a curious object and was bolted to the floor through the carpet. It stood by the window beyond the door to the dressing room. It was wooden and in some ways it resembled a simple bicycle saddle except that a shaft came from the front of it and ended in two round spars which were joined to it at right angles. The whole thing stood no more than a foot off the floor. By now Paula was so used to whipping posts and bars to hold her, as well as chains to hang her by, it didn't seem very imposing. But she did take full account of the wooden phallus which speared up from the seat and after the earlier events of the night she reserved judgement.

"It's a whipping stool. You can try it in a moment. But first tell me what that woman said to you at the auction today."

Paula was startled, she hadn't seen Sister Lavinia there. But she remembered the words and repeated them. The sister pondered for a moment.

"Hmm, I don't think she knows how thoroughly we work in the Church. But anyway if you're ever sold to her, you'll be able to draw comparisons."

She laughed but Paula found her earlier fears resurfacing. She didn't want to be sold. She wanted to stay where she was.

At last Paula's wrists were freed and her lead removed. And then she undressed Sister Lavinia. The memory of the last time she had done this, in the Games Room was still vivid. But this time when she helped the sister step out of her long skirt and Paula found herself face to face with her blonde thatch of pubes there was no hurry to whip her and return her to the brothers.

She felt Sister Lavinia's hand gently press her face forward. Inquisitively she let her lips press against the wiry hair and her nose drew in the perfumed musk of her sex. Paula was immediately aware of the contrast between this woman and the last man she had been with. Slowly she let her tongue probe for and find the lips, then Sister Lavinia parted her legs more and Paula was able to lick at the inner lips and find the nub of her clitoris. Her hands reached round the woman and held her buttocks as she dived in more deeply and lapped at the spicy moisture which began to seep from her. She pressed her tongue hard against the clitoris and felt it harden in its turn. She began to suck at it, drawing it out from its protective folds of sensitive pink flesh. Above her she heard the sister moan and sigh and probed farther in. Sister Lavinia tilted her hips and pushed herself at Paula so that she could get her tongue into her vagina and savour the full fragrance of the nectar which lubricated it. Eager now to bring her to a climax, Paula used her fingers to pull her lips apart and went to work, sucking and nipping at the clitoris while the woman's hands gripped themselves in her hair, her hips bucking urgently at Paula's lapping tongue. Suddenly she felt a spasm run through the woman's body, the hands gripped harder, Paula tried to bury her face deeper into the perfumed crack of her sex to suck at her entrance and with a shuddering cry she came while Paula licked and licked again at the flood of juice which poured over her eager mouth.

Paula held her tight while the shudders continued to run through her in the wake of her orgasm and sucked greedily at the pungent emission. But eventually she relaxed and Paula knelt back on her haunches in front of her. It was the first time she had had any sexual experience with another woman and felt that yet another bridge had been crossed to increase the distance between who she had been and who she was now.

"On the stool quickly now my Paula." Sister Lavinia's voice was husky and urgent.

Obediently Paula lowered herself onto the seat and allowed the phallus to ride up into her. She was wet and open, the frustrations of the evening and the sister's orgasm making her impatient for release. As her buttocks touched the seat and the phallus reached its maximum penetration she could feel that in front of its shaft, the wood had been cunningly carved into small protrusions which now pushed against her clitoris, especially when the sister told her to lower her legs so that her ankles could be tied to the bars which ran across the front of the stool. Then she was made to lean her body forward too, and pass her arms between her legs so that her wrists could be fastened to the same bars. She found she was bent forward as if in a rowing boat, with her knees up beside her elbows. But mainly what she was aware of was the fact that the whole of her back was exposed and bent forward. Her shoulders being pulled forward meant that the skin was pulled tight.

Sister Lavinia went into her dressing room and returned with a dog whip.

"The stool is a seldom used piece of equipment these days. But I like the way it exposes one so. It makes a thrashing much more painful."

Looking to one side Paula saw the naked woman stand over her and raise her arm. She was right. Not one millimetre of the lash was wasted, Paula felt every last piece of it bite into her skin. The sister started at the widest part of her back, her rounded shoulders and laid it on hard. Paula jerked and cried out at the very first blow. By the third she was desperately trying to wriggle away but to no avail. And at the fourth which cracked across the paths traced by two other lashes her body began to respond to her frantic writhings on the phallus. From then on each Smack! was answered only by hoarse grunts as Paula ground her clitoris down against the nubs of carved wood on the seat and felt the phallus spear deep up into her. The searing pain of the whip and her lowly position in front of it, only spurred her on. She put all the pent up excitement of the long evening into her gyrations and threw her head back to shout in triumph as at last the waves broke over her and the whip pounded down onto her. She felt her sex grip the shaft as it had longed to all night and go into helpless spasms of ecstasy, her stomach clenched to hold it still harder and shudder after shudder ran through her while she crouched so submissively in front of the whip. At last her head fell forward and she gasped out the last of her orgasm. The whip stopped.

"I'll let you have one more. And then tomorrow you begin to be trained to control your pleasure."

Before Paula could thank her she started again. This time it took longer for the pleasure she took in the pain to drive her to the heights. But then Sister Lavinia moved the lashes further down her back and allowed the whip to curve round her ribs and strike at the soft flesh on the side of her breast where it was swelled out by being pressed against the length of her thigh. This triggered her body once more and she began to buck and writhe again. Her hands gripped the bar to which she was tied and this gave her just enough purchase to bounce up and down a little, jarring the soft flesh of her open sex against the wooden nubs. Again she heard her almost animal grunts answer each Smack! as the leather cracked down on her naked back. Each bolt of pain it unleashed drove her to a crisis which left her soaked in sweat and sobbing with exertion.

When Sister Lavinia released her, Paula humbly kissed her feet in gratitude.

17.

Paula found that she now enjoyed all their training except for one part.

Although they no longer worked in the fields; they were not allowed to be idle. After morning prayers they would be taken to the kitchens or to the store rooms where the cleaning materials were kept. And for the whole morning they would labour under the watchful eyes of the brothers. After lunch they would report to Sister Helen for classes in deportment and dancing.

Paula had always enjoyed cooking and found it no hardship to work in the kitchens, particularly as the monastery used only fresh produce. Besides she knew how much a good meal meant to the new girls after their day's work. Most of her companions however had only ever microwaved food or eaten takeaways and she found herself frequently acting as assistant chef, helping them to master the arts of peeling and slicing vegetables, or cutting raw meat. She often earned the approval of whoever was overseeing them at the time. She was proud of this and it blinded her to a danger which was to take her by surprise in due course.

As for cleaning, they were all on a level playing field but Paula didn't find it too irksome.

Deportment and dancing she was naturally good at with an athlete's strength and instinctive timing. They were taught how to stand properly straight and how to walk in a graceful manner. Sister Helen employed suitably old fashioned methods to instil such old fashioned values. They spent hours parading up and down balancing piles of books on their heads. The Sister made liberal use of her riding crop around their thighs if they allowed any to fall. Paula usually escaped relatively unscathed, but could see how the rest of her group were being transformed. The purification process had hardened them physically at the same time as subduing them mentally, and it had also peeled off the outer shell of street wise defiance and rebelliousness. Their sufferings during purification had made them proud of becoming novices and of their slavery, just as they had Paula, and she could see how well they responded to the training. Almost daily they held themselves better, but it was the dancing which was the real revelation.

Sister Helen gave them long diaphanous gowns which were nearly transparent and which were split almost to the hip on both sides. All the girls loved them and hated having to take them off at the end of the lesson. But Paula couldn't help marvelling at their enthusiasm, considering how they had dressed in the past. And she was amazed at the gracefulness some of them attained. The sister would put slow sensuous music on her stereo system and take them through provocative steps which taught them to reveal tantalising glimpses of their naked bodies beneath the gauze of their gowns. They learned how the female body could sway and undulate seductively. And all these arts were light years distant from the coarse sexuality of selling themselves on street corners. Paula took to the dancing immediately, letting her imagination carry her away. She fantasised about what she was inviting from an invisible master and strove to make herself as desirable as she could, to induce him to possess her utterly. And it was this ability to transport herself which lent her dancing a quality which delighted Sister Helen.

But this too led to trouble in time.

Paula's immediate problem lay in controlling her pleasure. As Sister Lavinia had said, the next stage of their training, and it was conducted at the same time as their other instruction, was to be taught how to control their orgasms so that they would only come when they were allowed to. As they were now almost constantly in the presence of the brothers, they found that the men would take them whenever they liked. In the kitchens a girl would be bent over one of the tables, told to hitch up her dress and then whichever brother it was would simply thrust himself straight into her. Paula found the sight of a female body jerking in response to the man's brutal and uncaring thrusts, almost unbearably erotic. But if the girl gave any sign of pleasure she was immediately sentenced to contemplation time. As they had all been taught to enjoy being whipped, contemplation was used as punishment; and it was very effective.

But Paula took such intense pleasure in her submission that she came almost every time one of the brothers had her bend across a table or chair. Unfortunately the attractions of her body meant that they frequently took her and just as frequently she failed.

If she was summoned to a brother's room in the evenings, he only had to tie her and give her a few lashes before she was moaning with excitement at the prospect of feeling his shaft ramming into her after the whip had seared her into a state of uncontrollable arousal. It took only ten lashes sometimes to have her juicing and moaning helplessly. The whip and the hard shaft of a master's sex had been fused together in her mind and she didn't mind which they used on her.

As a consequence she suffered in the Punishment Wing repeatedly before she learned. Most often she was placed in the ankle pillory and hauled up by her feet to hang upside down. Every hour or so she was taken down to allow her circulation to recover and then she was hauled up again. But at last the days she spent in solitary and agonising confinement slowly began to have an effect.

Just how much of an effect however, she didn't find out until Brother Davis caned her.

He called her to his room one day after exercise but before they had been chained for the night. As Paula entered his room she immediately noticed the bed. Like Sister Lavinia's its posts were carved, but his ones had smaller figures carved in relief around the main shaft of the post. Each of the figures, and all of them were of naked women, were depicted in various attitudes of bondage to the post itself. Paula could pick out one hung by her wrists, another with her arms pulled behind her and bound on the far side of the post and yet another hung by her wrists again but with weights hung from her ankles. She could read the pain in their faces and could almost hear their cries for mercy, or at least the harsh attentions of the master who had strung them up.

Brother Davis lounged in a large old fashioned chair with barleytwist arms and legs, watching her reactions to the carvings.

"I hear you've spent a bit of time like that yourself just recently."

Paula hung her head. "Yes Master."

He stood up decisively. "Well I'm going to cane you tonight and we'll see how you're doing."

"Yes Master. Thank you Master." Paula kept her voice steady but her hands were trembling as she unzipped her dress and stepped out of it. She really didn't think she could hold onto her reactions under another caning from Brother Davis. He had always terrified and fascinated her, but had always seemed to take a special interest in her. Still if she could restrain herself now, she could do it anywhere and she really didn't want any more time hanging in the Punishment Wing.

He made her bend over in the middle of the floor.

To add to her problems, this was her favourite position. It was the one most used by the brothers to administer minor punishments on the spot. She loved the way her breasts swayed under her as she bent, and with her hands grasped round her ankles she could feel how her naked sex was ready to show him all too clearly how excited she was. And to cap it all he wanted her to count the strokes. If he had been able to read her mind he couldn't have devised a worse torture for her. It was those little touches of cruelty which set her pulse racing every time.

Crack! He struck without warning and all thought was swept away by the stab of pain which lanced through her.

"Aah!. . . .One! Thank you Master!" she managed to get out and then draw breath before the second stroke.

Crack! "Two! Thank you Master!" she managed not to scream and held the pain in, letting it flood through her but feeling it begin to lodge in her belly.

Crack! "Three! Thank you Master!" In despair she felt the familiar stirrings and a flutter in her exposed lips as they began to fill and open. She closed her eyes and thought of the sound of the door closing behind whichever brother had hung her in the Punishment Wing. She told herself to concentrate on the hours of lonely agony which would follow.

Crack! "Aah!. . . . Four! Thank you Master!" It had caught her by surprise again and the white heat of the pain and arousal nearly swept her thoughts away. But she hung on grimly, concentrating on the feeling of desolation it gave her to be left in solitary contemplation of her failings.

Crack! "Five! Thank you Master!" She heard her voice firm and calm. She was thinking of how she sat, naked on the cold stone floor of the Punishment Wing, waiting for her head to clear and rubbing at her ankles, knowing that yet another hour lay ahead of her. She was in control at last! The final lash cracked in and she counted it calmly. She could enjoy knowing that Brother Davis was caning her, and enjoy the caning, but she would only come later; when he gave her permission to.

He told her to stay down and pushed his fingers into her sex. She felt him stir the juices there and relaxed, allowing the pleasure to flow through her body, but keeping thoughts of the Punishment Wing firmly in her mind.

"Good girl! You enjoyed that, but not too much! Now we'll move on and see how you do."

He settled the cane across the tops of her thighs and made ready to slice it down hard so that it would crack across her sex lips. Paula knew that it would be all too easy to surrender to the bright bolts of agony as the cane licked at the very entrance to her sex but braced herself to fight.

She just had time to register the Swish! in the air behind her before the Crack! of the cane landing, the explosion of pain and her own scream seemed to happen all at once. As far as it could, her back arched and her head came up. She nearly lost her balance and staggered, but held on and managed to keep an image in her mind of the hated pillory closing round her ankles, as it surely would again if she surrendered to the sudden wave of heat which engulfed her sex as it was lashed.

Once more he took his time, laying the cane across her thighs and pressing it into the soft flesh of her lips. She felt him adjust his balance and settle himself. She could have screamed at him to get on with it, but he had no intention of hurrying. The torment of anticipation now added to Paula's problems. She was going to get at least one more right on her sex lips, and they were quivering with excitement at the prospect. Paula clenched her teeth and thought of the humiliation of having to go back to the room and tell the others she had been sent to Solitary again. That worked. He lifted the cane away and swished it in the air a couple ot times, so close to her that she felt the wind of its passage. She flinched each time, but kept her concentration. And when he finally did land the last lash, she managed to confine herself to a grunt as she acknowledged the impact and accepted the pain gladly, but didn't let it swamp her.

He let her straighten up and rub at her bottom for a moment before ordering her over to the bed. He had her kneel and bury her head in the quilt so that he had full access to her hindquarters which were raised up and offered to him. He could have spent some time getting his hand deep inside her, widening her, stirring her juices, playing with her clitoris as it engorged and then telling her not to come. And all that she could have coped with easily enough now. But she knew that Brother Davis was well aware of how her body reacted, and she wasn't surprised when he put his fingers into her only long enough to get them good and wet then thrust them roughly into her anus. Almost immediately he withdrew them and rammed his member in. Paula felt her tight little opening stretched wider and wider as the head of his sex pushed at it, the pain becoming more piercing by the second. She ground her teeth together and refused to admit that she was loving every moment of it.

The long hours of bleak pain in Solitary beckoned for a moment. But the very thought of them made her forget her own pleasure and concentrate on bearing down to help Brother Davis enter her. And as soon as she did, he slipped into her. He alternated between ramming himself in brutally hard and then withdrawing slowly. She loved both strokes but her obstinacy held firm; she wasn't going back to the pillory.

He came out of her before he reached his own climax and telling her to remain as she was he climbed off the bed. Paula's stomach lurched as she watched him fetch a riding crop from a rack by the bedhead. For a moment he stood in front of her and she drank in the sight of his muscular frame and the arrogant sex spearing rigidly up towards her. He smiled and flexed the crop, but said nothing before getting onto the bed and kneeling behind her again.

"We're going for a ride Paula. And you will be allowed to come, but wait for permission."

With the fingers of one hand he held her lips apart and pushed himself into her sex. She couldn't help moaning with delight this time as she felt her channel grip him eagerly and the sensitive tissues register his shaft's penetration deep inside. She was desperate to feel him come in there, to feel the member throbbing and pumping while the fluid spurted into her. But most of all, she realised, she wanted to hear his gasps of pleasure as he spent himself in her.

And of course he was the Master.

It was only right that if he was entitled to use her body in any way he pleased, it should be up to him when, or even whether she should be allowed to enjoy it. Anything else did not befit a slave. As soon as she had framed this thought, she knew that he could do what he liked with her, for as long as he liked. And if he didn't give his permission, she wouldn't come. It was so simple.

She was able to grind her hips hard against him so he could feel the depth of his penetration, and then sway them gracefully for his pleasure as her lips quivered round the head of his sex when he held it just at her entrance. And she was safe in the knowledge that she wanted to wait for his permission to let the flood gates of her own pleasure down.

At last she heard him groan and she held still for a

second. He had his hands gripped on her hips and she could feel the handle of the riding crop rubbing on her skin there and the tip pressed against her ribs. But now it was lifted away and she licked her lips in anticipation.

"I'm going you ride you now you bitch!" His voice was hoarse with excitement.

"I'm going to fuck you and whip you at the same time. But you can come and you can scream all you like."

He lashed down with the crop which caught her diagonally across her back and left a stripe of delicious pain stretching up from her lower ribs on one side to her shoulder on the other. But at the same time he slammed his pelvis against her and Paula felt him thrust even deeper inside her. Before she could even cry out in response to the first blow of crop and sex, the second was on her. Again the crop smacked across her back and again he drove into her with a force which set the flesh of her buttocks trembling. This time she cried out and lifted her head from the quilt to breathe in deeply. She could feel the fires beginning to rage out of control inside her. She had permission, and she was being fucked and whipped at the same time!

She screamed each time he lashed her and drove his sex into her. Frantically she shoved her hips back at him each time. She wanted him in deeper. She wanted the lash again. She got both, time after time it seemed. The livid pain across her writhing back joined with the molten cauldron boiling in her sex and she even heard herself begging him to go harder. And he did, until he was ramming into her so fast he couldn't wield the crop any more and just grabbed her hips to brace himself. She reared up and yelled as she felt him begin his release inside her. He grabbed a handful of her hair to brace himself better and that triggered the final explosion. In a frenzy of pumping and writhing their orgasms burst over them and they fell sideways onto the bed, Brother Davis's hand still clenched in Paula's hair.

Back in the novices' room, Paula lay face down on her bed while Linda rubbed cream into the weals left by the crop and the cane, and Paula told her that she had finally learned this ultimate obedience. She wouldn't be going back to Solitary again. Caroline looked over the partition when she had finished.

"So how did you manage when you were on the game?" she asked.

Paula tensed immediately. It was so long since she had thought about her cover that the question caught her by surprise. She played for time.

"How do you mean?"

"You couldn't go off like a bloody firework display with every punter. You wouldn't last two days if you did. But up till now every time one of the masters lays a finger on you, you go off like there was no blue touchpaper."

Alarm bells were ringing in Paula's mind. But Linda interrupted. "What're you trying to say Caroline?"

She came round the partition to stand beside Paula's bed. "All I'm saying is she's a bloody funny one to be on the game at all. I mean who was your pimp? We were all with Lucky right?" She looked round at the other girls and there was a murmur of agreement, even from Linda who stood up and moved away from Paula. "So who were you with? You don't look like one of us. You don't even talk like one of us."

"I didn't have a pimp. I was on my own and I'd just started." Paula tried to keep her voice calm and sat up to face Caroline.

"No. I don't buy that. Lucky wouldn't have stood for it. And how come you're so sodding good at the kitchen work and dancing and all those things. You're too posh to be a tart."

"I'm no better than you!" Paula retorted hotly.

"Maybe not better, but you're different. I don't know what you were, but you weren't one of us."

Paula knew she had to stop this before it went any further. There was only one way, and even then she had to be very careful. She jumped to her feet and pushed Caroline hard so that she staggered back.

"Listen you stupid cow. I worked on my own right? Just because you were too thick to keep the money you. . . ." It had the effect she wanted and she got no further. Caroline went for her. She had no science and Paula had to be careful to use none herself. Caroline leaped for her hair and yanked her head back so that they both fell onto Paula's bed. Her fist slammed into Paula's right breast and she gasped at the pain, but managed to bring her own fist round and into the other girl's stomach. She heard her grunt and the grip slackened on her hair. Paula took advantage and turned the tables by grabbing hers and pulling her head back to get on top of her. But she wasn't finished and as Paula straddled her she used the opportunity to bring her knee up into Paula's groin. It was a telling blow and knocked the wind out of her, making her double over and loosening her grip on Caroline's hair.

Now Caroline wriggled out from under her and began to rain blows down on Paula's back as she curled protectively round her pain and tried to get her breath back. They were wild blows but hurt nonetheless. Suddenly Paula uncurled, flung her arms round Caroline's waist and pushed, sending them both crashing onto the floor. Caroline clawed at her face but Paula grimly got a hold on one of her breasts and squeezed savagely, digging her nalis into the soft flesh. She screamed and tried to pull away, but Paula followed and let fly with a well aimed uppercut which slammed up between her legs and into her sex. That knocked the fight out of her long enough for Paula to turn her over, straddle her back, get one of her arms twisted up behind her and then, holding that with one hand, reach round and get a forearm across Caroline's throat and pull upward. She squatted across the naked back and for a second allowed herself to enjoy the helpless wriggling under her. Then she leaned forward and said, "if you work on your own. You learn how to look after yourself." She released her hold, stood up and just had time to be puzzled by the looks of terror in the other girls' eyes before she saw Brother Gibson.

They both spent three days in the Punishment Wing, in solitary confinement and were sentenced to ninety lashes.

Paula had had to blink back tears of dismay as she heard the sentence. Surely no-one could take that many? She had caught a glimpse of Caroline's face as they were led out of Father Burton's office. She too was pale and swallowing hard.

They were locked in different cells after repeated questioning had failed to drag from either of them the cause of the fight. They had stood before the Father's desk in the 'open' position and he had lashed the fronts of their thighs and their breasts with a crop. When that had failed Brother Gibson had slapped them both hard across the face repeatedly.

Paula knew that gang loyalty would keep Caroline silent. The church had forged them into a unit and although Caroline had been beaten in a fight it had been done fair and square. The others might distrust her, but if there was to be any revenge; then they would do it themselves. For the moment she was safe. That only left the punishment to deal with.

She was tied face first against a stone wall with her

arms and legs splayed. Her collar was chained so tightly to a ring slightly above her that she had to turn her face sideways. Her ankles and wrists were tied to rings with leather straps to keep her pressed hard against the stone and her labia rings were chained tightly to her ankles while her breasts were squashed painfully to the stone. She was taken down once a day for food and allowed to use a flthy pile of straw as a toilet. She was beaten three times a day by Father Burton. He used a very whippy cane and he used it across her shoulders and back as well as her buttocks and thighs. In silence he delivered ten lashes at a time, three times a day for three long days.

Paula learned something new while receiving the ninety lashes. Her reactions to being beaten depended on the sexual context. Father Burton entered her cell in his robe with his hood pulled up and the cowl hiding his face. He looked terrifyingly like a figure from the Inquisition. The cane he used hung by a short leather loop from a hook right beside Paula. It was no more than six inches from her outstretched right hand and she had no choice but to look at it during the long hours between beatings. But despite this cruelty she experienced nothing but pain throughout her ordeal. There was no stimulation, her body shrank in fear before the figure of Father Burton and before the prospect of the cane whistling across her defenceless flesh. And in her isolation and fear she could derive no pleasure at all.

After the very first lashing Paula thought she would die before she could complete her sentence. Just ten strokes had reduced her to whimpered pleas for mercy as her back seethed and boiled. And there were eighty lashes to go. Eighty! It was inconceivable! Under each beating she screamed until she was hoarse. And the agony grew worse each time, as new stripes were laid over old. She shook and trembled with exhaustion at the end of each lashing but had to watch helplessly as the Father's hand replaced the cane. Then he left her, unable to do anything other than stare at it and contemplate the agony of her next installment. By the end of the second day, even when she was taken down, she could hardly move for the pain. And there were still thirty lashes to go. It was a mountain she couldn't climb.

On the third day she passed out halfway through the midday beating. She was left to come round in her own time. And when she blinked her way back to agonised consciousness, Father Burton stood exactly where he had stood before. And he carried on. Paula stared in wide eyed horror at the cane when he left. There were ten more lashes to go, and she knew she couldn't survive. She shook and trembled uncontrollably. A whole afternoon lay ahead of her in which she could only await an agony she didn't think she could take.

On her final beating she begged him for mercy before he started. He listened to her pleas and promises in his usual silence, but when she had stuttered and sobbed her way to a halt; he began. She could hardly scream any more and simply cried as slashes of unbelieveable agony ripped over her. He took a long time delivering that final ten, giving her plenty of time to recover before laying on the next lash. It extended her torture and made sure she stayed conscious. Towards the end, in the long pauses between lashes, she felt something warm slowly oozing over her buttocks and shoulders. She realised that the skin had split at last. And when he replaced the cane she could see that it was smeared with red.

They were released that night but only allowed to return to their quarters when they had mucked out their own cells. Paula saw that Caroline was filthy and bedraggled, her head hung down and there was no fight left in her. I must look the same, she thought, and she determined never to go through anything like that again. Briefly the girls' eyes met and Paula could see that the same thought was in both their minds.

Back in the novices' room, there was complete silence when they entered. The brother who had escorted them left them at the door. They had both had trouble walking up from the Punishment Wing. They were stiff and racked with pain, as well as being weak from hunger and exhaustion.

Paula looked down the length of the room at the showers. They were one of the most welcome sights she had ever seen and she began to limp towards them. At exactly the same time Caroline did as well. They glanced at each other and slowly exchanged rueful grins, then they helped each other along. There were gasps and cries from the others as they passed and the extent of their punishment became plain. They stood next to each other while hot water washed over them and helping hands soaped carefully over their cuts.

Linda gently rubbed cream into the lesser of Paula's bruises when she finally eased herself down onto her bed. Nothing was said but Paula knew that although Caroline might have sown some seeds of distrust, it was a private matter; something between the members of the group. Both she and Caroline had kept faith despite the punishment.

It had cost her a lot but she had weathered the crisis.

18.

In the days that followed, the only concession made to the severity of the punishments which Paula and Caroline had suffered was that they were allowed extra rations at mealtimes to build their strength up again. They still had to take their four strokes of the tawse however.

News of the fact that they had been sentenced to ninety lashes must have gone round like wildfire Paula thought, and the dining room went silent at the first breakfast after their release. All the girls, including the initiates Paula noted, turned to look as Caroline with Paula behind her reached the sister on duty. Caroline stood hopefully in front of her for a second.

"What are you waiting for girl?" the sister asked coldly.

Paula saw Caroline's shoulders slump. Slowly her hands fumbled her dress up to her hips and she bent over. The sister wasn't satisfied and hiked the dress up farther to reveal the whole of her bottom. Paula heard a few stifled gasps from the initiates and for the first time wondered whether anyone had ever been sentenced to so many strokes of the cane. Caroline's bottom was a network of narrow, livid ridges and in places there were long scabs beginning to form over the cuts. The sister flexed her tawse and Paula could see her considering where to lay her blows. Caroline's hands were gripping the edges of the table so hard that her knuckles had turned white. Quite suddenly the sister lashed out and the tawse smacked across the middle of one buttock. Caroline let out an agonised screech and her back arched. The sister struck again on the other buttock and again Caroline screeched, but this time there was an audible sob at the end of it.

Paula swallowed hard. Caroline had come through everything she had and this was obviously just as bad as anything they had suffered to date. She felt tears come to her eyes. It wasn't fair! They had had their punishment. Why were they being punished all over again? The answer was obvious really, she thought gloomily. It was so that the others could see, so that no-one would ever dare to do anything like it again. She was roused from her thoughts by the third smack of the tawse. The sister had hit lower down on the buttocks and Paula could see that it had overlaid a place where two strokes of the cane had already crossed. Caroline cried openly and then wailed as the fourth smack came down on a similar place on the other buttock. She stood up shakily and went to get her food, wiping at her eyes.

Paula felt the whole room's attention now focus on her as she bent over and pulled her dress up. Like Caroline she gripped the edges of the table as hard as she could and gritted her teeth. The first stinging smack brought instant floods of tears to her eyes and it was all she could do not to scream. It revived all the agony of the caning and added its own distinctive broad sweep of fiery pain. The second one had her breath hissing out between her clenched teeth and her hips wriggling. The third and fourth simply made her scream with all her strength to try and dissipate the agony.

She, like Caroline was shaking and crying at the end. She wiped furiously at her eyes to try and see her way to where the food was. But once she had collected it and gone to her place, both she and Caroline had to stand up to eat.

As she ate Paula looked around at the other girls. Some of them were staring at her and Caroline with expressions of contempt. It was as if they were saying, 'that's what you get for being that stupid'. On the other hand some of the girls were looking at them with open admiration. Paula presumed that they were admiring the fact that the two of them had taken so many lashes. But underlying both reactions Paula could see the undercurrent of fear and awe at the devastating retribution which the masters had exacted.

For the next week, at the end of each meal, Paula and Caroline were made to strip and adopt the 'open' position by the door of the dining room so that all the others filed out past them and could get a good long look at their ravaged backs. Owing to the constant beatings with the tawse however, the damage to their buttocks was very slow to heal and it was nearly a fortnight before they could approach mealtimes without fear and trembling.

19.

Lights flashed and music thundered. It was a pounding, almost African rhythm, amplified to the pain threshold so that it was impossible to tell where the body ended and the music began. But Chief Inspector Margaret Barfield grimly held her ground against the swaying mass of women all around her and concentrated on the scene on stage.

The young priest had made his entrance and the women around Margaret had gone wild. The music had increased in volume and cages had been lowered from the flies. Inside the cages had been dancing girls, and it was these which held her gaze. They were naked apart from leather and chain harness and they danced with a wild abandon which set Margaret's heart thumping. She watched as their hips swayed and their hands snaked down their bodies to bury themselves between their wide-spread legs. Margaret felt her mouth go dry, they were lovely, big-breasted girls. One of them had black hair and for a moment she had thought it might be Paula.

WPC Cheever was her responsibility and she was determined to find her. She was sure the Church of Ultimate Purification had taken her, but no-one had been able to get any leads. They didn't dare go public and admit that they had lost a copper. The tabloids would have had a field day, and it could have put Paula in danger. So while her team scratched about for anything they could find, Margaret had taken it on herself to attend some meetings and services held by the Church.

When she had first come home and told her partner what she was doing, Lisa had gone mad and Margaret had taken some very severe punishment, but she had stuck to her guns. Lisa was very jealous and dominant, but Margaret found her dominance the perfect antidote to the pressures of a day of being in command herself, over both men and women. She had been very careful not to let on to Lisa how much she had fancied Paula, and made it a simple issue of police work. But even so, she could feel her bottom sting all over again when she thought about how Lisa's strap had ensured that she wouldn't stray.

But here was temptation. And the girls were so obviously submissive. Unfortunately it was the men to whom their submission seemed to be aimed, and Margaret had to remind herself that she was prepared to go wherever she had to in order to find Paula, and once rescued she would be only too glad to sleep with her.

The young priest was launching into some kind of sermon and she strained to hear above the noise. It seemed to be a tirade against the corruption of modern society, and how all the certainties of life had been swept away. She heard him proclaim the now familiar doctrine of the subservience of women as decreed by the Bible and how the Church of Ultimate Purification would rebuild society in accordance with the commandments. Women would stay at home, criminals would be punished, justice would be swift and terrible.

All around her Margaret could see the crowd of women responding. And she could understand why. All people wanted was to know where they stood, to have a rank, to have authority they could believe in again. And that desire was being focused through the handsome young man on stage, now being joined by equally well set up young men all in the robes of the Church, to whom the dancing girls made blatant invitations. Some of the women around Margaret were taking off blouses and hurling them at the stage. She saw some wriggling their knickers down and throwing them.

It had taken Margaret weeks to work her way here. She had attended small meetings and had dutifully lied about her belief in the inferiority of women and how attractive she found the Church's teachings. At last she had been allowed to attend this; what they called a sacrament.

The cages were lowered onto the stage and opened. As soon as the girls were released they fell to their knees in front of the men. The priest was saying something about training, but all Margaret could concentrate on was the sight of the girls' hands working at the fronts of the robes the men wore. A great sigh went up from the crowd as they saw the erect sexes rearing up in front of the girls' faces and then being taken into their willing mouths.

There was a surge towards the stage and Margaret began to elbow her way to the front of the crowd.

She had had sex with men plenty of times before she found that women turned her on more. And if she had to have oral sex with these men in order to find Paula, then that was what she would do. She held in her mind's eye a picture of Paula's pretty face. Her large eyes and mane of wavy black hair. And the inviting curves of her figure. She was certain that there were hidden passions in her and she was determined to unleash them.

And if she couldn't, a broad hint that future promotion prospects could be in jeopardy had done the trick with nearly a score of pretty young policewomen to date, it would work again.

She could probably arrange things again so that Lisa didn't find out.

Having fought her way to the stage, she held up her hands like the others, imploring the priest to take her. At last he noticed her and reached down, smiling. Up on stage and standing close beside him, Margaret could sense his extraordinary charisma. He radiated a kind of arrogant sexuality which she found she was helplessly responding to. The music pounded in time with her heart and the audience screamed and yelled. In front of her bodies swayed and joined in explicit acts of dominance and submission. The near naked females gleaming with sweat.

Margaret joined them and when one of the men turned to her she dropped to her knees. His member, shining with saliva from the mouth of another worshipper, jutted imperiously at her own mouth. She licked her lips and then opened them wide to feel the firm shaft slide towards the back of her throat. The salty male taste of the head and the vibrant life throbbing inside the rigid pillar of flesh, filled her senses. And suddenly this living shaft thrusting for her throat ignited a fire in her belly and eclipsed the dildo that Lisa wore and at which she had sucked so eagerly before.

She would find her lovely Paula and have her. But after that. . . . .?

20.

The Patriarch himself was coming.

Word gradually leaked down from the brothers that he was to pay a visit in only a week's time. At last Father Burton formally announced it after prayers one morning.

"He is to pay us the honour of staying with us for a few days. And we will show him how you have been rescued and redeemed, and now live only to serve the Church of Ultimate Purification. I intend to show him exactly how submissive you are to the work which he has begun, and which even now is gathering momentum in the outside world.

"In time to come the Patriarch will undoubtedly be remembered as one of the greatest men of this or any other day. So I cannot emphasise enough the honour which is to be ours. Work will start immediately on our preparations."

Paula couldn't help feeling a little sorry for the new girls whose promotion to the rank of novices would have to be delayed until after the visit. But mainly she felt sorry for herself. It meant that she and her group would not be able to become initiates either. She gazed enviously at the smart white dresses every day now, and dreamed of being able to wear the heeled shoes. But even in her dreams, she wanted them only to show off her submission more enticingly to the brothers. She knew the heels would accentuate the elegant length of her legs and the little white skirt would swirl around her loins so very invitingly. Now the brown shift she wore irritated her, and she could hardly remember the time when that in itself had seemed the ultimate luxury. The marks of hers and Caroline's caning had long since faded, even their buttocks now showed only the red patches left by the tawse. If there was any lingering distrust of her, none of her group ever mentioned it and Caroline seemed to be a firm friend if anything.

The novices were to dance for the Patriarch and Sister Helen began to drill them mercilessly. In the kitchens Brother Waite, the cook, began ordering massive quantities of food and the novices worked flat out each morning preparing a huge range of dishes under his direction which were to be presented to the Patriarch and his party.

It was the group he was bringing with him which provoked as much excitement as the man himself. It was rumoured that he never travelled without the members of his Inner Circle. These were the women who served him most closely and were the subject of envy and gossip. Sister Lavinia told them that some of them had once been sluts themselves who had been trained as they had been. Once Paula learned that it was possible to rise to the dizzy heights of serving the very man whose vision and power now controlled every aspect of her life, she knew what she wanted. Every other ambition she had ever had now seemed shallow. She had to become a member of the Inner Circle.

While every girl in the monastery was kept busy, the brothers themselves worked tirelessly. Lengths of timber piled up in the courtyard and the sounds of drilling and hammering filled the house. No-one would tell them what was being constructed but the knowing grins of the brothers left all the girls with a tingle of anticipation in their stomachs. It was bound to involve them in some way. Father Burton would want them to display their submission and the brothers were experts at devising ways of doing that.

On most nights now they were left to go to bed. Even the activities in the Lounge were restrained as the long hours took their toll on the men. But one night when Paula was sitting on her bed listening to Linda relay the latest gossip about the visit, Sister Lavinia came for her. She hadn't had

Paula since the night she had put her on the whipping stool and at the sight of her Paula's heart jumped a beat. She walked slowly along the room until she came to Paula's bed.

"Paula and Caroline, report to the Games Room now." She said.

All the girls exchanged glances. Why the two of them again? Paula stood up, her mouth suddenly dry. Sister Lavinia turned on her heel and they followed her out. They went in silence the whole way until she ushered them into the Games Room.

If Paula had been nervous before, her heart fell even further when she entered. No less than ten of the brothers were seated round the room. Some of them with initiates either on their laps or sitting at their feet. Brother Davis stood in the centre of the floor and he had a horsewhip coiled in his hand.

Sister Lavinia indicated that they should go to stand in front of him and then she left the room. All eyes were on them and no-one spoke as they came forward.

Brother Davis was in no hurry and let them stand, legs apart, hands behind their backs and eyes down, until he was good and ready. He walked slowly round them and only spoke when he stood in front of them again.

"Father Burton wants to make quite sure that before the Patriarch arrives, all the slaves are totally submissive to their masters and to the Church. You two are the only ones who've given us any trouble, so we are going to see if you've learned your lessons. Do you understand?"

"Yes Master," they chorused dutifully.

"Now as your offense was fighting. You are going to show us all just how much your punishment taught you to love one another and work in unity for the Church of Ultimate Purification. We are going to watch you while you do it."

Paula and Caroline exchanged sidelong glances. Paula had no idea what Caroline's experience with other women was, but her own was limited to her one time with Sister Lavinia. But here she was going to have to perform in front of an attentive audience.

"Strip!" He told them. Obediently they discarded their short dresses and stood naked. Brother Davis turned them so that everyone could see their backs. "Good as new," he observed, "so we've decided to whip you first, just to get you in the mood." Here he came close to Paula and fondled her left breast. "You always go better for a whipping."

Slaves who had suffered ninety lashes, he said, didn't need tying for the paltry ten he was going to give them. Instead they were taken over to the huge fireplace and made to lean over the bar at which Paula could remember so clearly being whipped before. They stood side by side and braced their hands on the mantlepiece. This left them nicely bent forward and Brother Davis gave them the ten lashes each which he had promised. It was the first time since their punishment that either had been whipped seriously.

He alternated between the girls, giving Paula one stroke and then switching to Caroline. Being whipped by the brothers again revived the pleasure Paula took in it. It was like being back in harness, this was where she belonged.

The sound of the whip cracking across her back, the bright shafts of pain as the lash curled lovingly around her ribs and made her breasts judder and ripple, all awoke the fires in her sex. She glanced over at Caroline as she got her lashes and loved the way her head went back and she gasped at each impact. The thought of making love to her in front of the men suddenly seemed exciting, she herself jerked under another lash and then watched Caroline's pretty little breasts sway as her stomach clenched when the long lash whipped round to bite into it. She saw Caroline look over at her and their eyes met while Brother Davis lashed at Paula's buttocks. They smiled at one another as he targeted Caroline's buttocks next. She closed her eyes briefly when the whip landed with a fleshy smack and Paula wanted to feel with her hands how the weal would trace a ridge across the smooth skin. The gasp Caroline made didn't sound like pain. And Paula herself found she had now to concentrate on thoughts of the long days of her punishment to prevent herself getting too excited. By the time they had each had ten lashes, they were both eager to please the brothers in any way they wanted. Just a little whipping, Paula thought, and we do anything. She couldn't prevent a delicious surge of arousal at that thought.

"Now," Brother Davis said standing back and coiling the whip neatly, "in the middle of the floor."

They stood facing each other. Paula could see how flushed Caroline's face was and knew that, like her, the thought of an audience didn't bother her in the slightest. She reached out and touched one of Caroline's nipples, the beating had made it hard and Paula rubbed it firmly, turning the metal of the ring where it pierced the pink flesh. Caroline came close and Paula pulled her hungrily towards her. They kissed, and their tongues quested deep into each other's mouths. It wasn't enough for Paula, she could feel the urgency in herself and she dropped quickly to her knees, trailing her tongue down the slender body until at last it found the bush of dark hair between her legs. Above her she heard Caroline moan and the legs parted further to allow Paula access. She pushed her mouth into the musky depths, using the rings in the labia to pull open the lips and savour the sight of the pink slit of her sex. Then she set about the soft inner lips, sucking and pulling, nipping at the swelling clitoris until Caroline cried out and Paula tasted the pungent juice of her arousal. She felt the girl's legs tremble and she sank down to her knees to join her and then she pulled Paula down to lie on the carpet.

As soon as Paula was on her back, Caroline was at her sex. She had never had a woman explore her there and arched her back in exquisite pleasure when Caroline's tongue began to repay her. She felt it lap and rub at her, persistently and patiently. She arched up even further to allow Caroline to get her mouth right to her hole and lick up into it. Caroline grabbed her buttocks and dug her fingers in, reviving the pain of the lashes and sending fresh waves of pleasure surging through her. Paula tried to reach down between her legs and press the girl's head even farther in but even as she did, several hard, rasping licks at her throbbing clitoris brought the bright tides of orgasm crashing over her. She writhed and bucked her hips as spasm after spasm swept through her before she finally lay panting on the floor.

But Caroline was impatient and knelt astride her quickly. She smiled down at Paula and mischievously pulled her arms up above her head and held them with her own hands while she moved up to kneel astride Paula's shoulders. Then she lowered her wide open sex onto Paula's waiting mouth. Held in a position which reminded her of being tied for the whip, Paula relished the sight of it descending towards her, its lips full and soft, swelling open to reveal the glistening flesh within. Caroline moved sinuously as Paula licked at her, sliding her pelvis forward to rub herself over Paula's tongue and let it probe up into her hole, then moving back to let her suck at her clitoris. And when Paula heard her begin her orgasm she worked even harder, mercilessly driving her on and making her cry and writhe above her. She delved with her tongue and felt the juice flooding from her to mingle with her own saliva and she pushed until her tongue ached and at last Caroline arched rigid for a second, gave one long cry and then collapsed and lay beside her. They lay for a moment face to face, then Paula tentatively licked at the shining fluid spread on Caroline's cheeks. To her delight she tasted the pungent musk of her own arousal where it had oozed over the other girl. She began to lick more eagerly and Caroline began to stir, realising that she too could taste herself off Paula's face.

In only a few minutes of frantic licking and kissing Paula could feel her sex stirring and churning again, the lips quivering. But she wanted to use fingers now as well. She turned herself and knelt over Caroline. Her legs were spread wide over Caroline's face in complete abandon and Paula reached down to plunge her fingers into the warm moistness of another woman's sex. She pushed them in as far as she could and watched as Caroline's hips rose to meet them. At the same time she felt Caroline's fingers probing her, twisting and turning in her to stir the juices and set yet more of her nectar flowing. Both vaginas made hungry slurping noises as the fingers worked in them. With a moan of gathering ecstasy she bent forward and buried her face once more deep in the soaking darkness between Caroline's legs. She wriggled her hips to settle her own sex more closely over Caroline's mouth and set about bringing her to another peak. She knew her position meant that she was totally exposed. Her crouching posture stretched her buttocks tight and her lips would be opening eagerly right above Caroline's face. She felt the girl reach round the backs of her thighs to hold the lips apart and then her tongue began to lap once more.

Both girls had been so transported by their passion that they had forgotten their audience. But now, from the corner of her eye Paula saw Brother Davis come to stand beside her. Trailing from his hand she saw a dog whip. He raised it and Paula gave a cry of shock as he lashed her across her buttocks, only inches from Caroline's mouth working at her sex. She felt Caroline wrench her buttocks apart to let the whip bite into the soft skin at the next lash, under the constant rasping of a tongue against her clitoris and the sharp stabs of pain from the whip Paula was driven to a peak of blinding passion. Her face was buried in the writhing, flooding gash of Caroline's sex and the taste filled her mouth while her buttocks burned under the whip and her sex rippled and churned under the caresses of Caroline's tongue. She nearly fainted at this third orgasm which exploded and burst inside her to leave her twitching and helpless in its wake.

For a moment she went totally limp and felt herself being rolled onto her back. When she opened her eyes it was to see Caroline's buttocks over her and her swollen sex lips. Without even thinking she reached up and pulled them closer so that she could repeat the experience for her. She pulled the cheeks of her bottom apart and frantically ran her tongue up and down the length of the slit. Just above her was the tight closed bud of Caroline's anus and she was about to reach for it with her tongue when Brother Davis began to wield the whip again. Fascinated and thrilled she watched as the lash cracked across Caroline just inches from her mouth. Even though they were pulled taut she saw ripples run through the cushions of flesh at each lash and felt the girl jerk in response. One more time she delved with her tongue and took a cruel pleasure in driving her remorselessly on to those heights which she herself had just reached.

When the nectar of Caroline's delirious ecstasy lay thick over Paula's tongue and the whip had ceased to lash at her, she too fell limply onto her side.

For a long time they lay side by side, heads at each others sexes, bewildered and amazed at their own passion.

But eventually Caroline's hand found one of Paula's breasts and began to stroke it. Paula groaned, she couldn't take any more. But she had to. They had passed this test and the brothers weren't about to waste two whipped and aroused slaves with sexes wide open and vaginas desperate for filling.

Neither of them could remember how many men took them that night, but Paula counted at least two who rammed themselves into her anus. And the sprays of sperm pumped repeatedly into her mouth left her with a delicious taste of mingled male and female climaxes.

21.

On the day of the visit the girls were all mounted and displayed by early afternoon.

The new girls were displayed on the huge wooden X which had been constructed in the main hall. It started at floor level and went well above the galleried landing, supported by thick ropes mounted high on the wall. The brothers lowered it to the floor to put nine of the girls on it. Each limb of the cross had two girls tied firmly to it one above the other. They were tied full length, arms and legs stretched out, feet and hands together while a thick belt at their waists, tightly cinched around the timber of the cross held their bodies parallel to the wood. In the centre of the display was a girl tied spreadeagle fashion. When they had all been mounted, the brothers hauled on the ropes and the living cross, formed by naked female bodies, rose up to stand at the back of the main hall towering some thirty feet above the floor. The last girl of the group was tied to her own cross which was hoisted up above the entrance to the gallery along which Paula's group was to be displayed. And as they were marched past to take up their places they couldn't help gasping at the spectacular sight.

At first Paula couldn't make any sense of the preparations which had been made for them. There were ten thick lengths of timber spaced out along the corridor and jutting straight out from the same wall at slightly less than shoulder height, the ends had been planed into dome shapes and covered in leather. Each girl was stood in front of a timber with her back to it and her arms spread and chained back behind her. Her ankles were then spread and forced back against the wall and chained tightly as well. The timber post jutting out into her back below her shoulder blades supported her but forced her upper body out and left her leaning out into the corridor as though she were the figurehead of an old sailing ship. With her arms spread back and stretched apart, her breasts were prominently displayed, and to further emphasise this effect each girl was gagged with a long leather strap, fastened not at the back of the head, but to studs set in the length of timber. This forced her head up and back, pulling the breasts even further up and ensuring that no screaming could spoil the harmony of the display. And before it was her turn to be gagged, Paula managed a look up and down their line. Twenty breasts were all prettily thrust out and ten naked bodies were splayed open. Once they were all gagged, the reason for it became clear. A flex was run down the whole line and a small crocodile clip attached to each nipple ring. A second flex ran along the line as well, this one attached to each labia ring and a smear of electrolytic cream on the sex lips themselves ensured good conductivity. The finishing touch was provided by delicate silver bells hung from each ring at both nipples and labia. Brother Gibson connected the transformer at one end, ensured that each flex was correctly looped to its terminal and experimented with delivering shocks of varying severity until he found the right setting for the rheostat.

The effect they wanted was to make all ten bodies jerk and stiffen at each shock so that all the bells would ring. Shocks could be delivered either at their sexes and breasts simultaneously or separately, the trick was to find a setting which could deliver a shock repeatedly without making any of the girls pass out.

Paula felt each hammer blow at her sex strike up into her stomach sickeningly, while the ripples that ran through her breasts seemed to make her teeth rattle against her gag. But after five or six experiments a level of supportable agony which set all the bells jingling had been established.

They were left to await the visit for an hour or so and Paula found herself moistening in the familiar way as she thought about how cruel and complete the preparations had been.

At last they all heard the scrunching of gravel at the front of the house as the car carrying the Patriarch and his party arrived.

Father Burton and the entire staff had gathered in the hall. Paula heard his voice raised in greeting and heard it answered by a voice even more resonant than his. She could make out some words which were congratulating everyone on the magnificent display in the hall, and then the party entered the gallery along which she and her group were displayed. By swivelling her eyes to the side, Paula saw them arrive. First came four women. They had to be part of the Inner Circle, they were dressed in beautifully tailored sheath dresses which were split up to the hip on one side, and as they moved the material parted to reveal a tantalising glimpse of long, elegant leg. Behind them came Father Burton and the Patriarch himself.

Paula just had time to register his tall powerfully built figure and strong face with the most piercing blue eyes she had ever seen, before Brother Gibson began the display.

Helplessly she jerked and writhed under the shocks, shrieking silently into her gag. Her hips bucked and her stomach spasmed, her shoulders shook and her back arched in agony. Time and again the shocks came, sometimes just at her breasts sometimes at breasts and sex together. The bells jingled prettily as the ten girls stiffened and slumped helplessly.

When at last they stopped it took a few moments for the red mist of pain to clear from Paula's vision. But when it did the Patriarch was standing nearly in front of her.

He was laughing delightedly. "What a charming display Father! You have excelled yourself!" he said. He waved casually at Brother Gibson and immediately the shocks began again. Paula thought she must pass out this time, but after only three or four they stopped again. Some of the bells continued to ring as girls slumped against their bonds but then there was silence and Paula looked again at the man for whom she and all the rest suffered. He radiated power, simply dressed in an immaculate dark suit and white shirt, there was no mistaking who was in command.

His eyes seemed to bore into each girl as he walked slowly down their line. When he came to Paula she met his gaze.

Here was all the power and cruelty which she had come to need. All the power which she had thought belonged to Father Burton and the brothers was only a pale reflection of his brilliance. She would obey any command he gave her, obey any command any of his servants gave her, but somehow she had to get close to him. The piercing blue eyes drilled into her and seemed to see her willing submission because a slight smile twisted at his lips before he passed on. She marvelled at his economical movements, so strong and so utterly self confident.

He was power personified. He was the Church. And Paula wanted to be nothing but a tool for his use.

He passed on and behind him came the four women he had brought. They too gazed at each girl, but with cool contemptuous smiles. The last one, a tall blonde, stopped for a long time at Paula and stared hard at her. And as Paula stared back she realised that she knew the woman. She had seen her somewhere before, but she couldn't think where. As she searched her memory though a small knot of fear began to form in her stomach.

The woman herself obviously couldn't remember where she had met Paula, and looking thoughtful she moved off. Soon the whole party had gone into the room prepared for them and where the initiates waited to serve them. Two of the brothers took Paula and her group down and allowed them only a couple of minutes to recover before hurrying them back to their quarters. Sister Helen was waiting for them with their dancing costumes and there was no time to nurse aching breasts and throbbing sexes. They drew on the thin gowns, brushed their hair and went back.

The party, along with Father Burton and several senior brothers and sisters were seated in small groups around the edge of a luxurious drawing room that none of the girls had been in before. The initiates were either on all fours with their backs providing footstools for the men and women seated beside them, or scurrying carefully on all fours between tables with trays strapped to their backs from which drinks were taken.

Paula glanced hurriedly round at the scene as her group took up position in the middle of the room. She noticed the blonde woman looking hard at her again. The music started and Paula focused all her attention on the dark figure holding court in front of her. She let her imagination tell her she was dancing on her own and for him alone, and she knew her body was giving a blatant display of submissive need and invitation. She swayed and writhed seductively as she had been taught to but knew she was bringing to the movements every bit of passion she could conjure up. And for a moment, when the music stopped and all the girls knelt with their legs apart and their hands high above their heads, she thought that she had succeeded in catching his eye. She stole a glance and saw him looking at her. But then he turned to Father Burton and she saw the colour drain from the Father's face. The blonde woman leaned over and there was a whispered conversation between the three of them.

And as she watched Paula suddenly felt her world fall apart. She saw the blonde woman in profile and knew where she had seen her before.

22.

Sick with terror Paula stared down at the carpet. But then the Patriarch spoke.

"You! Come here!" His voice brooked no argument.

She looked up again hoping desperately that he meant one of the others. He didn't. Shakily she got to her feet and approached him. The blonde was staring at her in open triumph now, Father Burton was white with fury and the Patriarch had a closed, unreadable expression. He gestured her to her knees again when she reached him and then stood up to tower over her.

"Your name is Paula, is it not?"

"Yes Master."

"WPC Paula Cheever. You are a spy and an informer against us." His voice was flat and unemotional, yet it conveyed to Paula depths of anger and cruelty which turned her stomach to water.

"Master, I am not a spy." She managed to whisper.

Her thoughts were racing and raging against this twist of fate. Just as she had found the core of her new identity, the man she knew she wanted to give herself utterly to, her past identity which she had thought finally buried, returned to haunt her. The blonde woman's name was Maria Hegarty and two years ago Paula had played a large part in having her arrested for running a brothel. Again Paula had been in plain clothes, Maria had got six months and must have gone back on the game when she got out and been picked up by the Church.

"You are a policewoman. You are a spy." He stated facts. His voice was so resonant and strong, his personality so overwhelming that Paula had to struggle against admitting any crime he accused her of.

But she wasn't a policewoman, not any more. And she wasn't a spy.

Hopelessly she murmured, "I am not a policewoman Master. And I am no spy."

"Liar!" The blonde shrieked.

Paula glanced up sharply and saw the Patriarch hold up a hand angrily to silence her. Then the hand descended and dealt Paula a blinding blow across her face. The rings on his fingers slammed into her and she felt her mouth fill with the warm salt taste of blood as she fell. She hit the floor and dazedly tried to wipe at her mouth but two of the brothers suddenly held her arms in their powerful grasp and hauled her up. She saw Father Burton's face in front of her. He seemed to have controlled his fury but ground out his words between clenched teeth.

"Put her under the Punishment Wing. She can rot there until we decide what to do."

There was a door leading out from one of the rooms in which Paula had endured a day's comtemplation. She was taken through this and down some steps into a maze of cellars. At the door of the farthest one the two brothers who held her tore off the gown in which she had danced and pushed her in naked. It was nearly pitch black and there was only straw on the stone floor. But they weren't finished yet. One of the men switched on a dim light and Paula saw the other lift a metal grating in the floor. She began to scream and beg but only received another blow to the face. They lifted her easily down through the hole and let her hang at the full extent of her arms, holding her only by her wrists. And then they let her drop. She fell only a foot or so but it might as well have been a mile. The grating was closed above her and she heard a padlock clamped into place. Then they left her and turned out the light in the room above as they went.

Once her eyes became accustomed to the dark, she realised it wasn't total. There was a small, filthy little window set in the wall of the cellar above her and this let in just enough light for her to be able to make out her surroundings. She was in a pit barely big enough for her to lie down in. There was some old, stale straw in one corner and down one side of her prison ran a shallow gutter, presumably for her waste. A word came back to her from history lessons at school, 'oubliette'; a pit into which prisoners were thrown to be forgotten about until they starved to death. Were parts of the monastery old enough for this to be a real one? It did the job even if it wasn't authentic. And would they leave her? No, she was sure that the Patriarch would want to get out of her all the information he could. She shuddered at the implacable willpower she had sensed in him. She had no information to give him. But she knew that the Church had members in the police and she was sure that even now Maria's story was being checked and her own identity established. Besides the girls in her group would confirm that they all thought she was different in some way. And Brother Davis would remember his first misgivings about her. She sank down miserably in a corner and tried to curl up on the straw to keep warm. At last she fell into an exhausted sleep.

She was woken by the light being turned on in the cellar above her and the grate being unlocked and lifted. Paula blinked in the light and saw a ladder being lowered, Father Burton's voice told her to climb it. She emerged into the cellar and saw the brothers preparing it for her. New chains were being attached to old rings set in the walls and their strengths tested. Already some hung from the ceiling and all Paula's terror returned. Father Burton smiled as he saw her look about her.

"You are right to be terrified. We know quite well who you really are and all that remains is to know who you were to report to, and how. The Patriarch himself intends to get the information from you."

Paula could only drop to her knees, "Please Master! I am not a spy!" she begged.

Father Burton's only response was to gesture irritably to the brothers that they should begin. Her wrists were fastened together behind her and at the same time a chain was clipped to the catches on her restraints. The chain ran through a ring in the ceiling and two of the brothers simply hauled her up by it. Paula screamed as she never had before. It felt as if her shoulders were being torn from her body as her arms were pulled up behind her and her whole bodyweight came agaist them. They pulled her up until she was hanging some four feet off the floor. Through her tears and screams she became aware that the Patriarch stood in front of her.

"Paula Cheever. In the words of an older and more crude movement than mine. I am going to put you to the question. And I will go on asking it until I think I have arrived at the truth. Who were you to report to and how were you to contact them?"

Paula could hardly speak from pain, all she could do was scream out again that she wasn't a spy. Again and again he asked her the question and she shrieked out her denial until merciful darkness claimed her.

When she came to, she was lying on the cellar floor exactly where they had let her fall, her arms still tied behind her. One of the brothers stood over her and glanced down impassively as she stirred and moaned. She heard him leave and slowly managed to lever herself into a sitting position by using the wall. Her shoulders ached savagely and she was nearly sick with fear of what they would do next. She cried until they came for her again.

The Patriarch watched while she was laid on the floor and chains attached to her ankles this time. She begged them for mercy but they ignored her and pulled her up so that her legs were raised and spread, only her upper back remaining on the floor. The Patriarch came to stand beside her and she looked up into his implacable face. The bitterness of having the man she wanted to serve believe her to be a traitor was unbearable. She glanced up the length of her body and saw the brother who stood beyond her wide spread thighs, and she saw his whip. She groaned.

The Patriarch repeated the question. Paula gulped and braced herself before repeating her denial. Immediately she heard the Swish! of the whip and it lashed into her wide open sex. It was a heavy, many-thonged whip and its impact drove all breath out of her. It seemed to crush the tender flesh between her legs and its weight on her stomach almost winded her. The Patriarch waited patiently until she had got enough breath back after screaming, and then asked her again. She sobbed out her denial and then bucked and twisted in her chains as she was whipped again. As when Father Burton had condemned her to the cane, her fear outwieghed any pleasure.

How she would have loved to have been able to tell the truth and be believed. Then she would have welcomed this pain at the hands of the Patriarch. But as it was all she could cling to was the hope that if she kept up her denials they might be forced to believe her.

Again the question and again the denial. Swish Smack! Her left inner thigh blazed with pain this time and she arched frantically until only the back of her neck touched the floor.

Swish Smack! Her right thigh this time and she screamed again.

Slowly it ground on. She passed out and they gave her time to recover before starting in again. The question, the denial; Swish Smack!

Despite the cold she was sweating with pain and hoarse with screaming. Her sex had been pounded into a kind of total white hot agony which was all she could see or feel. She shook and trembled but croaked out her denials, stubbornly clinging to the truth. She was no spy.

The brother who was whipping her came to stand at her head. Now the lashes bit into the crease between her buttocks and made her anus sting and blaze. But still she denied and still the dreadful whipping went on until all she could do was shake her head dumbly in denial and then moan as the whip smacked home again, her body too exhausted to even writhe anymore.

At long last the Patriarch stopped it and ordered her to be lowered and released. She lay with her legs spread as they fell from the chains, sobbing brokenly. She felt the Patriarch's shoe dig contemptuously at her ribs.

"If anyone wants this slut, help yourselves."

At this final devastating cruelty Paula's spirit nearly broke. What really hurt, even above the scarlet agony which consumed her body, was his anger with her. Her Master believed she was his enemy and she had no way of demonstrating her willing submission to him. Everything would be misinterpreted as stubborn loyalty to some other cause.

She had no time to dwell on her misery however. The time they had spent whipping her wide open sex had inflamed the brothers. One of them dragged her over to the pile of straw and lowered himself onto her while she lay on her back. Her body arched and she managed one more shriek as he thrust in between her tortured lips. The channel of her vagina was dry and it was some time before he was able to get full penetration, but once he did, her body reacted on its own. And while she lay groaning under his weight he took his pleasure with her, reaming her out and then spurting his seed into her in the casual way she so loved. The second one turned her over and raised her haunches before ramming into her back passage. Again she shrieked as the tortured flesh was stretched but then she had to moan once more in helpless pleasure as the inner membranes were stimulated and then flooded with his spend.

She lay motionless for a long time after they went. But eventually the door opened and Caroline came to kneel beside her. She brought a bowl with cold wet flannels in it and pressed them gently to Paula's weals. She brought food and water as well and she urged her to make a confession. She knew Paula was no spy, she said, she could have saved herself that terrible caning if she had told Father Burton that it was she, Caroline who had started the fight. Paula knew the trick - hard and then soft - wear them down. But she couldn't explain the truth to Caroline either, it would seem like a partial confession and they would come after the rest of it just as hard. And Caroline left her with a pitying look. The brothers returned and lowered her back into her prison.

She had no real way of measuring time in the dark. They left her a blanket and she slept, curled protectively around her throbbing sex. At some point food came and was lowered in a bucket which was hauled up again when she had eaten the bread and drunk the water. She slept again, food arrived again, and so it went on until her pit stank and she itched constantly from whatever was in her straw.

She began to sink into a stupor, she ate what she was given, she used the wretched gutter and she dozed. Time ceased to exist, the dark, the stench and the cold were the only realities. It was only much later that she learned she was down there for a week before being brought up again. She could hardly climb the ladder and sank down exhausted at the top. She noticed the men shrink from her and knew she must stink of her own filth. They only stayed long enough to ask whether she was ready to confess, listen to her refusal and say she was to be kept up here until her next appearance before the Patriarch, an appearance which would be made much more pleasant if she would stop being so stubborn. She shook her head and crawled over to the wall, to which her wrists were chained, when they told her to, and then they left. Caroline appeared again with warm water this time and sluiced off most of the filth. She told her they had something special lined up for her next time, but Paula could only shake her head again and she left, angry at Paula's stupidity.

Whatever they had lined up for her, she thought, they wanted her in reasonable condition for it now that deprivation had failed to break her. She got real food regularly and Caroline gradually combed out and washed her hair each day. She gave up trying to get Paula to confess and gave her the news instead.

The Patriarch was staying on to deal with Paula himself and some new women had joined the monastery. They were volunteers she said, not rescued sluts like the others, but women who wanted to join the Church. They served of their own free will and were housed separately. They went out of the monastery to work for the Patriarch, but served like the other girls when they were in it.

When she was taken out for questioning for the last time, Brother Davis came for her. As he knelt beside her to unchain her wrists she realised there was some pity in the way he looked at her. That scared her, this was the man who had first trained her, whose arrogant cruelty had excited her. She had never seen him look at any of the slaves with pity before, no matter how savagely they were being treated.

"It would be better if you confessed now. The Patriarch has sent the volunteers out to work for the day; he says they are not ready to see what he intends to do to you."

Paula felt her legs tremble and her mouth went dry. What was left that they could possibly do? But whatever it was she had no choice but to take it.

23.

Naked and led by a chain clipped to the rings at her belly, Paula was led into the courtyard. Brother Davis allowed her to stand for a moment and blink owlishly until her eyes became accustomed to the daylight. It was an overcast day but to Paula it felt like brilliant sunshine which hurt her eyes. But eventually she was able to see what was in store for her.

"The Patriarch wants to make quite certain you haven't got any accomplices here." Brother Davis whispered.

She saw that the whole monastery had been gathered to watch, presumably in the hope of flushing out an accomplice by the severity of the treatment which was to be handed out to her. Even in her terror she felt the familiar comfort of her admiration for the brutal logic.

There was a scaffold. It must have been built specially and stood where the whipping post normally did. It had a platform and above the platform rose a post. From the post a short beam protruded at right angles which was braced so that it would hold her weight and from this beam hung a simple rope. All the girls and the staff were lined up in two rows in front of it, but they had been kept well back.

Brother Davis tugged her forward by her leash. She followed on legs which would hardly support her. By the time he led her up the steps and onto the platform where the Patriarch waited, she could hardly see through her tears.

"Who were you to report to and how?" he asked immediately.

She sank to her knees, "Please Master! Believe me, I am no spy!" she begged one last time.

"How can you be anything else?" he asked.

Paula could only shake her head once again.

"Take her up." He ordered calmly.

Sweating and shaking in terror Paula watched while her normal wrist restraints were removed and long ones, almost the length of her forearms were buckled on. Steel loops ran down the insides of them and through these the end of the rope was first threaded, down one arm, up the other and then securely knotted back on itself. Brother Davis and Brother Harris hauled on the other end of the rope until Paula hung by her wrists, well clear of the platform, and then they tied it off. She swung helplessly and as her body turned on the end of the rope she saw the horses.

Four of them were lined up at the far end of the huge courtyard, they were each ridden by a brother, and each brother held a horsewhip.

Paula began to scream. The Patriarch climbed down from the platform and stood in front of it with one arm raised. He glanced up at Paula, his face expressionless, and then he dropped his arm. The first rider put his heels to his mount and over Paula's despairing wail, there was the sound of hooves beginning to pound.

Paula closed her eyes but still heard the hooves closing in on her and then with a rush of wind and the horse's breath snorting just below, it was on her. And so was its rider's whip. A lightning bolt of blinding pain struck across her stretched breasts and a thunderous Crack! half deafened her. Her body spun helplessly at the end of its rope and shock made her open her eyes wide. As the scene around her revolved crazily she heard hooves again, this time she craned her neck desperately to see where the horse was but it was too late. It was on her and its rider's whip cracked across her buttocks. The force of it made her body sway as well as spin this time. She put her head back and screamed as a pain so sharp as to be almost numbing engulfed her. She screamed again and was still screaming when another thunderous

Crack! exploded across her lower stomach. Her legs bicycled wildly in mid air trying to stabilise her body. The courtyard and its surrounding buildings blurred past her eyes as she spun and then the fourth horseman arrived. Whether it was one of the more openly sadistic brothers or whether his aim was just poor, Paula had no way of telling but his whip snapped around her thighs and wrapped itself tight. She screamed as a band of white fire engulfed her legs and then she choked on the scream as her legs were pulled after the rider for a second, which nearly wrenched her arms from their sockets. And when the whip did fall away, her body swung like a pendulum and spun at the same time.

The four horsemen were now gathered at the opposite end of the courtyard to the one from which they had started. They came back. But because her body was now moving so much, as she herself frantically squirmed, Paula suffered lashes to virtually any and every part of her body. Of the next batch of four, one landed fully across her middle back and left her gasping for breath and again set her swinging madly, one caught her round the waist and spun her, one hit her breasts again. The last one, as her legs splayed and struggled in mid air, struck round one thigh and bit deep into the soft flesh at the top. It robbed Paula of any remaining breath and the onlookers saw her gape helplessly in agony and then they saw her cruelly wrenched by one leg in the wake of the horse.

When two batches of four lashes each had been delivered and the horses were back where they had started, Paula was taken down. She lay on the platform, sobbing and heaving for breath. Her whole body a sea of agony from wrists to ankles.

The Patriarch came to stand over her. He asked her his question and she gave the denial which by now was the one thing she had left to cling to. He knelt beside her and held her chin so that he could look into her eyes. She blinked away some tears and tried to look back. His face was troubled, it seemed to Paula that the light of self belief which had seemed to stream from him before was being dimmed by a cloud of doubt and she hated the thought that she was the cause.

"It must go on!" He spoke quietly to her, grinding out the words, but she knew he meant them as much for himself as for her.

Of course it had to go on. He had to be seen to be in control. Paula herself wouldn't have it any other way. If she could only think of a means to convince him of the truth and save them both from this impasse. . . .

"I understand Master." She said at last.

His fierce eyes held hers. A small smile touched his lips briefly and set a fire raging in Paula's body more bright than any pain from a whip.

"We will talk again later." He said quietly and then stood up and gave the order to take her up again.

Although it felt as if her arms were being held by red hot pincers and she faced another savage flogging, Paula's heart rejoiced. Somehow she would convince him of the truth, and in the meantime she knew that the show had to go on, otherwise the whole edifice he had created would crumble.

Joyfully she prepared to play her part, and when the next lash struck the pain which ripped across her buttocks and hip joined in the molten eruption her master's smile had started in her belly. Her body's spinning meant the next lash cut across her pubis and the cry she gave in response was one of wild abandon. She was being whipped again, but for her master's sake this time; and there was only one way she would respond to that.

Even as she gazed up at her wrists and the taut rope which held them, she imagined what it would feel like to have the Patriarch take his pleasure with this body which was being tortured for him. The whip smacking deafeningly across her breasts and wrenching at her nipples before falling away only served to make the juices flood into her yearning vagina more urgently. A further explosion of pain across the fronts of her thighs made her sex ripple with longing for him.

Back the horses came, and made her twist and swing helplessly, but she tried to press her legs together to feel as much of her pleasure as she could while she cried out and writhed for her master under the repeated blasts of the whips.

She wasn't put to the question this time. They made one more pass and inevitably, as she felt her very vulnerability propel her to a shattering climax, she felt the first warm trickles down her flanks. And Paula experienced a breathtaking pride at this proof of how she had suffered for the man who was in all senses her master.

When they took her down finally and her head cleared, it was Brother Davis's face she saw looking down at her with disbelief. She realised that she was lying with her legs open and he had seen how her sex lips were open and glistening, full with desire and pleasure. She gave him a secret smile and crawled after him on all fours, her body raging with fires inside and out. Dimly she heard everyone being dismissed and at last she was back in the cool darkness of the Pen. Brother Davis led her to the shower room and allowed her to collapse. She lay in a heap and let the cold water he flung over her sting and soothe her at the same time.

Eventually she managed to prop herself up into a sitting position and sat gasping, dripping and exhausted on the concrete floor. Brother Davis gave her some time before he and his companion picked her up, their strong hands gripping her under her arms. They dried her with the rough towels, but with a gentleness they had never shown before, and then they half led her, half carried her along the corridors towards the Punishment Wing. Just as they approached the door and Paula was able to stand while Brother Davis fumbled with the lock, she heard footsteps approaching and heard voices.

And she heard one voice in particular.

Brother Davis glanced at his companion and then at Paula's battered body.

"Better get her in. I don't think volunteers are ready to see her just yet."

Even through her pain, Paula was listening intently to the approaching sounds. The volunteers who Caroline had told her about! And, yes, in amongst the voices, there was one she knew well.

She was hustled inside before anyone came round the corner, but it didn't matter. She was smiling as they led her away. Just as the door had closed behind her, she had heard the voice one more time.

There could be no doubt. Paula knew that her trial was at an end.

She allowed herself to be taken quietly to her cell and chained by her wrists, sitting against the wall again.

"Master?" She asked Brother Davis as he was about to leave. "Please could you tell His Reverence that I am ready to tell the truth now."

He allowed himself one of his quick smiles. "At last." He said and then left her. Paula stretched herself painfully and then, calm and proud, she let the darkness of exhaustion close over her.

24.

Paula was roused by the sound of her cell door opening and the Patriarch entering. He came to stand over her.

"Well?" He stared down at her, his dominance radiating from him once more and setting Paula's pulse racing immediately.

"Master. I will tell you the truth."

She told him the whole story and he stared at her when she finished. She saw fury and disbelief in his face, as she had known she would.

"You expect me to believe that? That you are here because of a mistake?!..... an accident?!"

"No Master. I don't expect you to take my word alone for it. That's why I couldn't tell you before. But now there is someone here who can confirm it. Now there is someone here who really is a spy."

"Who?"

"There is one of the volunteers, a woman who probably calls herself Margaret."

He thought for a moment. "There is one by that name, yes."

"Her real name and title is Chief Inspector Margaret Barfield. She is my superior officer. She will have come here only to find me, and once she has found me; she will betray you Master."

There was silence and then he squatted in front of her and held her face again. "And you would betray your own colleague?"

"Master I was never a spy and I have become your devoted slave. This is the only way I can prove it to you. And she was no friend of mine."

Paula told him about Margaret Barfield's method

of procuring bedmates by blackmail.

"And if you send Sister Lavinia to question her," she concluded, "I think you will save time and maybe find you have another good slave. She will thank me for it eventually."

"You are either the most devoted servant the Church has ever had, or you are a very dangerous enemy indeed Paula Cheever. Which are you I wonder?" Again that cloud of doubt on his face. She hated to see it, and hated herself for being the cause.

"Give me any test Master."

He gave a short bark of laughter. "I thought I already had. Now I am not so sure. But we will question this woman," he stood up and made to leave, "and I will keep you very close to me, where I can watch you. Very close indeed."

"Yes Master!" Paula smiled delightedly up at him.

Sister Lavinia looked at the figure before her. The woman was naked and hung from chains connected to her wrist retraints and mounted at the tops of two tall, wooden, whipping posts, set in the floor of a dungeon just a few doors away from where Paula was being kept. The chloroform was beginning to wear off and slowly her legs began to take her weight. She was hooded and gagged, the hood covering eyes, ears and nose, leaving only small holes below the nostrils. The gag was a stout wooden one attached to leather straps, it would give her something to bite on during the torture she was about to undergo for the next two days at least. That was how long Lavinia had been given to get a full confession from her, and she intended to enjoy it.

The body she was about to work on was a good one, large breasted, good skin and muscle tone, perfect material for what Lavinia had in mind. She experienced a momentary pang of regret that it wasn't the lovely Paula she was being given a free hand with, but this one would do well enough.

The victim began to panic as she surfaced to blind darkness and constraint.

Lavinia moved forward and undid the fasteners over the ear pads.

"Chief Inspector Barfield?" She whispered.

The figure went into paroxysms of terrified writhing.

"Paula's told us you see. Now all we need is confirmation from yourself. But unfortunately for you, I'm in no hurry. So for the next two days you'll stay gagged. I don't want you spoiling things by telling me everything before I've had my fun."

The figure trembled visibly and tugged at the chains.

Lavinia stepped back and ran a practised eye over the equipment the brothers had installed. Yes, there was plenty to work with and smiling in anticipation, she began to strip. She preferred working naked, she could move more freely she found. The blouse and long skirt were removed and neatly folded on the top of a whipping trestle, but the thigh length leather boots remained, Lavinia always felt they terrified the victim more; especially on those occasions when she was given a man to work with.

She removed Margaret's hood. The large brown eyes stared about her and a muffled moan came from behind the gag.

"Well we may as well get started," Lavinia told her briskly, "and the first thing we'll do is get your lovely legs open."

While Margaret struggled and kicked, Lavinia set about chaining her ankles wide apart, fastening them to the bases of the two posts between which she was mounted. With women she felt it was vital to get their legs spread straight away, it made them feel so vulnerable, even more so than a man, in her opinion. And ignoring the desperate snortings and muffled cries from Margaret, Lavinia sauntered over to a whip rack and made her selection. It was a particularly flexible crop with a very large flap of leather at the top. Lavinia had no intention of starting with the usual targets of back or buttocks. No, with a spy to work on her first taste of the whip was going to be agony; and from then on it would get worse.

    She explained this to the sweating, spreadeagled prisoner and then began. The crop whistled down across the upper curves of the large breasts. It bit deep into the pillows of fatty flesh, momentarily forcing them down the rib cage, but when it was lifted away they bounced and joggled very prettily as the victim straightened and locked rigid, eyes wide and staring in incredulous agony. The white line of the lash immediately began to darken and fill. A second lash cracked down across the nipples with pinpoint accuracy, the leather flap smacking wickedly into the nipple farthest from Lavinia. Calmly Lavinia walked to Margaret's other side and repeated the lash so that the other nipple got the same treatment. The victim's struggles were now so violent that accuracy was difficult so she concentrated on the main meat of the breasts, four more to the upper slopes and then six slicing uppercuts to rip into the soft underflesh. Margaret was rigid on her toes by now, her head back, breath snorting through her nostrils as she breathed between screams, saliva dribbling from around her gag and every tendon strained to snapping point. She held at a peak of agony just long enough for Lavinia to get one more snapping blow in across the nipples. Then she broke and abandoned herself to the agony, a long shudder went through her as her wailing reached a new pitch and urine spurted down her thighs. Lavinia watched in satisfaction.

She herself had reacted similarly the first time she had undergone breast torture. And she expected a similar reaction to occur several more times before she finished, she picked up a handful of straw and wiped the inner thighs dry. It was time to move on she felt, the breasts were nicely tenderised for the constriction and beating she had in mind for the next day. She replaced the crop and allowed Margaret to slump in her chains and recover herself just a little before she started in with the whip she chose next, it was relatively short but with many lashes, all knotted at their ends.

    She stood directly before Margaret this time and gave her plenty of time to look at the whip and sob with terror before she sliced it up into the wrenched open sex. The knots in the lashes gave them just the right amount of weight to lay themselves along the soft groove of the sex and then wrap up into the buttock crease and slam home on the anus.

    Margaret took two and then passed out. Lavinia waited patiently, moving the breast stocks out into the room so that Margaret could get a good look at them before experiencing them. After a few minutes she came round again and Lavinia continued where she had left off. Her victim's struggles became a demented frenzy as time after time the lashes snaked up along her sex. Lavinia worked slowly now, letting the searing agony be absorbed from each lash before the next was laid on. She admired the muscles of the thighs as they strained rigid to try and lift the body away from the pain, and after ten lashes she was impressed by the fact that she hadn't passed out again. Tough, she thought, good material to work with.

    When that bout of torture ceased, Lavinia left her for quite a long time and then went to cradle her head and stroke her hair, congratulating her on her endurance. She felt this was essential, if the victim, especially a woman felt that her suffering was being paid attention to and enjoyed by the woman inflicting it, then a sort of bond, partly exquisite humiliation, partly perverse pleasure would be forged between them and ultimately the submission would be more complete.

However she got a shock when she moved to attach different chains to Margaret's ankles and hauled them up behind her until her legs were spread and raised so that her body was spread eagled parallel to the floor. She ducked under one leg and stood so that she could see the ravaged sex spread out before her at eye level, livid welts crossing and scoring the tender labial flesh, but between them she could plainly see the coral pink gash of her inner flesh and it was gleaming with the secretions of arousal. Incredulously, Lavinia poked two fingers into the horizontal vagina and they slid in easily, delving into a moist channel which contracted eagerly around them. Lavinia laughed and went to stand in front of Margaret, whose head hung down. She grabbed her hair and wrenched it to bring her face up. The woman's pain glazed eyes blinked and focused groggily.

"You're loving every minute of this aren't you slut?"

Slowly the head shook.

"Well in that case you're really going to hate the next thirty six hours. I'm going to hang you in agony - this is just a taster by the way - I'm going to use the breast stocks and whip your lovely tits when they're purple anf full of blood. You'll undoubtedly wet yourself again under that torture. I'm going to stretch you on the rack and cane your back until you're raw. And during all those I'm going to coat the biggest dildo you've ever seen with a special ointment I've got and plug your arse with it. Believe me you'll think I've put a red hot poker up there. But of course if I take your gag off and you confess, then you'll miss out on all that fun."

She reached round Margaret's head and undid the gag, easing it out from between her clenched teeth. It was a risk, she knew, the slut might really confess and then she would have to give her back to the Patriarch.......well after another hour or two, and then she herself could confess that she hadn't handed her back straightaway and she would undoubtedly be condemned to a session down here with one of the brothers. She always enjoyed those, so whichever way things went, she would get something out of it. But she needn't have worried, Margaret took in several deep gulps of air and then spoke in an agonised whisper.

"No you bitch. I won't confess. Not yet. I need it all........everything. Whip me good and hard, I've got a lot to confess and you're going to earn it........every bloody word."

Lavinia laughed in delight. "I see we understand each other perfectly. Very well let's enjoy ourselves." She let the head drop and took a cane from the rack, showing it to Margaret.

"Before I leave you to enjoy your suspension for an hour or so, I'll cane you."

Margaret's head nodded.

"Very well, and you have my permission to scream, seeing as you're not going to confess until we've both enjoyed this, I'll leave the gag off."

"Do it hard ......you bitch. Torture me properly............Aaaaargh!"

Lavinia swung her whole weight and strength into the stroke which lashed across her buttocks. Even suspended in her chains Margaret managed to writhe under it and the next ten, until finally she slumped into unconsciousness. Lavinia left her for a while, savouring the prospect of how gratefully the slut would kneel before her and thank her for her punishment when it was all over.

She came back an hour later and took her down, leaving her plenty of time to writhe on the floor and recover before she began the next torment. When her preparations were complete she came to stand over her victim again.

"Well Chief Inspector. Shall we proceed, or will I have to gag you to stop you confessing?"

Margaret turned over onto her back and stared up at Lavinia

"No," she whispered. "It was good, but not good enough. You'll have to work harder."

Lavinia was delighted and set to work willingly. She hauled Margaret to her feet and supported her as she led her over to a wall. Once there she fastened Margaret's arms to the stone, down by her sides, she used a collar mounted on the wall to immobilise her head and then spread and chained her legs. Next she clamped pegs onto her already swollen nipples, fetching gasps of pain from her victim. The pegs were attached to thin nylon cords which Lavinia fed through runners at the tops of the whipping posts. Then she attached weights to them until Margaret's ample breasts were pulled cruelly out into grotesque points and she was whimpering and squirming in her bonds. She left her for the rest of the afternoon.

When she was taken down Lavinia gave her only a few minutes to cradle her ravaged breasts before dragging her to the rack and stretching her out on it face down. Once she was tied down and stretched taut she fulfilled her promise of the caning to her back. Working steadily down from the shoulders Lavinia laid the lashes on very slowly, allowing Margaret every opportunity to savour each explosion of pain and driving her, howling to three of the most shattering orgasms Lavinia had ever seen a woman attain under punishment. At last she put the cane down and leant close to

Margaret's ear to whisper to her what she would face the next day.

Margaret was covered in sweat, her hair was soaked and matted, her gleaming body heaved with sobs and gasps of agony and the aftershocks of ecstasy, but Lavinia noted the small nod of complete agreement when she laid out her plans for her. Then she slackened off the tension slightly and left her for the night.

The next morning Lavinia began by coating a huge dildo with a special cream which would irritate and burn the tender membranes of her rectum. She pushed it roughly up into the tight anal entrance, and then shoved again until it was fully embedded in the body. Almost immediately, Margaret began to buck and squeal. Lavinia had quite a struggle to move her back to her chains and tie her so that she could constrict the bases of her breasts with straps. But she had time to recover and watch as Margaret writhed and arched under the twin torments, screaming till she was hoarse. At last the breasts were just in the right state for her to begin, an angry and congested purple colour. She used the crop on them again. And when she had finished she decided that it was time to apply the final touch. Margaret was beyond words now, a limp and savagely marked figure hanging in chains. It would take only Lavinia's last cruelty to make her feel that she had been well enough punished. Two of the brothers came to help and the three of them mounted Margaret on her back on an X shaped table, whose arms supported her limbs and trunk but left her head hanging down and her sex available between her wide-spread legs. The sight of Margaret's devastated body and her own panted admission as she was tied down that if she was whipped as hard as she deserved to be this time she would confess, had both men eagerly erect. They positioned themselves one at her head and one at her crotch.

"Beat me and fuck me hard! Hard as you can........I need it....." Margaret gasped, lost in a delirium of humiliation and submission, as she saw what was in store for her. She managed one last shriek as Lavinia began, but then could make no more noise.

Lavinia stood beside her exposed crotch, stomach and cruelly striped breasts and wielded a heavy crop in a steady rhythm of Swoosh! Crack! Margaret's body bucked wildly at each impact but one of the brothers had rammed his erection into her gaping mouth while the other had pushed himself deep into the moistness of her vagina. In a parody of passion the body on the table shook and rippled under the triple impacts of the two men thrusting and the whip lashing across her. Lavinia had counted only ten lashes before one final spasm ran through Margaret, bowing her tortured body up off the table and locking it rigid for a long second while the men both released themselves into her and pumped their hips mercilessly at her helpless form and she passed out.

As was her custom, Lavinia had worked naked. Now the sight of Margaret's final torture had her breathing hard as her stomach rippled and churned with need. Her left hand made its way down to her crotch and she gazed longingly at the men.

"Brothers, I must confess too. I harboured thoughts of delaying her confession so that I could enjoy myself, while the Patriarch waited."

The brothers smiled at her. And while Margaret lay unconscious they put her in the ankle pillory, one which Paula had never experienced, it spread the victim's legs to a joint cracking extent. But before they hauled her up they tied her hands behind her and anchored her wrists to a chain which was mounted in the centre of the beam of the pillory, and then they shortened it.

As a result, when she was hoisted up, Lavinia's body was bent back in a taut bow as she hung head down. They pulled her up to a height where her mouth was available for use, and while she sucked eagerly on one brother, the other plied the whip on her stretched stomach and breasts. But once the brother who was using her mouth began to thrust into her to achieve his release the other shifted his target and lashed Lavinia between her legs, bringing the whip slamming down onto her open lips and fetching muffled squeals of agonised ecstasy from her as she drank in the spend which flooded her throat.

Then the men changed places and repeated the process, laying on another ten lashes after the second dose.

And when Lavinia had shrieked and shuddered her way through forty lashes they let her down and released her to lie in a delighted and sweat-soaked heap beside her victim who still hadn't stirred.

Some minutes after the men had left, Lavinia climbed slowly to her feet and dressed, then she held smelling salts under Margaret's nose till she came round, huddled on the floor.

"Now then Margaret my little bitch. Crawl to me and lick me or I might put the gag back and carry on."

Finally Margaret shook her head.

"No, no more." She groaned. "Not yet." She crawled to her new mistress and kneeling up painfully began to lick at Lavinia's crotch, while she held her skirt up. Margaret put her tongue out as far as she could licking at the livid traces of the whip and passionately tasting the juices which were seeping from the vulva and licking at the hardened clitoris until Lavinia groaned in delight.

Lavinia stroked her matted hair while she worked,

"Now we both know what we like, don't we Margaret?"

Margaret broke off long enough to whisper, "yes, mistress."

And when she had at last satisfied her, Lavinia let her confess everything and there was a lot that even Paula didn't know, involving corruption and perjury apart from blackmail.

Paula sat in her chair by the infirmary window and gazed down longingly over the courtyard. They had put bars up at the window and the door was locked and guarded, but she was mending fast and wanted only to be back in the monastery again. But she never would be, she knew that now. She was different from the others after all. She could see Caroline and the rest of her group, wearing the longed for white dresses of the initiates now. She herself was kept naked until the Patriarch decided what to do with her.

She heard the bolts on the outside of the door being pulled back and the key turning in the lock. The Patriarch entered and Paula immediately stood and adopted the respectful pose she had been taught. As always he moved with economical grace and the bearing of one born to power and crossed the room to stand in front of her.

"In the Inner Circle Paula, you kneel with your legs apart and your hands clasped behind your head."

She obeyed even before the meaning of his words had sunk in. But when it did she couldn't help looking up in disbelieving joy. He was smiling at her and she bathed in the warmth of it.

"With a little help from Sister Lavinia the woman called Margaret has unburdened herself of her sins. Of which there were many. You were right on all counts. . . . She responded well to Sister Lavinia and is making good progress.

Father Burton has high hopes of her. Now you may stand and show me how your marks are healing."

She stood and turned full circle so that he could see how the bruises were fading and how the cuts were healing without scarring. When she faced him again he ran a hand slowly across the smooth curves of her breasts and let his fingers trail across the sensitive flesh of the nipples. Paula felt her chest go so tight she could hardly breathe. Her breasts felt taut and full while her nipples sprang out hard and red almost at once. She could hardly believe that at long last her Master was touching her.

"You are very beautiful Paula. And the Church needs the services of beautiful women."

His index finger was tracing a line down between her breasts and across her stomach. She could make no reply.

"Kneel down." He told her.

She knelt in front of him and at his command opened his clothes to free his sex. It wasn't fully erect, the hood of soft skin still covered the head. Very gently she leaned forward and let her tongue probe. To her delight she felt him begin to stiffen immediately and as she closed her lips over the top of the member she felt the foreskin peel back and the head emerge. It throbbed and grew in her mouth until it filled her to capacity and still it grew until she had to stretch her lips to their fullest extent before he was fully erect and her cheeks puffed out as she fought to contain his massive sex. When she took her mouth away to run her tongue down the shaft she was thrilled at the length and size of it. She let her lips and tongue kiss and caress the huge purple head until it shone with her saliva, her hand gripped the shaft and she relished the iron hard strength and power of his erection. And as she sank her head over the tip once again, her darting tongue tasted the salty pearls of his fluid which were beginning to appear at the slit. She began the rhythmical movements of her head, up and down which would bring him to his climax. She could hardly wait until she felt the force and volume of his come, she was sure it would be awesome as he spurted himself into her. And at last when she felt the pulses begin to run through the huge member and felt it swell even more she pushed down further still, until she felt him at the back of her throat. But she was too desperate with hunger for the taste of his sperm to care. The floods which finally erupted into her satisfied even her appetites, spurt after spurt slamming against the back of her throat and joyfully she swallowed time and again until she had gathered every last drop.

As soon as he withdrew from her he told her to undress him and by the time she had, exploring him with her mouth at every opportunity, running her tongue across the broad and muscular chest, letting it delve deep between his legs and in between the hard curves of his buttocks, he was erect again. He took her on the bed and Paula moaned in almost a delirium when she felt his fingers part her lips and begin to toy with an already throbbing clitoris and then push up into her flooding vagina which was trembling with longing. Then at last she felt his huge erection push into her, spreading her lips and seeming to rub every nerve in her channel to the very point of explosive release.

When he reached full penetration he stopped for a second and smiled down at her before beginning his withdrawal and then thrusting in again.

There was no need for any words now. All that needed to be said had been said on the platform while Paula was undergoing her worst torture.

They understood each other perfectly; the ruthless master and the woman born to serve him.

Paula arched her back in yearning for him to start

and wrapped her arms tightly round his back. Then he began. Thrust after thrust rammed into her quivering sex and her body surrendered to a series of silent detonations which ripped her senses apart and filled her brain with whirling patterns of ecstasy. She hardly felt him reach his climax, the ones he drove her to were so shattering. But when Paula at last lay quiet and content, still quivering and feeling littlle ripples and spasms run through her, her Master cupped her left buttock in one hand and told her he would have her branded there.

She was taken to his private residence, a huge house in the Midlands, staffed by the Inner Circle. It had extensive cellars which had been converted to dungeons which shamed the ones at the monastery. Paula saw every conceivable device for discipline on display, but each room was comfortably furnished and carpeted for the comfort of those who would watch. The day after her arrival she was tied face down on a table like the one on which she had been ringed. Beside it a white hot brazier glowed. From the coals Paula's Master took the incandescent iron, forged in the shape of the X and held it firmly down onto the flesh of her left buttock which sizzled and bubbled. As she arched against her bonds, Paula just had time to smell her own flesh roasting before she passed out.

Two weeks later she returned to her own flat. A car came for her and she was delighted to see Brother Davis driving. The farther they got from the Patriarch's house however and the nearer they got to her own, the more Paula became depressed. She had to go back into the world for a while. There was a cover story to be put about, questions to be answered, but she had to do it on her own. And she had been so used to being with others so intimately for so long. At the Patriarch's house, on the rare occasions when he didn't want her, she had slept with the others, even Maria. Now her clothes felt constricting and uncomfortable, especially her bra.

And against the fabric of the seat she could feel the brand on her buttock; a symbol of comfort on the one hand but also a reminder of where she really belonged. When he had seen her off the Patriarch had assured her that when it was safe for her to return, he would contact her. Until then she had to operate on her own and make no attempt to contact him.

When Brother Davis dropped her off outside the flat which she had left so long ago he tried to encourage her.

"The call will come Paula. You can rely on that." She was grateful for his attempt to cheer her up.

The days which followed were grey and lifeless. She felt lost and adrift, she had no desire to be independent again; quite the reverse.

Mainly her time was taken up with debriefing. She and the Patriarch had decided on a story which would account for Margaret Barfield remaining undercover for the next two months; she was gathering evidence against the Church, having used her trusted status within it to secure Paula's release. Paula's story was that she and the others had only been encouraged towards a reformed lifestyle. While her brand had been healing, she and her master had rehearsed details day after day until she was word perfect. The debriefing was conducted for ten days by a hard faced inspector from another division and by a female inspector from a division in the north, Laura Patterson. She gave Paula the hardest time, picking over details, time after time until she wanted to scream.

On a Friday afternoon they finally thanked Paula for her patience and thoroughness, said that there might be a commendation for the way she had handled the situation she had found herself in and that that would be all.

Paula went to the ladies' toilets washed her face, combed her hair and set about repairing her make-up. She had just finished and was looking at herself in the mirror when she saw Inspector Patterson enter and come to stand beside her. They were alone. In the mirror Paula saw the Inspector's eyes fixed on the reflection of her own. But as Paula watched she saw the Inspector's hand reach down and across to lightly touch Paula's buttock directly over her brand. Rigid with shock and fear, Paula felt the fingers probe for and find the grooves carved by the red hot iron, and they traced the shape of the X. She swallowed hard and turned to face the Inspector, who was smiling at her. But the Inspector merely took hold of Paula's nerveless right hand and guided it to her own buttock where her fingers in their turn traced out the X beneath her clothes. Paula breathed out and sagged against the vanity unit in relief. Laura Patterson laughed.

"You know how thorough He is. He couldn't take any chances. But you handled yourself well and tomorrow there will be a car for you, you can post your resignation from the house. He has work for you."

He needed her! Paula's spirits soared, she was going back to where she most wanted to be. Gratitude towards this woman, herself one of the Inner Circle, who had given her the news flooded through her.

"Now," the Inspector went on, "I'm staying in town tonight. Why don't we have dinner together?"

Paula looked fondly at her kindred spirit. She would gladly do anything for her.

"Your place or mine?" she asked.

25.

Paula stretched luxuriously in her bath and enjoyed the feel of the warm water flowing round her body, especially between her legs. She reached down and opened her lips with the fingers of one hand to let water circulate more intimately. Laura had been an energetic lover.

They had dined at her hotel but Laura had insisted that they return to Paula's flat afterwards. Her reasons only became plain later. She brought with her a sports bag and from this she first of all took a letter. Paula had opened it curiously and read it with gathering delight. It was from the Patriarch; from her Master.

> 'My Dear Paula,
>
> Please accept my congratulations for having completed your debriefing successfully. By now of course you will have met Laura properly and I hope you will forgive my having kept an eye on the progress of the debriefing. It was not that I didn't trust you; I think we have passed that stage. Laura was more in the way of being an insurance policy in case the going got rough, but she assures me you coped magnificently. She has another function to perform however.
>
> Although I have had you whipped more than any other member of the Inner Circle, I have never whipped you myself. When you return here tomorrow I intend to remedy that. In the meantime I would like you to enjoy Laura. I send her to you as a gift, one that you have more than earned. In addition she has been instructed to offer herself to you in ways which will help you with the work I need you to undertake.
>
> Enjoy.'

Laura had waited until she had finished reading and had then taken from her bag a riding crop which she handed to Paula. With hands which trembled from excitement, Paula had taken it and felt its strength and flexibility. Laura had smiled,

"Where's the bed?" she asked.

She had undressed quickly and lain down on Paula's bed, stretching her arms up to grasp the headboard. Paula had undressed more slowly, savouring the anticipation. How many times had she seen submissively offered female flesh tremble and judder under the whip, how often had her own? But now, by her master's express command she was to experience the thrill her own body provided for those to whom she offered it.

She let her hand run caressingly down the shaft of the crop while she looked at the naked woman in front of her. Her eyes travelled from the rounded pillows of her buttocks to the slender waist and then up along the curves of her back and shoulders. And the brand she wore declared that it all belonged to whoever her master wanted to have it.

Paula's heart leaped with joy at the first lash. She laid it hard across Laura's bottom and watched hungrily as the flesh rippled and her head jerked up. From then on she had gone to work in earnest and Laura told her later that it was one of the hardest beatings she had ever had from another woman.

And Paula knew exactly what her master had meant. She now fully understood the excitement her submission caused and would now be well aware of the effect she could have on anyone he wanted to give her to.

The car had come for her the next morning and

Brother Davis had driven her again. They were equals now but Paula was still grateful for his early awakening of her submissiveness. When they said goodbye, she reached across the car and took his right hand, bringing it to her lips and kissing the palm gently. This was the hand at which she had first suffered, this hand had wielded the first whip she had ever felt.

She worshipped only one man, but Brother Davis had played a large part in bringing her to the realisation that she needed to worship a master. They exchanged a smile and Paula hoped she might be allowed to see him again one day. But when the car drove away and she turned to see her master waiting for her, all thoughts of anyone other than him immediately vanished.

He had shown her the room which was to be hers from now on. On her first visit she had stayed in the various girls' rooms but the thought that she would have one of her own had never entered her head. The bathroom in which she was currently relaxing was itself bigger than the grandest hotel room she had ever stayed in, and more luxuriously appointed. But better than that, spread out on the bed next door was the most beautiful scarlet silk dress. And best of all she was to wear it for her master at dinner that evening.

Bathed and relaxed, she took her time applying perfume under her breasts and between her legs. She took an age to apply exactly the right shade of lipstick and the right amount of lip gloss, in exactly the right way and only when she was quite certain that she looked as good as she could did she slip the dress over her naked body. The neckline plunged right down between her breasts, while over them it clung and moulded itself faithfully to every contour. Like the dresses the others wore, and which she had admired at the monastery, it was split right up to one hip. She walked and twirled in front of the mirrored wall of her bathroom and admired the way the material concealed and revealed by turns. But the crowning glory to her mind, were the fine chains to be worn at wrists and ankles, they had delicate silver bells attached, slave bells, which tinkled softly at every movement. Round her neck she wore a silk choker which matched the scarlet of her dress.

She dined alone with the Patriarch that night.

When she descended the main staircase and entered the dining room, he was waiting for her, immaculate in evening dress. He had even kissed her hand. But then he had stunned her as he led to the table.

"In your honour Paula, I have provided some entertainment. I think it will put us both in the mood for what we know is to follow." He told her. She looked towards the other end of the long dining table and saw one of the other girls hung by her wrists from two chains which came down from the chandelier above her. Paula couldn't tell which girl it was because she was hooded completely, the hood even incorporating a gag. Her nipples were clamped and weighted with heavy spiked balls.

"I'll have her whipped while we eat." The Patriarch said. Paula knew that the other girls would have envied this one the chance to display the pleasure she took in his total dominance. But even so the casual cruelty set Paula ablaze, as it always did, and even as she took her seat she found herself pressing her thighs together to try and stop the juice of her arousal soaking her dress. At a signal from the Patriarch another girl stepped forward and placed herself behind the chained one. She held a whip, Paula noted that it was not a particularly severe one, having many lightweight lashes, but it was one which a girl used to being beaten with heavier whips could take almost indefinitely and enjoy.

The Patriarch waved a hand as the girl who was waiting on them poured his wine.

"Indefinite number of lashes. Bring her round as necessary."

The meal began to the heady sound of leather smacking on female flesh, and being answered by muffled grunts which slowly changed to groans of pleasure. As time went on there were more and more pauses while the chosen girl writhed and shook as orgasm after orgasm pulsed through her. Then the remorseless rhythm of the whip would start again, and Paula was deeply impressed by the girl's ability to maintain consciousness under the barrage of ceaseless stimulation.

Despite the arousing spectacle of the whipping girl twisting and writhing at the end of the table, Paula couldn't take her eyes off her master. She breathed in every detail of the way he so casually and gracefully accepted the subservience of those around him. She hung on his every word as he told her about his plans for reforming the evils he saw around him. All the time her arousal was being racked up by the steady Thwack! Thwack! of the whip on the body of one of his devoted slaves and she knew what she was waiting for above all. To belong to him utterly at last.

After a long meal, fine wine and a glass of brandy, the Patriarch waved at the girl who was handling the whip. It fell silent and at last the stretched body in chains was allowed to slump forwards as it was taken down. But he and Paula were looking only at one another.

"I will whip you now Paula." He said quietly.

"I know Master." She replied.

He took her to one of the basements and watched as she let the dress rustle slowly to the floor and lie at her feet.

She raised her arms obediently as he buckled restraints onto her wrists and then tied her wide-spread arms to a steel bar and hauled her up till she hung in agony a foot above the ground. And then he whipped her. He used a long whip similar to the horsewhips she was accustomed to, but this had a lighter lash which prolonged the ordeal and slowed the long climb to ecstasy.

Paula felt as though a dam had burst inside her at the very first lash. She had waited so long, she forgot all her training and let her excitement grow as it would while she writhed and screamed under her Master's relentlessly steady lashes. Her sex lips quivered and fluttered with longing for him, her belly burned with arousal and her breasts felt as tight as drumskins while her nipples thrust out in rock hard little points. She counted the lashes out loud and came at the fifteenth. He stopped and let her get her breath back before he continued. Another climax ripped through her at twenty five and at thirty lashes she went rigid as the brightest explosion of sensuality she had ever known burst deep in her belly and she almost fainted before he released her.

He took her on the carpeted floor of the room they were in and his powers of self control drove Paula wild with desire. He took her first in her anus until she came again as the huge shaft stretched her tissues to tearing point, and his hands cupped her breasts and stroked her weals. Then he turned her and used her belly until she was limp and inert, just crying out as one orgasm after another shook her in every limb and her body jerked helplessly as he drove into her time after time. And only when he finally withdrew from her gaping sex did he allow himself his release. He rolled onto his back, grabbed her hair and thrust her face down onto his still, rock hard shaft. He pumped his seed deep into her throat and Paula, lost in an erotic dream and sucking on the huge member which had plundered her back and front passages and which now gagged her, distantly heard his cry of joy and swallowed as fast as she could with the very last of her strength until he slid out of her and she fainted.

A week later she performed her first task for him. The Patriarch summoned her to his office one morning and showed her a file. She was amazed to see that it concerned a very senior government minister.

"There is some legislation going before Parliament in the near future and this man can steer it through. It will greatly benefit the Church, therefore we must make sure we control him so that he does exactly what we want. I am going to offer you to him Paula."

"Of course Master."

"Men who are already corrupt are easy to corrupt even more. That's why the Church needs the services of beautiful women. Let this man think he controls you Paula, let him think you are his slave. And he will be our slave."

"The Honeypot, Master." Paula said laughing.

He smiled at her and reached out to put his hand up her short skirt. He stroked the slit of her sex affectionately but wouldn't be distracted. "Precisely Paula. The Honeypot. Now look at these and see what it is he likes."

She looked at the sheets of the dossier. The research was thorough, it even stated that the riding crop was his preferred instrument of discipline but there was something else. And just as she was about to turn and ask her Master, he placed a handful of long, thin needles on the desk.

"These," he said, anticipating her question, "he likes to use these. They can be inserted into the flesh in various sensitive spots. They cause a lot of pain but leave virtually no trace."

Paula reached out and touched the wickedly sharp points.

"It will be something new Master." She said smiling at him.

The minister was invited to dinner that night and she sat next to him. When his third glass of wine had been drunk she leaned towards him and placed her hand over his. He turned to her and Paula watched as his gaze travelled down her cleavage and then along her naked arm until it got to the chain at her wrist and the bells.

"I've listened to some of your speeches in the House," she said, and then spoke softly, "I would say you have a .....needle sharp wit."

She looked steadily at him and he looked back for a long time. "Do you take an interest in politics..... at the sharp end?" He asked finally.

Paula laughed huskily, the fires in her belly igniting at the thought of her master giving her to this man to do as he pleased with. "I'm sure I could be made to." She said.

Here is the opening of our book for next month, LITTLE ONE, by Racheal Hurst , writer of "Confessions of Amy Mansfield.

ONE

"No, don't. Please don't!"

Susan's whisper was urgent, nervously appealing rather than protesting as she shuffled on the bar-stool, almost forgetting herself and pressing her knees together. She knew that any plea or protest she might make would be ignored. She also knew that he understood the perverse thrill that underlay her blushes when he showed her off like this.

His hand carried on up her leg anyway, as she knew it would. Past the top of the black, seamed nylons Michael required her to wear these days, softly over the bare flesh of her inner thigh, on and up. There was not even the flimsiest of barriers to his progress because he did not allow her to wear panties any more.

"Relax, little one" Michael whispered, his mouth close to her ear, his breath warm on her neck. "Make room."

Desperately embarrassed by the presence of an audience, yet totally unable to resist either Michael or the lurch of heat growing in her belly, Susan parted her knees a little more to allow his insidious hand access. She knew Michael was only showing off his ownership and was ashamed of her reactions to it. What he was doing was deeply humiliating, yet the very brazenness of it set off sparks in her nerve- ends.

His hand delved. She tried to hide her reactions. She always did, but not too much. Once, when she had succeeded really well in keeping quiet, he had pinched her clitoris hard between his forefinger and thumb just as she was starting to come, and made her wail, and drawn attention to her and, shamefully, doubled the intensity of her climax. Already several faces in the bar-room had turned towards them, and conversations had got quieter.

Michael caressed her knowingly and insidiously, and she melted. She tried desperately not to come. Tried to forbid the flush she knew was sweeping from her cheeks to the vee of her collarbone and down towards the neckline of her 'little black dress'. She fought to control her breathing as he worked her up. Fought to control the unwilling, eager, rippling movements of her body on his wonderful, terrible hand.

Conversations in the bar had become tense whispers now as groups of eager men, and women who were either embarrassed or even more eager, watched Susan shudder into the orgasm she tried to hold back, and failed to disguise. At least he did not pinch her this time.

Oh, how she wished he wouldn't do this! Wouldn't show her off this way. But at the same time it was what she wanted. She didn't know why. Just that he was he, and she adored him, and he had taken her under his wing, wrapped her in his charisma - made her feel that she belonged; belonged with Michael and to Michael.

"I love you," she whispered as Michael slipped his hand out from under her short skirt. She was already holding the tissue with which, as she had done before, she would surreptitiously wipe his fingers clean of her juices.

This time, though, instead of lowering his slicked hand into hers, he raised it. Raised it to her lips. For a moment she froze. It was only a moment, but was long enough for her to see the flash of triumph in his eyes. She leaned forward and began to lick his fingers, desperately aware of the audience all around, knowing that later on he would spank her for her hesitation.

His gaze held hers, cool, knowing, unutterably penetrating. She felt the eyes of the people in the bar watching her clean his fingers with her tongue. To them, she was no more than an obedient pet, a creature, a slut; a sort of outlandish cabaret. It did not matter. That is what she was. His creature. His worshipping pet. His slut. Tears brimmed on her eyelashes. She didn't know whether they were tears of love or tears of shame.

It didn't matter.

Love burns, he'd said, when she was falling under his spell. Love demands. She told him she loved him. He smiled, that smile of his which cut through her sinews and made her no more than a rag doll.

"I love you," she whispered when Michael moved his fingers away from her mouth and at last let her wipe them on the tissue.

She was desperately aware of the tension in the whispered conversations in the bar. A woman's high-pitched laugh pierced her like a shard of ice. For a moment she wanted to curl up and die, then, perversely, she felt a flush of pride. The woman's laugh had been shrill and nervous. Let her laugh! It was not she who Michael had fondled. She was not the lucky one! Susan focused her eyes on her drink. The ice had melted as she had melted, and what was left of the orange juice was now mostly water. She wanted to leave the bar, to get away from this sea of strangers to which he had displayed her for his amusement and theirs. She wanted to make love, to feel him moving in her body, to breathe his breath and feel his power. But she knew they would not leave until he was ready. It was part of his game.

Michael told her to order fresh drinks. This was another part of his game. Melt her; show her off; then make her look at and speak to the barman who had watched her submission. She saw the mixture of speculation, scorn and lust in the barman's eyes as she ordered. "A large Armagnac please, no ice, and an orange juice, with ice." Michael did not allow her alcohol. The shadow of a grin flickered across the barman's face as she took the banknote out of her purse and passed it across the bar. He stared openly at her breasts rather than her face. She knew what he was thinking, and blushed. She was thinking it too, or rather feeling it. The main reason she wanted to get away from the bar was so that she could make love to Michael. The barman knew it. His glance told her that given half a chance he would drag her round behind the bar and fuck her. She looked back to Michael, who smilingly sipped his Armagnac and glanced at his wristwatch.

Later, she stood quietly in the corner of his living-room, waiting. This was another one of Michael's games. She knew that soon he would fuck her, would let her writhe on his bed with her feet clamped around his waist and her pelvis bucking, would allow her body to demonstrate its lust for him; perhaps even allow her to stay all night so that she could make love to him again and again. But he would keep her waiting. As she faced the wall she wondered whether he would test her with one of what he called his 'variations', those escalations of his demands with which it amused him to make her demonstrate her love and submissiveness. Early in their relationship, after hardly more than week in fact, he had said he would like her to shave her pubis, while he watched. It had been desperately embarrassing. Before she met Michael she had been shy; still was come to that. But when he had turned his request into a teasing challenge to her professions of love for him, she had complied. It was the strangest experience. Susan was blushing with terminal embarrassment as she took off her clothes and parted her knees, but at the same time something primeval seemed to be waking in her. Somehow, what she was doing became a conscious exhibition, and at the same time something almost impersonal. She did not understand it; all she knew was that, by the time she finished with the scissors and lather and safety razor and rinsed and dried herself, she was so ready that the very touch of Michael's hand as he smoothed her with talcum powder set her undulating into a sudden, volcanic orgasm that went on and on as Michael pushed her back and penetrated her with a single, glorious thrust. It did not last long, for Michael too had become aroused by Susan's performance. Afterwards, on his bed, he let her re-rouse him with her mouth - something he had taught her how to do and a skill which she now rejoiced in - and they made love again and again.

The next escalation was the exhibitions in bars, like the one earlier this evening. The first time he did it she had wanted to die. She could not really handle it even now. In private doing anything he wanted, caressing his penis with her lips and tongue and fingers, caressing him and being caressed in her turn was one thing. Being made a show of in front of strangers, being brought to orgasm on his hand, was quite another. Yet she had never once been able to stop herself coming as he fondled her. And the more she tried to hide it, the more subtly obvious it became.

He wanted to show her off. Maybe being shown off only added to the primeval fulfillment she felt at being his; his to do with as he wished. In a way, she rejoiced that he thought her worth showing off. She waited, facing the wall, still fully dressed but knowing that that would soon change. She heard the chink of bottle against glass and the glug of liquid. In her mind she saw him pouring Armagnac into a cut- crystal tumbler. She felt as well as heard him sit down and sip from the glass, light one of his small cigars, watch her. She kept very still. She could feel his eyes and his cool smile. She waited eagerly for his order to take her clothes off, even though she was sure the first thing he would do would be to spank her. He did not spank her very often, but when he did the sex afterwards was always even more intense than usual.

"You were very good this evening, little one." His voice was like oiled silk.

"Thank you, Michael." She caught her breath because this was a dangerous beginning.

"But you did make a slip."

"I'm sorry, Michael."

"Do you know what you are apologizing for? What your little slip was, pray tell?"

Her mind whirled. When he got silkily sardonic like now, he could become very demanding, and her punishments more testing. Once, he had made her go to the office wearing a tight jersey frock and no underwear at all, and it had been a day of excruciating leers and wolf-whistles and snide comments from the other women. She took a breath.

"I got embarrassed. In the bar. When you wanted me to lick your fingers. They were all looking!"

There was a long silence, as though he was considering her excuse. Then . . .

"Of course they were all looking. That is the whole point." His voice had taken an edge now. She continued facing the wall, wondering where this was going to lead. It was different from before. Nerve-wrackingly different. He did not tell her to take off her clothes and come to his bed on her knees, as he usually did at this point and as she longed for him to do. He did not make love to her and send her body wild. Instead, he told her to call a taxi and go home, and to return on Monday

evening, when he intended to cane her for her lapse. Shaken, Susan did as she was told, 'phoning for a cab and then facing the wall again while she waited for it to arrive. He did not want her! Her body, already throbbing in anticipation of the sex she ached for, became chilly. She felt goose-pimples on her back. Her mind went blank, shying away from this new escalation in the demands of the man she adored. He was going to cane her! She gave an involuntary shudder. The first time he had spanked her had been enough of a shock, but afterwards he had fucked her so hard it drove away any semblance of pain. But that was only with the palm of his hand. Later, he had used his slipper and then a hair-brush, and that had been so painful that even the sex afterwards hardly made up for it. How much worse would a cane be!
"Oh, and don't touch yourself in the meantime," was his parting
instruction. Susan knew exactly what he meant, and blushed.

TITLES IN PRINT

Silver Moon

ISBN 1-897809-03-4	Barbary Slavegirl	*Allan Aldiss*
ISBN 1-897809-08-5	Barbary Pasha	*Allan Aldiss*
ISBN 1-897809-14-X	Barbary Enslavement	*Allan Aldiss*
ISBN 1-897809-16-6	Rorigs Dawn	*Ray Arneson*
ISBN 1-897809-17-4	Bikers Girl on the Run	*Lia Anderssen*
ISBN 1-897809-20-4	Caravan of Slaves	*Janey Jones*
ISBN 1-897809-23-9	Slave to the System	*Rosetta Stone*
ISBN 1-897809-25-5	Barbary Revenge	*Allan Aldiss*
ISBN 1-897809-27-1	White Slavers	*Jack Norman*
ISBN 1-897809-29-8	The Drivers	*Henry Morgan*
ISBN 1-897809-31-X	Slave to the State	*Rosetta Stone*
ISBN 1-897809-36-0	Island of Slavegirls	*Mark Slade*
ISBN 1-897809-37-9	Bush Slave	*Lia Anderssen*
ISBN 1-897809-38-7	Desert Discipline	*Mark Stewart*
ISBN 1-897809-40-9	Voyage of Shame	*Nicole Dere*
ISBN 1-897809-41-7	Plantation Punishment	*Rick Adams*
ISBN 1-897809-42-5	Naked Plunder	*J.T. Pearce*
ISBN 1-897809-43-3	Selling Stephanie	*Rosetta Stone*
ISBN 1-897809-44-1	SM Double value (Olivia/Lucy)	*Graham/Slade**
ISBN 1-897809-46-8	Eliska	*von Metchingen*
ISBN 1-897809-47-6	Hacienda,	*Allan Aldiss*
ISBN 1-897809-48-4	Angel of Lust,	*Lia Anderssen**
ISBN 1-897809-50-6	Naked Truth,	*Nicole Dere**
ISBN 1-897809-51-4	I Confess!,	*Dr Gerald Rochelle**
ISBN 1-897809-52-2	Barbary Slavedriver,	*Allan Aldiss**
ISBN 1-897809-53-0	A Toy for Jay,	*J.T. Pearce**
ISBN 1-897809-54-9	The Confessions of Amy Mansfield,	*R. Hurst**
ISBN 1-897809-55-7	Gentleman's Club,	*John Angus**
ISBN 1-897809-57-3	Sinfinder General	*Johnathan Tate**
ISBN 1-897809-59-X	Slaves for the Sheik	*Allan Aldiss**

Silver Mink

ISBN 1-897809-09-3	When the Master Speaks	*Josephine Scott*
ISBN 1-897809-13-1	Amelia	*Josephine Oliver*
ISBN 1-897809-15-8	The Darker Side	*Larry Stern*
ISBN 1-897809-19-0	The Training of Annie Corran	*Terry Smith*
ISBN 1-897809-21-2	Sonia	*RD Hall*
ISBN 1-897809-22-0	The Captive	*Amber Jameson*
ISBN 1-897809-24-7	Dear Master	*Terry Smith*
ISBN 1-897809-26-3	Sisters in Servitude	*Nicole Dere*
ISBN 1-897809-28-X	Cradle of Pain	*Krys Antarakis*
ISBN 1-897809-32-8	The Contract	*Sarah Fisher*
ISBN 1-897809-33-6	Virgin for Sale	*Nicole Dere*
ISBN 1-897809-39-5	Training Jenny	*Rosetta Stone*
ISBN 1-897898-45-X	Dominating Obsession	*Terry Smith*
ISBN 1-897809-49-2	The Penitent	*Charles Arnold**
ISBN 1-897809-56-5	Please Save Me!	*Dr. Gerald Rochelle**
ISBN 1-897809-58-1	Private Tuition	*Jay Merson**

UK £4.99 except *£5.99 --USA $8.95 except *$9.95